I'll Call You
MINE

SHARON L.
CLARK

Dedicated to all the authors, artists, and creatives who may think it's too late.

"We are the music makers, and we are the dreamers of dreams"

from Ode by
Arthur O'Shaughnessy

ONE

You are mine.

You've always been mine, even though you deny it. Our bond is unbreakable, born of the stars and designed by the universe, and we are both powerless to escape it. When will you stop fighting your fear and surrender to destiny?

Waiting for you has been so lonely. At times I'm convinced you are close to grasping the infinite depth of our connection, but then you drift away again, just out of my reach. My love for you, my insatiable hunger, burns brighter than a thousand suns, threatening to consume me from the inside. But I know the certainty of our future together, and it sustains me as I wait for the perfect moment to reveal myself to you.

FOR NOW, I'LL BE PATIENT. I'LL WATCH, AND I'LL YEARN, AND I'LL DREAM OF HOLDING YOU IN MY ARMS. BUT I WON'T WAIT FOREVER. WHEN THE TIME COMES, REST ASSURED I WILL DO WHAT HAS TO BE DONE TO MAKE YOU SEE ME.

NO ONE WILL EVER LOVE YOU THE WAY I DO, AND THERE WILL NEVER BE ANOTHER WHO WILL BEGUILE ME SO COMPLETELY. I HAVE BEEN UNDER YOUR SPELL FROM THE MOMENT YOU FIRST SMILED AT ME, AND I HEARD MY NAME ON YOUR LIPS. I WON'T GIVE UP UNTIL I POSSESS YOU, BODY AND SOUL. AND WHEN THE TIME IS RIGHT, I'LL COME FOR YOU.

SOON.

Katie Parker refolded the worn pages and tucked them in the pocket of her purse. She knew the words by heart, having read and re-read them over the last several weeks. Even now, every line made the hair on the back of her neck stand on end.

"Ladies and gentlemen, welcome to beautiful Iowa, where the time is 4:17 p.m., and the temperature is a pleasant sixty-two degrees. We'll be taxiing to the terminal in just a moment. Please lease remain seated until the captain turns off the fasten seatbelt sign, and thank you for flying with us today."

Passengers all around her stood and stretched, pulling their carryon bags out of the overhead compartments, laughing, and talking. Cell phones were turned back on, filling the air with the dings of incoming messages, and calls were made to loved ones, letting them know the plane had landed. People stood in the aisle or crouched in front of their seats, waiting for a turn to escape the cramped airplane after the four-hour flight. But Katie hadn't moved, barely registering the motion in the cabin. Her hands were clasped in her lap, just trying to keep her anxiety in check. Would anyone notice if she didn't get off the plane? Maybe she could stow away and disappear in whatever city was the next destination.

The knot she'd been carrying in her stomach since leaving San Francisco tightened into a hard, dense ball now that the plane was on the ground. When she moved to the coast for college seven years ago, there had been an air of excitement and a promise of a wonderful life ahead of her. Fear and dread were her ruling emotions now, and there was no way to ignore the dark cloud she had brought with her.

Whether moving back to her hometown was the right move remained to be seen.

Katie hefted her carryon bag over her shoulder and checked her cell phone again. The fact that she hadn't heard from her brother only made the knot in her stomach tighten. Her arrival was right on time, and she was positive he knew when to expect her. It's fine. He's fine. Squaring her shoulders, she made her way to the baggage claim and watched as the suitcases, boxes, and golf clubs slid down the ramp to join the carousel of luggage.

The last week of packing had been a whirlwind of emotion, and her nerves were still raw. Pressing her back against the wall, Katie scanned the faces that passed, getting more concerned with every minute that ticked by. Had something happened to him? She'd kept her plans secret from everyone except her closest friend Charlotte, but it wasn't out of the question that she'd been followed, anyway. Closing her eyes, Katie pushed against the dread creeping up her spine.

From the far side of the carousel, a smattering of laughter started up, and it didn't take Katie long to see why. As her suitcases came into view, so did her brother. Nick was squatting between them on the black conveyor belt, grinning at his cleverness like a Cheshire cat. His bright blue eyes, so much like hers, sparkled with mischief while Katie's face burned a bright red.

"Oh my god, Nick, get down. You're going to get us in trouble." He was drawing too much attention, and she didn't know if she could manage any more anxiety at this point. "People have been arrested for less."

She swatted his leg when he was within arm's reach, but he rolled away and hopped to the floor with a bow. The other passengers milling around chuckled and shook their heads at his antics. Now that he'd pulled off his little trick, his smile softened, and he opened his arms.

With no hesitation, she buried her face against his shoulder, and they held each other tight for several minutes. Nick rocked Katie while she tried not to dissolve into a blubbering mess in the middle of the terminal.

"Are you okay?" He kissed her forehead then held her at arms' length, scanning her face carefully.

Katie sniffled and rubbed her eyes, bloodshot with sleepless nights and far too many tears. "Oh, yeah, just tired." As Nick gave her another tight squeeze, she was grateful for the momentary chance to hide her face from her overprotective brother. She bit her lip and took a deep breath before plastering on a bright smile.

Nick slung his arm around her shoulders and steered her toward the exit. "Then let's get you home where I can dazzle you with my newly discovered cooking prowess."

———

The weather in Enderlin was mild for this time of year, so Katie hung her hand out the open car window. The cool, crisp spring air smelled fresh compared to San Francisco, and she couldn't get enough of it. As they drove into Enderlin, Iowa, a wave of nostalgia washed over her. The town square where she spent most of her teen years boasted one of the most beautiful City Hall buildings in the state of Iowa, surrounded by several unique shops. It was home to everything from a small movie theater and a hardware store to a photographer's studio and a soda fountain. People strolled along the sidewalks, in no hurry to go anywhere, looking in the windows and holding hands while talking. Everything was so relaxed here. Katie could feel the stress melting away with every mile that passed.

Turning onto the street of her childhood, a pang of sadness tightened her chest. She loved coming home, loved seeing the two-story blue house, the wrap-around covered porch, and the gingerbread scrolling. On every other visit, the big yards, towering oak trees, green grass, and white picket fences soothed her. This time was different. She wasn't home for a birthday or to recharge with the people she loved.

She was running. Hiding. This new reality made the idyllic scene around her take on a sinister shade.

Nick helped her carry her bags up the stairs to the bedroom her parents never had the heart to change. The same comforter of purple irises covered the bed, a solid purple dust ruffle hiding the box spring. There was her white desk, her stuffed animals piled in the corner, the pictures of all the big cities she planned to live in one day: New York, Paris, San Francisco, Tokyo.

That was always a big difference between Katie and her brother. She couldn't wait to get out of Enderlin, to see the world and experience everything life had to offer. Nick, on the other hand, was perfectly content to live his life in their home-town. It wasn't that he was afraid to leave or didn't have big plans for his life. Before he'd turned thirty, Nick started his own business on the town square, designing and building high-end furniture. His talent and work ethic had earned him a flawless reputation all around the Midwest, and he was in high demand. At least that was the excuse he used to explain why he was still single.

After unpacking and tucking the suitcases in the closet,

Katie laid back on the bed, gazing at the ceiling. Nick laid on his back next to her.

"How are you?"

She sighed. "Fine."

Rolling onto his elbow to face her, Nick scoffed. "Sure, you are. Come on, level with me. How are you, really?"

All her emotions rushed to the surface, and she feared she would fall apart if she acknowledged them. Instead, Katie kept her eyes trained straight up.

"I'm a mess, Nick. I don't know what the hell is happening, and I feel like I'm walking through someone else's nightmare. It's all spinning around me, and I can't focus on any one thing long enough to make sense of it."

Nick took his sister's hand. "Kat—"

She shook her head. "Don't. Please don't spit platitudes and clichés at me right now. A year ago, everything was perfect. Well, not perfect, but I was relatively happy. I liked my job and made good money; I thought I was in love. I had a good life in one of the best cities in the world. Now…" Her voice broke. "I'm unemployed, I left my best friend two thousand miles away, and I found out that Derek, my 'great' boyfriend, had been taking credit for all my work before he up and vanished, so I don't even have the reputation I earned. Did I mention that I've got a lunatic stalking me? Because there's that, too."

Nick squeezed her hand in the silence. Then he jumped up and pulled her to her feet.

"Okay. You need a distraction, stat. A distraction that includes beer, pool, loud music, and not sitting here stewing."

Katie shook her head. "I don't know, Nick… Is that a good idea with everything that's been going on?"

He spun her around and steered her down the hall. "You're in Enderlin, in a town with maybe fifteen thousand people, in the literal middle of nowhere. Plus, I'll be right there. I think you owe yourself one night to relax and decompress. Let's go grab a couple of greasy burgers and a few drinks. Maybe we can hustle some poor sap at the pool table and get your bad-bitch mojo back."

Katie shot him a withering look over her shoulder. "God, you're weird."

But a night out might be exactly what she needed. She had been cautious when she left San Francisco, trying to erase any trails that would lead to her. Maybe, for the first time in months, she could let her guard down and relax. Besides, ruminating over recent events wouldn't fix anything. Not tonight, at least.

She perked up as an idea came to her. "How about Maxie's?"

"I'm already getting an Uber."

"Great. Their burgers are the best, and right now, I'd love a normal pub that hasn't turned into some trendy nightclub or pretentious martini bar."

Nick locked the front door behind them, and the siblings sat on the porch, enjoying the spring breeze. "You've met Max, right? Do you think that will ever happen in a million years? I'm sure it's written into her will that it can never be 'rebranded,' or she'll come back and haunt the place."

A warm sense of peace stole over her at the thought of seeing some familiar faces and forgetting about the recent nightmare she'd been living. "Then, by all means, let's relive some memories."

The two entered Maxie's, classic rock blaring over raucous laughter and conversation. Smoking in bars had been outlawed many years ago, but the phantom smell of cigarettes from decades past still lingered. Cheesy velvet paintings and Bob Ross-style landscapes hung on the walls, the same as the last time Katie had been there.

"Katie Parker?"

No sooner had they stepped inside than a young man with cropped blond hair and a round, familiar face stopped them. He wore a gray suit with a loosened tie, and the look on his face was one of utter shock. "Wha—How are you here? Didn't you move to San Francisco?"

Katie leaned into his welcoming hug. "Well, if it isn't Cael Green, almost exactly where you were the last time I saw you." She kissed his cheek. "It's been a minute."

"Hey, man." Her brother stepped forward. "Good to see you."

"Yeah, you, too." Cael shook Nick's hand but barely looked at him. "Katie Parker, you are a sight for sore eyes! How is it that every time you come back to town, you get better and better looking?"

Blushing, she shrugged, trying to think of something to say. But before she could respond, his watch pinged. He took a quick glance and groaned. "God, I wish I could stay and catch up, but I was just on my way out. If I'd known you were coming—"

"Don't worry about it." Katie waved him off. "Kinda want to spend some time with my brother tonight, anyway. But hey, I'm sure we'll run into each other again soon, small town and all."

With a bright smile, Cael nodded. "I'd like that. Have fun tonight."

"I'm glad to see you and Cael Green are still such good friends." Nick steered them toward the bar.

Katie shrugged. "I don't know that I'd say *good* friends. We seemed to run in the same circles, and he was always pretty nice to me growing up and every time I saw him when I came home. But enough about Cael; you promised me beer and pool. I'll even buy the first round."

With local craft beers in hand, Nick and Katie wound their

way to the pool tables in the back of the bar. "Why don't you rack 'em up, Kat? I'll be right back."

She felt a clutch in her ribs, and she looked over the crowd. "I'll come with you."

Laying a hand on her shoulder, Nick shook his head. "I'm just going to the bathroom and I sure as hell don't need your help. You'll be fine, I promise. We don't want to lose the table, so just chase everyone away."

She rubbed her sweaty palms on her jeans and took a deep breath. It was fine, she'd be fine. No one knew she was coming here. No one but Charlotte, and Katie knew she'd take that information to the grave, if need be.

After a healthy swallow of liquid courage, she pulled out the triangle, arranging the balls just right. When she was satisfied they were snug and ready for play, she hefted a couple pool cues to find the best weight and balance. Anytime she played against her brother, she did everything she could to gain an advantage. He was the one who taught her not to take anyone at face value, even him.

"I can show you the trick to the perfect break if you'd like."

A deep voice from behind her caught Katie off guard, and she whirled around, ready for a confrontation. But instead of the monster of her nightmares, she found herself looking into a pair of striking green eyes. The man before her didn't seem dangerous but her heart was still racing, and her ability to speak vanished.

He was tall with broad shoulders, a neatly trimmed beard, and thick, dark hair. And when his mouth lifted into a lopsided grin, her heart skipped out of beat.

"Wh—What makes you think I need you to show me anything?"

He chuckled and leaned in closer. "Maybe it was just wishful thinking so I could have a chance to talk to you."

"Why?"

He blinked at her question. "Why what?"

"Why did you want to talk to me?" She swallowed the anxious butterflies and raised an eyebrow. "Do we know each other? Or were you coming to explain the rules of a game I've been playing for half my life?"

Katie's heart was hammering in her chest, and she was sure he could hear it. What the hell was going on here? Despite the way he'd surprised her, there was no reason for her body to be reacting like this. He locked his penetrating gaze on her, sending a jolt from her head to her toes; whether it was from fear or excitement, she wasn't quite sure.

Just then, Nick rounded the corner and clapped the stranger on the shoulder. "Back off, Collins. You're out of your league here."

"Hey, how's it going, man?" The two shook hands and the stranger locked eyes with Katie, making the blood rush to her cheeks. "So, who's your new friend, Nick? I don't think I've seen you in here before."

"This is my sister, Katie, just moved back from her adventures in San Francisco. Kat, this is Ben Collins, one of Enderlin's most eligible bachelors—after yours truly, of course." He laid a hand on his chest and gave a slight bow.

"Oh, is that what you are?" Katie finally tore her eyes away and bumped him with her hip.

Ben laughed and she had to fight the urge to step closer to him. "Well, I didn't mean to interrupt. I'll let you get back to your game." Again, he caught Katie's eyes. "I hope I'll see you around."

With that, he turned on his heel and headed to the front of the bar, glancing back several times. Katie watched him walk away, her heart thudding each time their eyes met.

Nick nudged her with his elbow. "Put your tongue back in your mouth, Kat. You're embarrassing me."

"Ha. Ha." Katie continued to prepare the table. "You want me to break, or what?"

"Please, do the honors."

Katie chalked her cue, lined up the shot, and with a loud crack, sent the balls scattering across the table, sinking two of them in the process. Nick groaned.

"Damn. You've been practicing."

"Nope. Just natural talent." Katie lined up the next shot, dropping two more balls while Nick looked on in feigned despair.

"This is the last time I let you break," he muttered.

Movement on the opposite side of the table caught her attention and she glanced up. With a pretty blonde hanging on his arm, Ben Collins strolled into her line of vision. Their eyes locked and he winked, making Katie skip over the top of the cue ball, missing the shot entirely. She scowled, and he responded by flashing her a satisfied smile.

Nick nudged Katie aside. "It's about time. Get out of the way, Kat, I'm running this table."

She blushed and took a long drink of her beer, trying to calm her nerves. True to his word, Nick was sinking every shot, catching up in no time.

"And another...oops, there goes that one. Want me to drop yours, too?"

She caught Ben watching her while the blonde prattled on, his eyes lit with smug amusement. Those deep-set, almond-shaped eyes mesmerized her. She took in his long, dark eyelashes, the laugh lines crinkling the corners, his slightly tousled hair. He looked like he had rolled out of bed and ran a hand through it with perfect results. It wasn't until Ben raised his eyebrows in a playful smirk that Katie realized she'd been staring. Her cheeks burned, and she turned to watch her brother, who was now strutting around the table, putting on quite a show. But his cockiness became his undoing, and he flubbed an easy corner shot.

"Ha!" Katie laughed, relieved at the distraction. "Well, well. See how the mighty have fallen."

Nick hung his head and dragged his cue behind him to the

table, where he raised his drink to the ceiling in a mock salute. "Ah, well, it was lovely while it lasted."

Katie kept her head down, resisting the urge to see if Ben was still watching. When she dropped the eight ball and won the game, her brother let out a theatrical groan.

"And that, dear brother, is how winners play." She slung her arm around his shoulders and kissed him on the cheek. "Aw, let me get the next round as a consolation prize."

Waiting at the bar, Katie's attention kept drifting across the room, to Ben. He smiled easily and laughed freely with the people in his group, rousing Katie's curiosity further. God, he wasn't her type at all, but she couldn't take her eyes off him.

She shook herself. What the hell was she doing? There was a madman still out there somewhere, and the last thing she needed was a charming stranger to complicate her life further. She had no business flirting with men, especially not one with a Manhattan-sized ego. No matter how drawn to him she was.

Katie took the beers back to her brother, who shook his head as she approached. "Don't go there, Kat."

"Go where?" Her eyes grew wide. "I don't know what you're talking about."

"Right. You two have been eyeballing each other since we got here. It's gross." He stuck his tongue out at her.

She swatted him. "Not eyeballing."

"Don't insult my intelligence. Everyone in this place sees what's going on. You keep gawking at him all doe-eyed and dreamy, and he's undressing you with his eyes. It's disgusting."

She leaned on the pool cue while her brother worked his way around the table. "Not that the thought ever entered my mind, but why shouldn't I 'go there'? What's wrong with him?"

Nick didn't look up from his shot. "I don't know. It's not like I think he's dangerous or anything. But all the women in this town pant after him, and I think it goes to his head, you know? Be careful."

"Don't worry, I will. But who says I'm the one who should be careful?" She batted her lashes at Nick while he mimed throwing up.

They played a couple more rounds of pool, then switched to darts. The night sped by with drinks, laughter, and conversation with old friends who had found their way to the bar. Despite her best intentions, Katie continued to look for Ben, to see who he was talking to and what he was doing. If she was honest with herself, she just wanted to look at him again. The beer was affecting her, she reasoned, and it was possible she had exaggerated how attractive he was. She wanted to double-check, just to be sure.

Coming out of the bathroom a while later, Katie ran into a solid wall of human, the collision almost knocking her to the floor.

"Oof!"

Two large, warm hands caught her around the waist, keeping her upright. "Whoa, steady there."

She'd automatically grabbed onto the stranger's shoulders, her body pressed against his, realizing too late whose embrace she'd fallen into.

"Well, hello again." Ben Collins peered down at her and laughed. "I knew you'd end up in my arms one way or another."

Katie gawked at him, failing to string two words together. She was too captivated by his smile and those amazing eyes and distracted by the heat blooming in every place their bodies touched.

"You okay?" He chuckled, snapping her out of her stupor, heat racing through her veins. She grabbed his wrists and extracted herself from his embrace.

"I'm fine."

He stepped back. "I hope we're going to keep literally running into each other, Katie Parker."

Narrowing her eyes, she cocked her head and her pulse jumped. "I didn't tell you my last name."

"You're Nick's sister. It seemed obvious."

"Maybe I'm married."

He laughed. "You're not wearing a ring. I looked."

"Maybe it's being cleaned." She scowled up at him, her cheeks burning. "You don't know everything."

"I know I'd like to see you again." Ben lifted her hand, brushing his lips across the back of her wrist. "Well, it was indeed a pleasure meeting you, Miss Parker." With a wink, he strolled past her and back toward the bar.

Katie stared after him, openmouthed, until Nick appeared and flung an arm around her shoulders. "What was that about?"

Katie shook her head. "Um, I don't think I know. But hopefully, I won't have to worry about running into him again."

Nick threw his head back and guffawed. "Oh, right. As if that's what you want." He puckered his lips at his sister. "You were laser-focused on him all night. And you can bet your ass he saw it, too. I can guarantee that is not the last you've seen of Ben Collins."

———

People were talking and laughing all around him, but Ben wasn't listening to any of it. Instead, he was searching the crowd for one woman that he couldn't get out of his head.

He noticed her the minute she walked into the bar, but it was talking with her that had really gotten his attention. Within thirty seconds of conversation, she'd called him out on his game and had rendered him speechless. That never happened. Not to him.

Something about Nick's sister had him feeling off-kilter,

and he couldn't put his finger on exactly why. She was certainly beautiful, there was no question about that. Long, dark hair smoothed away from her face into a neat ponytail, white tank, red flannel, slim jeans: there were half a dozen other women in there dressed similarly. But none of them had a pair of blue eyes that pierced him like a laser.

He couldn't keep from checking throughout the night to make sure she hadn't left. It was easy to spot her every time, too. Even across a crowded bar, her eyes were like a beacon, especially when she was smiling and laughing. It seemed half the patrons knew her and were glad to see her. They stopped by the pool table to give her a hug and engaged her in conversation at the dart board. The way she interacted with everyone as though each one was a dear friend made him smile. Either she was a genuinely kind person, or she was the best grifter out there.

Occasionally, though, he caught some signs that her confidence wasn't much more than a façade. She scanned the crowd every few minutes, a frown creasing her brow. Was she waiting for someone? If she was, it didn't seem it would be a happy reunion. Breaking eye contact with whoever she was with, her whole face would tighten, mouth pressed in a razor-thin line. And then the tension was gone in the blink of an eye.

The contradiction of vulnerability and strength in this woman was intriguing. He wanted to talk to her, to learn as much about her as possible: What did she do for work and for fun? What made her leave San Francisco? And how would it feel to have her in his arms again?

Physically running into her by the bathrooms had been pure coincidence. That little bit of contact, though, had made his stomach flop and his heart race, like he was a lovesick teenager. Seeing her rosy cheeks and the defiant shine in her eyes was so much more of a turn-on than he would have expected.

But Ben walked away from their exchange confused and

unsettled. What had been a clumsy attempt to fluster her had only managed to get *his* pulse racing and his curiosity piqued. The rest of the night was spent trying to catch a glimpse of her again, to find another opportunity to talk to her, but it never presented itself. Disappointment weighed him down until he just wanted to go home.

"Hey Benny." Cindy, the sweet blonde who'd been keeping him company earlier sidled closer and wrapped her arms around his waist. "I've got some good tequila at my place. Why don't we move the party over there?"

Any other weekend he would have been happy to take her up on her offer. Cindy was beautiful and easy-going, but right then he was yearning for more than just a good time. He kissed her forehead and hugged her. "Thanks Cin, but I'm gonna have to take a raincheck."

Her shoulders dropped as he walked away alone, but all he could think about was a certain dark-haired beauty with brilliant eyes he was sure were full of magic. Nick had been right; she was way out of his league.

Besides, he'd likely never see her again, anyway. And that was probably for the best.

TWO

With Nick doing paperwork at his office the next morning, Katie decided it would be a good opportunity to reacquaint herself with her hometown. She tucked a whistle and pepper spray in her running belt, just as she had for months, and stepped outside, filling her lungs with fresh air. It had been a long time since she could get out and run without feeling the need to look over her shoulder with every step. And she was going to take advantage of that freedom.

She had forgotten how green Iowa could be. It was a definite contrast to San Francisco, where you had to go out of your way to find open space. As she jogged, a slight breeze made the leaves on the towering trees dance. Families walked with their children or their dogs, people mowed lawns or tended to lush gardens, washed their cars, chatted with neighbors.

Derek would have hated it here. Anywhere that wasn't a big city held nothing but hicks and hayseeds and wasn't worth her ex-boyfriend's time. Having grown up in San Francisco and traveled the world, he entered every room like he owned it, and he made it very clear that he was only allowing other people to share it with him.

Crossing through the park in the middle of the square, Katie turned back toward home. She should have known something was off with him, that things weren't quite what they seemed. But anytime they were together, it was hard to see past the brilliant glow of his good looks and charm. Derek had an amazing energy, and it was impossible not to gravitate toward him.

Kind of like Ben Collins.

Katie shook her head, a wave of irritation sweeping over her. She did not want to think about Ben, to picture his smile and deep, penetrating gaze. It was challenging to push away the memory of his arms around her, so close that it would have been effortless to lean forward and kiss him.

If the gods answered prayers, Ben Collins wouldn't cross her path for a long while, if ever. A romantic entanglement was at the bottom of her to-do list. She needed to get her head right first, neutralize the threat in San Francisco, and move back to the coast where she could rebuild the life she always wanted. Then Ben Collins wouldn't be an issue.

Back at the house, Katie grabbed the mail before trekking up the driveway. The short workout had done wonders for her mood, and she was full of energy for the first time in weeks. As she approached the door, however, something caught her eye, slowing her steps. The porch railing obscured her view, but she hoped against hope that she wouldn't find what she already knew was there.

The skin between her shoulder blades prickled into gooseflesh, and she spun around. She was positive she was being watched, that someone was skulking in the shadows, just out of sight. On shaking legs she scrambled up the steps, pressing her back to the wall. When she saw what was waiting for her, her hand flew to her mouth.

In front of the door lay a bouquet of yellow roses, the stems wrapped in thick black ribbon, with a familiar yellow envelope nestled among the ominous blooms. Katie froze, her legs like lead as panic clawed up her throat. She scanned the bushes, the street, the driveway and grasped her can of pepper spray. Suddenly every face she'd passed on her way home flashed through her mind; had one of them been Him? Was He watching her now, drinking in her terror?

All she could think was that she had to get inside, she had to get out of sight. Keeping her back to the wall, she crept along the porch, stepping gingerly over the unwelcome gift. There was no way she was going to touch that envelope. She knew what it would say—what they always said—and she couldn't read those words again.

With her legs threatening to buckle under her, she stumbled from the porch and dashed to the back of the house. Every fiber of her being was convinced her tormentor was only steps away, reaching out to grab her, and she flung herself against the back door with a wail. Her keys jangled in her shaking hands as she fumbled with the lock, cortisol and adrenaline flooding her system and pushing her to run, just run. Every sound was menacing; she craned her neck over her shoulder at the imagined breath in her ear, the steps of an invisible threat drawing closer and closer. Katie's stomach was roiling, her heart beating faster and harder against her ribs as hysteria threatened to overtake her.

Finally, the lock turned, and she burst through the door, slamming it behind her and sinking to the floor. Her body racked with sobs, there was nothing she could do but give in to the terror that was choking the life from her.

This should have been her safe place. Leaving San Francisco should have afforded her a reprieve from the torment she'd been living with, but she hadn't escaped anything. Trembling, she scrambled through the house, shutting the blinds and the curtains, checking the locks as she went. There was no way she was taking a chance that He was watching from outside the house, waiting for the perfect opportunity to make His move.

Katie crouched against the wall where she could see the front and back doors and shot a frantic text to her brother.

KATIE:

When will you be home?

It only took a few seconds for him to respond.

NICK:

About an hour. Everything okay?

Katie fought back tears as she typed out her reply.

KATIE:

Yes. Maybe. Idk. Just scared.

In less than a minute, Nick was calling her cell.

"What's going on, Kat?" he demanded when she answered.

"There was a—I found something on the front porch." She drew in a wavering breath. "He knows I'm here, Nick."

The line was silent. When her brother spoke again, his voice was tight and low.

"Lock the doors. I'm on my way."

———

As soon as Nick was home, Katie let the tears flow.

"It's okay, Kat. You're safe." He kissed her forehead. "I promise."

"You can't promise that. Hardly anyone knew I was leaving, much less coming here. How could He know?" Her voice dropped to a whisper. "How did He find me?"

Nick guided his sister to the couch, keeping a protective arm around her.

"God, Kat, I wish I knew."

She groaned and put her head in her hands. "What do I do?"

"Get the sheriff involved, let his office work with the San Francisco police to track down possible leads. After that, live your life like normal, I guess. We'll be careful, take precautions, and the police will find him and stop him. Okay?"

Katie drew in a deep breath to quell her mounting despair. She wanted to burrow under the covers of her bed and never come out. Ever. "I don't think I have a choice, do I?"

Nick stood and held Katie's arms, pulling her up with him.

"Gather everything you've gotten from this creep, and I'll call Sheriff Jacobson. Do you have the other police reports?"

Katie nodded.

"Great. You can tell him everything that's happened and see what he has to say."

———

Sheriff Jacobson read the latest letter and grunted. "Can you think of anyone who would do this?"

Katie and Nick shared a glance, and she sighed. "I don't know. Maybe. My ex-boyfriend, Derek, wasn't too happy with me before he dropped out of sight."

The sheriff's eyebrows shot up, and he paused in his notetaking.

Running a hand through her hair, Katie frowned. "I'm not even sure what to think. Derek was stealing my work, taking credit for it, and when I confronted him, he—well, he didn't take it very well and he threatened me. But the notes and gifts were showing up before then, so who the hell knows."

She rubbed her arms to dispel the chill that had settled under her skin. When she told Derek it was all over—their relationship, him stealing her ideas—he reacted badly, to say the least. Banging on her door in the middle of the night, accosting her in the halls at work, even going so far as to break into her place and threaten her. She called the police, but he disappeared before they got there and hadn't been heard from since. His apartment hadn't been touched, his cell number was disconnected, and his bank and credit cards left no trace. While she was afraid of him and what he might be capable of, they had been together more than a year, and a small part of her was worried about him.

Nodding, Sheriff Jacobson jotted down a few more notes. "Any idea where he might be?"

"No. He hasn't been seen in months."

Nick looked at his sister with pursed lips. "How do I protect her, Sheriff? Can your people keep her safe?"

The sheriff locked eyes with Katie. "We'll do everything within our power, but you need to be proactive and not take any unnecessary risks. When I get back to the station, I'll reach out to the detective in San Francisco so we can coordinate efforts. Keep us informed of anything—*anything*—out of the ordinary that happens, okay?"

Katie nodded and tried on a weak smile. "I will. I just want this to be over."

———

After scouring several employment websites, Katie submitted applications for everything from Graphic Artist to Marketing Director to Administrative Assistant. A local printer looking for a new account manager was the only response that resulted in an interview. It wasn't an Art Director position like she had held in San Francisco, but beggars couldn't be choosers.

Katie took a deep breath and walked through the front door of Dixie Printing. She was met by a young redhead who flashed a bright, perfect smile. "Good morning, I'm Jocelyn. How can I help you?"

Katie returned the smile. "I'm Katherine Parker. I'm here for an interview with Dixie."

Jocelyn nodded, making her loose curls bob. "Of course. I'll let her know you're here. Please, have a seat." She picked up the receiver and pressed a few buttons. "Hi, yeah, Dixie, your appointment is here." There was a pause, then she muttered, "I know, but I'm not calling you 'mom' at work. It's totally unprofessional. Okay. Thanks." She smiled at Katie again. "She'll be right with you."

After only a minute, a tiny woman with gray-streaked red curls like Jocelyn's marched into the lobby. She made a beeline for Katie, her hand outstretched.

"Hi, I'm Dixie. Come on back, and let's get started."

Dixie led her to a large office behind the reception desk, shutting the door behind them. "Please, sit, make yourself comfortable. Katherine, is it?"

"Katie is fine, thank you." She perched on the edge of the chair, hands clasped in her lap, back straight, and waited.

"So... How are you enjoying Enderlin, Katie?"

"Oh, I love it. I grew up here, and my brother and parents still live in town."

"Is that what made you want to leave a beautiful city like San Francisco?"

Katie hesitated, unsure how to answer without explaining everything that had happened in the last year. Images flashed through her memories—that final demeaning proposal to the board, Derek's brazen smile, his angry hands on her body, his kisses chasing the pain, fighting to keep the bile from rising in her throat.

"My position at Barnaby Marketing had...changed in recent months, and it was no longer someplace I felt I could really grow. It seemed an ideal time to move home and reconnect with my family."

After about ten minutes of typical interview back-and-forth, Dixie picked up Katie's resume and drummed her fingernails on the desktop. "You applied for the Account Manager position, but I don't think that's the right fit for you."

Katie deflated and dropped her gaze. "Well, I appreciate your time and thank you for meeting with me. Please keep me in mind if you think you can use my services down the road." She stood and reached out to shake Dixie's hand, but the diminutive older woman just stared at her.

"Where are you going? I said you weren't right for *that* position. But I want you onboard, of that I am certain." Dixie cocked her head, sizing Katie up. "In fact, I know the perfect place I can use you."

Katie smiled, excited by the twinkle in Dixie's eye.

"We have one account marketing rep, but he's buried. I love his work. He's brilliant with an insane work ethic, but he's stubborn, and I don't want him working himself to death —which is where you come in." She flashed a bright smile at Katie. "You can do it all—budget, design, lead a team, build a campaign. I want you to share the load and be another bright young mind to dangle like a carrot in front of prospective clients. What do you think?"

As Dixie explained the position, Katie's excitement grew. It sounded like the perfect opportunity for her to showcase her skills and still learn more. An exhilarated smile broke across her face. "What do I think? I think I'd like to know when I can start."

THREE

Monday morning, Katie was up before the sun. The excitement of a new job paired with the fear of being thrown into a building full of strangers had kept her awake, her stomach churning. She hadn't outrun anything by coming home, she'd simply brought it with her. Knowing that He could follow her anywhere, could be anyone, made her want to lock the doors and burrow under the covers forever.

It was an enticing thought, but she knew she had to do something to keep from retreating into her own mind. Wading through the rising panic at the realization that she was powerless, being hunted even here, was enough to drive her crazy.

She'd spent an hour on the phone with her best friend Charlotte Saturday night, trying to convince herself she was doing the right thing.

"Listen, darlin'. Everyone is doing what they can to get this creep. I'm in touch with San Fran police here, you've got Nick watching your back, and damn it, this sicko's got to fuck up sometime." Her voice softened. "No one's going to let him get to you."

Katie twisted her hair around her finger and sighed. "I know. You're right, I know that logically in my head. But I can't shake this feeling of dread that something's coming. Something really terrible."

"Oh, Katie. I wish I were there to just wrap you up in a big hug."

That made Katie smile. "I wish you were here, too. But I wouldn't be much company, unfortunately."

After hearing the latest gossip about Charlotte's coworkers and making nebulous plans to see each other soon, Katie hung up feeling only slightly better. There was nothing else she could do for the time being. Until the police tracked down the stalker and he was removed from her life, she didn't really have any viable options. So, she'd keep moving forward while constantly looking over her shoulder and hope that her pursuer would be caught—before he caught up to her.

———

After showing her around the building, Dixie led Katie to the break room. "Are you ready? I scheduled a staff meeting for first thing this morning, so you'll meet everyone at once."

Katie's stomach knotted, but she answered with as much confidence as she could muster. "Absolutely. From what you've told me, I don't have any reason to be nervous, right?"

Dixie raised her eyebrows but said nothing. People started trickling into the room, where they poured steaming mugs of coffee before gathering at the tables, talking and laughing. At Barnaby Marketing, the men were young, wearing expensive suits and ties, and the women mirrored them to fit in. But in that break room, Katie was surrounded by friendly faces of all ages, shapes, and sizes, exuding a comfortable and welcoming air. Every one of them, from the white-haired old man in denim and an ink-stained factory shirt to the bubbly young receptionist, Jocelyn, made eye contact as they entered the room. Some of them examined Katie with brief curiosity but then smiled and continued their conversations.

When Dixie started the meeting, Katie's gaze drifted over the faces surrounding her. Were any of them familiar? Had she spotted a flash of that shaggy brown hair behind her on the BART? Maybe she recognized that smile in the back of the room. Taking a deep breath, Katie tried to swallow her anxiety. She could do this.

After covering a few more staff announcements, Dixie motioned for Katie to stand next to her. "Everyone, I'd like to introduce you to Katherine Parker—Katie—the newest member of our marketing division. She just moved back here from San Francisco, where she worked for the prestigious Barnaby Marketing firm. Be sure to find Katie later today and introduce yourselves, make her feel welcome. As always, put your best foot forward, and let's continue to be the best in the Midwest."

Katie's heart jumped into her throat as a door flung open across the room, banging against the wall. Before she could pinpoint the source of the sound, Dixie called out to the latecomer.

"So good of you to join us, Mr. Collins. You almost made it this time."

Collins? Katie's head whipped around, and her stomach dropped. *Oh no.* The Mr. Collins that had just blown in was *Ben* Collins, the handsome stranger from the bar. She turned her back and started rearranging the creamers and sugar packets on the counter. What the hell was he doing here?

"Ben, I have found the answer to all our problems. Fresh from San Francisco, I present to you a bona fide marketing professional to take some of the weight off your shoulders."

"That's...fantastic." The tightness of his voice told Katie he thought it was anything but fantastic. "Thanks, Dixie."

Katie's belly was flipping, her heart racing, but she fought to keep her nerves under control. It sounded like Dixie had hired her to work with Ben. And he wasn't too pleased about the arrangement.

Well, tough shit. Curving her lips and squaring her shoulders, she pivoted slowly to face her new partner. When she reached around Dixie and offered Ben her hand, she had to admit a sense of satisfaction—and a thrill—ran through her at his slack-jawed expression.

"Good morning, Mr. Collins. I'm Katie Parker. I believe I'm the 'solution' Dixie referred to." She paused, watching his eyes widen as the realization sank in. "Nice to see you again."

Ben stared at Katie's hand, his lips pressed into a thin line. Looking back and forth between them, Dixie's furrowed brow smoothed into a smile.

"Ahhh…so the two of you have already met? Splendid."

Ben plastered on a smile and grasped Katie's hand. "Welcome to the team. I, uh, look forward to working together." She narrowed her eyes, keeping the smile on her own face and matching the intensity of his grip. Their eyes locked with a silent challenge passing between them, neither willing to relent.

"Let's break it up, kids," Dixie said. "I don't need you two starting a full-fledged arm-wrestling match. Ben, you know I adore you. Because of that, I have hired a partner with some great experience and brilliant ideas. I know the two of you, together, will build an unstoppable marketing department."

Ben opened his mouth to protest, but Dixie held up a hand.

"For today, I would like you to show Katie around your neck of the woods, so to speak, and help her settle in. Katie, Ben will show you where everything is and answer your questions about Dixie Printing." She glared at him, daring him to contradict her. "And he'll be happy to help you with anything you need. Right?"

"We'll play nice, Dixie. I promise I won't break her." He flashed a brilliant smile that Katie felt all the way to her toes. "At least not today."

———

Ben waited for Dixie to leave the room before turning his attention back to the problem at hand. How the hell did the one woman he couldn't stop thinking about end up as his new partner? He was being punished. That was the only explanation. He looked her over, hoping to find some flaw to counteract the image of her he'd burned into his mind. But no, she was just as captivating as the night he first saw her. He'd be damned if he let her know it, though.

"Right. Let's get you set up then, Ms. Parker. This way."

She trailed him to his desk, where he shuffled around some papers, trying to think about how to approach this situation. He was an adult; he could work professionally with her— couldn't he? Knowing she was standing just a few feet behind him, waiting, threw that assumption into doubt.

Besides, he didn't want nor need any help. So what if she came from some big-deal firm out west? He'd worked for a big-deal firm out east. Dixie was overreacting, that's all. Everything was well under control.

From the corner of his eye, he watched Parker as she waited and caught something he probably wasn't supposed to see. Her gaze was on him, her lip trapped between her teeth and that same light he'd seen at the bar shining in her eyes. So it hadn't just been the beer, then. That little nugget of information, that she seemed to feel whatever this was between them, got filed away for future use. If she wanted to play cool and collected, he was going to have a little fun at her expense. He buried his face in a file so she couldn't see the mischief in his eyes.

After a couple more minutes, she cleared her throat. He jumped theatrically, as though he'd forgotten she was there. She did not look amused, which greatly amused him.

"Which one of these should I use?" She indicated the three empty cubicles.

"Makes no difference to me. Pick whichever you want."

Pretending to be engrossed in his email, he watched her contemplate her options. And she was contemplating.

What Ben assumed would be an eenie-meenie-miney-moe decision appeared to be puzzling her. Parker stood at each desk, turning to look around the room before moving to the next one and doing the same thing. He couldn't tell what she was looking for: the easiest access to the bathroom? The best view out the window? Some kind of feng shui vibe?

She finally seemed to be satisfied with one of the workstations and set her bag on the desk. Ben saw an opportunity to tease her a little, and he took it before his common sense could stop him.

"No, not that one!"

She jumped away as though the desk had burned her, then glared at Ben while he laughed. "Hilarious."

Ben chuckled. "I couldn't resist. That desk is fine." He piled up the papers and files he'd been looking over and leaned over the top of her cubicle, his arms crossed.

"I suppose I should help you set up and show you where everything is."

When she swiveled in her chair and looked up at him, he caught a glint of challenge in her blue eyes, and his stomach flipped.

This was going to be trouble.

She smoothed her hair and faced him, one eyebrow raised, her shoulders squared. "Lead the way."

Before she had a chance to stand, Ben moved into her workspace, squatted at the keyboard, and started to pull up the system. He realized his mistake almost immediately. It was impossible not to be aware of the heat radiating from her body, the scent of her perfume. This close to Parker, the brilliant color of her eyes was breathtaking. He found his gaze drifting to her lips over and over, wondering how soft they would be.

His daydream was interrupted, however, when he saw the

corner of her mouth twitch, and it was clear she'd caught him looking. *Damn.*

She cleared her throat and rolled her chair out of the way. "Sorry, was I crowding you?"

Ben hated the way his cheeks were burning—and how smug she looked that she had caught him admiring her. This was not a position he was used to being in, and it set his teeth on edge.

"It's fine. You'll want to take notes on how to navigate the system until you're comfortable." When she didn't move, Ben raised an eyebrow. "So? Write this down?"

When Katie's eyes flew wide and she tried to drag her bag out from under the desk, he felt like a jerk. Ben straightened with a sigh. "Right. I was going to show you where to get supplies." Backing out of the tight space, he tipped his head toward the door. "Follow me."

At the end of a narrow hallway, Ben held open a door and waved her in.

"Thanks," she murmured and crossed the threshold. When the door closed behind them, she froze and looked around. "It's a little cramped in here, isn't it?"

"I prefer to think of it as 'cozy'." He heard her sharp intake of breath when he brushed up against her and felt the electricity spread over his own skin from the contact. It chased up his arm to his brain in a split second, making it hard to think clearly. How had he forgotten how small this closet was? And what made him think bringing her here was a good idea?

Ben started pulling things off the shelves, reaching over her head and around her, standing so close he was sure he could hear her racing heart. It took a second for him to realize it was his own heart making so much noise, and it was galloping along at an alarming rate. The crowded space suddenly felt like a sauna, making it hard to breathe. When he saw the beads of sweat forming along the curve of Parker's neck, he had to fight the urge to follow their track with his fingertips.

"What do you think you're doing?" She crossed her arms and glared up at him.

Ben focused on Parker's face, hoping his expression was calm and neutral while he grabbed random things from the shelves around her without looking. He noticed that she kept licking her lips and looking at his, and it dawned on him that she was just as affected as he was. The corner of his mouth lifted which only seemed to incense her.

"Are you trying to intimidate me because I didn't fall all over you at the bar?"

"What?" Ben snorted. "Don't flatter yourself."

But he wasn't entirely sure that wasn't the truth behind this little exercise. There was a part of him that desperately needed her to want him. Was it strictly his ego making him behave this way? Or was it that he felt disoriented around her, fascinated by her, and it was crucial that she feel the same way around him?

He went back to gathering supplies, tossing them into a box by the door. Snatching it from the floor, he thrust it into her arms. "I don't know what men you're used to dealing with, but some of us *can* resist you." Ben held the door open, forcing her to squeeze past, dangerously close to him.

He watched her walk down the hall with the box in her arms and as soon as she was out of sight he fell back against the wall. What the hell was he getting himself into?

———

Her heart was beating so hard she could feel it from her fingertips all the way to her toes. The box shook in her hands as she slid it onto her desk and dropped into her chair. Her knees were weak, and her mouth was dry; what in the world was he trying to do? And why the hell did she let him affect her like that? She needed to get it together.

Blowing out a slow, cleansing breath, she started sifting

through the box. Soon her drawer was filled with paper clips and fasteners, highlighters, and yellow legal pads. She frowned when she reached the final items, however. Lying at the bottom was an assortment of bizarre articles: a paperweight shaped like a frog, a desk calendar of kittens and motivational sayings, a banana stress ball, and a roll of 'Great Job' stickers.

"What in the world?" she mumbled. She shook her head and grinned. Maybe she wasn't the only one thrown off her game.

"Ready to get started?" Ben rolled his chair close to her desk and settled back with his hands clasped behind his head. Equally irritated and intrigued by how cool he seemed toward her, she didn't trust herself to speak, so gave him a quick nod.

"You'll get a lot of emails that don't pertain to you, so I'd recommend flagging them right away." He pointed at the screen with a smirk. "For some reason, the Press Floor copies everyone in on their messages. If you'd like to spare yourself an unending stream of groaner dad jokes, I'd flag them now."

She had no trouble navigating the basic programs as she'd worked in most of them before. But when they got to the time-tracking system, Katie faltered.

"God, I'm sorry," she groaned, dragging her hands down her face. "I know it isn't difficult, and I should be smart enough to figure this out."

"Don't beat yourself up, Parker." Ben waved a hand in the air. "This is not the most user-friendly program out there, and you've been in it for all of twenty minutes. Cut yourself some slack. You're doing great."

When he smiled, a tingling warmth spread through her chest. *Keep it together, Katie,* she scolded herself. *You know better.*

"Thanks. What kinds of services will we be offering the clients?"

"Pretty much everything: design, content writing, websites."

Katie rubbed her hands together. "Now, you're talking. I may be clumsy in this program, but I'm a virtuoso in design software."

"Oh?" Ben regarded her with raised eyebrows for a moment, then rolled his chair back and crossed his arms. "Let's see what you've got, hotshot."

He laid out challenges for her in a variety of applications, testing her knowledge, and Katie enjoyed it more than she expected. From copy edits in Microsoft Word to graphics updates in a variety of Adobe suite applications, each challenge was more involved than the last. He quizzed her on creating website widgets, building social media slide shows, and interactive contact forms. She felt a smug satisfaction when she checked the final item from the list, asking, "Do you want this video rendered for web or 4K broadcast?"

"Color me impressed, Parker," he mumbled, shaking his head. "You certainly know what you're doing. Glad to have you aboard."

The little bit of praise made her glow. "Thanks." Her stomach growled, and Ben smirked even as she stared at him, wide-eyed and appalled.

"You're right. It's time for lunch. Thanks for the reminder." He rolled his chair back to his desk. "See you back here in an hour."

While she was disappointed that Ben didn't invite her to have lunch with him, she was also relieved. Katie wasn't quite ready to venture out into town, even if she wasn't alone. Instead, she'd brought some leftover pizza from home, perfectly content to tuck herself into the corner of the breakroom and simply observe. Even the thought of being out in public with a group of strangers, well-meaning as they were, brought the familiar panic back to the surface, making her nauseated.

It won't always be like this, she reasoned. Once she was settled, once she knew her way around better, once she was no longer looking over her shoulder for the boogeyman, she could spend more time making friends.

At least that's what she told herself.

When she returned to her desk, Ben was leaning back in his chair, tossing a blue racquetball while he seemingly contemplated the ceiling. She peered around the edge of her cubicle, watching. What made him tick? At the bar, he came off as pompous and conceited, apparently not used to hearing *no*. From Dixie's description, Ben was a hard worker, brilliant and driven, and painfully independent. The time they'd spent together that morning told her he was funny and patient—nothing like her initial impression of him. These conflicting glimpses of his personality only had Katie more intrigued.

He was engrossed in the ball's progress, chewing his bottom lip. Staring at his mouth, she caught herself wondering if his lips were soft, if he sang along with the radio, what his favorite food was, and if he snored.

Suddenly, she realized Ben was looking directly at her. His eyebrows were arched, and his arms crossed, while the corner of that mesmerizing mouth lifted. "Something you want, Parker?"

She blushed at his teasing implication and cleared her throat. "Just wondering what you're working on. Maybe I can help."

Ben shrugged and pushed out of his chair. "I suppose I can show you what I've got in the works." He led her to a large cork board with papers tacked up haphazardly and waved an arm. "It's all right here."

Walking her through all the clients, Ben explained each business, which ones had transitioned into full marketing portfolios, and who he was still trying to get on board. He showed Katie the editorial calendars he had put together, the designs he had created, and every campaign he had built from the ground up. As he talked, she watched his eyes light up.

Excitement and pride tinged his voice as he moved from client to client, genuine enthusiasm in every word.

With each detail he shared, Katie was more impressed by what he had accomplished. The things he had put in motion would have taken three departments at Barnaby Marketing—which the client paid for dearly.

"You did all of this alone?"

Ben shrugged. "I put together a template of sorts with the first job and tailored it to fit everyone after. It wasn't a lot at the beginning, but gradually my hours got longer, and the deadlines got pushed further out." He sighed then glanced at Katie from the corner of his eye. "I mean, it's fine. I love the work, but it may be good to have another set of hands."

Reading different papers on the wall, lifting some to see what was on the paper underneath, Ben nodded to himself then motioned for Katie to follow him back to their desks. He rifled through some files and held one out to her.

"Can you go through these notes and create a spreadsheet? We need to see at a glance each company name, the main contact, phone, and email, what their business does and what marketing, if anything, we've done for them."

She frowned at the papers in her hands. But before she got upset, she reminded herself that it was her first day and someone had to do the drudgery. "Sure. Let me know if there's anything else I can help you with."

FOUR

Ben tried to keep his eyes on his work, but the woman on the other side of the room kept drawing his attention. He hadn't expected to see her again so soon, and certainly not in his office first thing on a Monday. Not that he was complaining.

It had been hard to hide his surprise when she ambushed him that morning and even harder to keep from showing her how glad he was to have her there.

The gods were definitely smiling on him. Either that or playing a cruel joke.

Dixie said she was looking to hire someone, so that was no shock. But why did it have to be Katie Parker? Why couldn't it have been some paunchy, balding old man who would eat lunch at his desk and complain about his bunions?

Ben stole another peek at his new distraction, sitting rod-straight in her chair, not a hair out of place, her clothes impeccable. She was lost in the task at hand, the tip of her tongue pressed to her upper lip in concentration.

Jesus. What was he going to do?

Parker was not the type of woman he was generally attracted to. Any given weekend, Ben could be found at

Maxie's telling lame jokes to a giggly blonde and impressing her with stories of his old life in Boston. It never took much to get and keep their interest. He didn't suggest after-hours dalliances, but he also wasn't one to turn down an invitation. It worked out well because they both knew what the encounter was: a distraction and a bit of fun, no strings attached.

"Something you want, Collins?"

Parker's voice jolted Ben out of his reverie, and he realized he wasn't peeking anymore. He was flat-out staring. And the way she threw his own teasing words back at him set the tips of his ears on fire.

Well played.

"Nope. Just wondering how things are going over there. Any questions?" He saw her eyebrows dip for a fraction of a second, but her smile stayed in place. There was no way she bought that.

When she turned back to her work, he stood at the corkboard, breathing deeply to stop his heart from racing the way it was. If his back was to her, he couldn't stare, right? Ben took some papers off the board and pretended to read them.

His mind wandered over the course of the day, recalling every interaction, every time he brushed up against her. Like when he chased her out of the supply closet: he hadn't meant to pin her against the shelves. In his defense, it was a tiny space. Smiling to himself, he pictured the defiant glint in her striking blue eyes as she refused to let him fluster her. Ben had never been one to back down from a challenge, and Parker was definitely a challenge.

He turned slightly, keeping his head down to appear engrossed in whatever was in his hands. Parker was no longer typing but reached her hands in the air, her head tipped back with her eyes closed as she stretched. The innocent movement had him thinking some very devilish thoughts about the way her arched back pulled her blouse tight against her delicious curves. Then she smoothed her already-neat hair and ran her fingers through her ponytail. He was spellbound.

With a shake of his head, he turned his back to her. No. She was off limits. Romance wasn't something he did anymore, and sex with coworkers was always a bad idea. He'd stick with the shallow hook-ups that didn't involve putting his heart on the line. It would be better for everyone involved if he kept his distance and ignored his attraction to Parker. Stabbing the papers back in place on the board, he frowned.

That might be easier said than done.

———

Katie scowled at her monitor. It was the end of the day, at the end of her first week, and all Ben had been letting her do was data entry and filing. It frustrated her.

The mess on the corkboard told her there was plenty of creative work to do. Ben was following up on leads every day, and she could hear him promising clients that he'd start working up promotions or campaigns as soon as possible. And yet, day after day, he was handing her busy work and then ignoring her.

"Hey, we're still on for drinks tonight, right?"

Thankful for the distraction, Katie turned her attention to the athletic blonde who had just perched on the edge of her desk. "You bet we are." Patsy Ryan had taken on the role of Katie's friend almost as soon as they met. She was loud and fun, and to be honest, Katie wasn't sure she had a choice in the matter of their friendship.

Patsy leaned in and lowered her voice. "They hired some new blood over at MachineWorks, and I heard a rumor they might be at Maxie's tonight." She rubbed her hands together. "I think we need to be there to give them a real friendly welcome."

Laughing as Patsy went back to the production floor, Katie

was glad to have her around. She said what she thought, never mincing words, and had a deep repertoire of colorful phrases. Thanks to her, Katie felt at ease in no time, even if her work so far was less than fulfilling.

After Patsy's departure, Dixie appeared at Katie's desk. "How's the first week going? Settling in all right?"

Ben called out from near the corkboard. "It's going great. She's doing good work, and everything is running smoothly."

"Thanks for your input, Mr. Collins, but I was asking Katie. Looking at your project board, you could give her a new job every day for a month and still not catch up." She smiled at Katie. "That's a good problem to have, though."

With a snort, Ben grabbed his coffee mug and strolled out of the room.

Dixie turned her full attention to Katie and raised her eyebrows. "So? How do you think it's going? Ben literally could be on fire, and he'd tell me everything was fine."

Katie laughed at that image. "That sounds familiar. Maybe Ben and I have more in common than I thought." At Dixie's knowing smile, Katie blushed, then cleared her throat and showed her scribbled notes. "He was very thorough in walking me through the system, giving me background on the clients. I'm impressed with the amount of work he's done alone."

Dixie nodded. "Ben doesn't give himself enough credit, and he sure won't accept any praise. How are you two coming on the Green's Spices marketing plan?"

Frowning, Katie tried to remember if that was one of the clients on her spreadsheet. "Oh, um… I'm not sure I'm familiar with Green's. I've been working on filing and building spreadsheets to organize all the client information." Dixie shook her head, trying to hide a smile, and Katie's heart sank. "What?"

At that moment, Ben sauntered into the office, stopping

mid-stride when both women turned their attention to him. "Uh-oh. I don't like that look. What's going on?"

"Correct me if I'm wrong, Mr. Collins, but weren't you supposed to bring Katie in on the Green's Spices account?" Dixie crossed her arms and waited.

"Right. Well, I, uh, didn't think you'd want to jump straight into such a big undertaking your first week, and so I was giving you time to…acclimate yourself, first. Don't worry, Dixie, I've got a good start on it." He wouldn't look Katie in the eye, instead occupying himself with the files on his desk.

"Thank you so much for your consideration." Katie heard the sarcasm dripping from her own voice, so she clasped her hands in her lap and shut her mouth before she said something she couldn't take back.

"You need to put that plan together next week. Drop it for today—it's late, and I want you both to get the hell out of here." Ben was on the receiving end of a very pointed look as Dixie walked out. "That means you, too, Collins. Go. Home."

———

Katie slammed into the kitchen, startling Nick.

"Jesus. Trying to give me a heart attack?" He nearly dropped the apple he'd been eating but, after scrutinizing his little sister, took on a softer tone. "Wanna talk about it?"

Katie plopped onto one of the barstools, folding in half to press her cheek to the cool countertop. "No." She raised her eyes. "Yes."

The words spilled out in a rush. Katie described the last few days, about how she had seen a hint of humanity in Ben that first day and how excited she had been to get back into doing marketing work.

"Apparently, we were supposed to be working up a plan all week, but he gave me busy work to keep me out of the way while he worked on it alone. I haven't even been given a chance to prove myself, and I'm being handled. What an asshole."

Nick picked at the label on his beer bottle as he listened to her rant. When she finished, he cleared his throat. "Katie. I've known Ben for a while now, and he's a good guy, no matter how hard he tries to hide it." He held up a hand when she tried to contradict him. "I'm not saying what he did wasn't shitty—it was—but I doubt it was malicious."

"Well, then either he thinks I'm incompetent, or he doesn't want to share his toys. Regardless, I'm tempted to knock that smile off his pretty face."

Nick nearly choked on his beer.

"What? What's so funny?" Katie demanded.

Nick shook his head. "Jesus, Kat. How is the sexual tension at this level already? I mean, you guys barely know each other."

"Don't be ridiculous." But Katie's cheeks burned at the accusation. Ben was attractive, she wouldn't deny that. And he occupied her thoughts far more than any of her other coworkers. But that didn't mean she wanted to sleep with him, did it? When his crooked grin and flashing green eyes popped into her mind once again, she took a drink and fumed. "He dislikes me for whatever reason, and I think he's a jerk. I mean, why would he do that? I'm capable of doing the work, and I'm good at what I do."

Nick squeezed Katie's shoulder. "Try not to let him get to you. Call him out on his shit and make him give you legitimate work. He'll learn quick enough that he has no idea who he's messing with."

FIVE

Monday morning, Katie arrived an hour earlier than usual. As she had hoped, Ben was already at the corkboard.

"Good morning," she called.

Ben turned, a wicked smile creeping across his face. "So, you came back."

She stared him down with her arms crossed. "You can't scare me off that easily. I'm here to do a job, and I will do that job." Katie unbuttoned her blazer and turned to the mess on the wall. "Now. Let's see if we can make some sense of this nightmare. Then we can attack each campaign, in order, with a plan."

She tried to remove a few pages, but Ben slapped his hand over them. "This wall makes perfect sense, and I don't need you screwing with it. I have everything right where I want it. I'll let you know when—and if—I need your help."

Refusing to back down, Katie held his gaze with a sweet smile, pulling the papers out from under his palm. "Obviously, Dixie thinks I can improve things, or she wouldn't have hired me. You don't have everything under control, as evidenced by the hodge-podge of crap pinned here. I can have this organized in a couple hours, so it makes sense to rational people, not only you."

Ben's smile twisted into a frown. Katie brushed her bangs out of her eyes and cocked her head, all humor gone. "I can always wait until you leave the room."

He sized her up, eyes narrowed, weighing his options. "You wouldn't dare."

She leaned in. "Are you sure about that?"

After a moment's pause, he snarled, "Fine." Ben slumped at his desk, his back to the wall—and to Katie.

A couple hours later, he turned back to her from his work. "How's it going?"

"Why don't you take a look."

When Ben looked over the corkboard, his mouth dropped open. His shock both irritated and thrilled her; on one hand, he hadn't thought she could do it. On the other, though, she'd managed to stun him speechless.

Katie would take that win.

She'd organized the papers into multiple columns, each one identified by the client's name with the editorial calendar pinned at the top. Below that was the information on their respective projects, starting with the most recent.

Ben walked along the wall, nodding his head in approval. He took a few steps backward, hands on his hips, and stared at it long enough to make Katie nervous.

"Well?"

He sighed dramatically, rolling his eyes. "It's amazing." He turned to Katie and shrugged. "I'm impressed. Thanks, Parker."

"You're welcome." Katie smirked. "Was that painful? Are you okay? Maybe you should lie down."

"You're going to rub this in, aren't you?"

"Oh, yes. Every chance I get." She laughed. "Come on, don't pout. Let me buy you lunch."

Ben held the door for her. "After you."

The two walked along the city square to where a couple of food trucks served a growing crowd of people. Katie bought them each a sandwich, and they found a bench in the park across the street.

"So, you were at Barnaby Marketing when you were in San Francisco?" When Katie nodded, Ben added, "That's impressive. How was it?"

She chewed while she thought about how best to word an answer. "It was not the right place for me. Don't get me wrong, I enjoyed the work, and they are certainly a prestigious firm that looks great on a resume. It's just…" Her time there was a sensitive subject. It wasn't as simple as talking about an ex-employer. Her reasons for leaving went well beyond dissatisfaction with her pay. Attempting to change the subject, she blurted, "Tell me about you. Did you come to Dixie Printing with a plan to start a marketing department?"

"Oh no, not at all," he scoffed. "I had just moved to Enderlin and was working as an account manager, trying to keep clients happy and grow the bottom line. One day, I made an offhand remark about how the client could extend their reach and bring in more business by adopting a few simple techniques. They loved the idea, Dixie saw the potential, and here we are a year or so later. It was all a happy accident but well worth it. I mean," he paused, peeking at her with a roguish smile. "It drew *you* here, didn't it?"

His comment surprised and confused her. Before today, he had seemed largely uninterested in her presence. Was he throwing her a pickup line? Their eyes met briefly before she looked away, trying to hide the blush that crept into her cheeks.

Maybe there was more to Ben Collins than charm and a devastating smile. One thing was clear: Katie was in trouble.

SIX

At her brother's urging, Katie signed up for a self-defense class in a nearby town. She had envisioned lots of yelling and punching and flipping willing male assistants to the ground. Instead, this course took a new approach called 'empowerment self-defense' that blended traditional with verbal moves.

"I'm not saying we won't be teaching you the best way to knee an attacker in the groin." The instructor, Carly, shrugged. "Because we most definitely will be teaching you the best way to knee an attacker in the groin." There was a smattering of nervous laughter before the room turned serious again. "Non-fatal violent attacks are perpetrated by strangers in only thirty-eight percent of cases. In seventy percent of homicides, however, the victim knew and trusted her or his killer. That's why we are here to empower you to recognize, defuse, and escape dangerous situations."

Katie was able to lose herself in the class and reclaim a sense of control she'd been missing for quite a while. Carrying pepper spray was all well and good, but the role-playing they did to practice defusing a situation was even more valuable to her, and she couldn't help thinking that these skills might have helped in her volatile relationship with Derek.

Nick insisted on taking her to and from class, and the drive home was always hard for her. Knowing that her life was at stake took a toll on Katie, and during that ride, her mind plunged into what-if scenarios. No matter how hard she tried, she couldn't keep from imagining the myriad ways her stalker might come after her—and wondering if she'd be able to escape when he did.

"You're quiet." Nick's voice jolted her out of her thoughts. "What's on your mind?"

"Nothing, I'm just wiped out." She knew better than to talk to Nick about her anxiety. If he knew how worried she was, he would insist on following her everywhere, neglecting his own life to act as bodyguard for her. He had a hard time turning off his inherent Big Brother setting. No, it was better to wallow alone in her worst fears, without dragging him into them.

The tires on the road were the only sound for a few minutes, then Nick cleared his throat. "Have you heard anything from San Francisco?"

Fiddling with the zipper on her hoodie, Katie shook her head. "No. Nothing. Do you think it *could* be Derek? I mean, he was livid when I ended things."

"I don't know. You were getting letters way before you met him, right? Seems pretty unlikely."

"You're right. I know you're right, but the thought that it could be anyone and I'd never see him coming is horrifying." Just talking about the uncertainty of it all made Katie's stomach churn, and she squeezed her hands together to keep them from shaking. "The whole idea that someone I may or may not have even met thinks they know me and feels a sense of ownership over me makes me want to throw up. At least if it was Derek, I'd know what to expect."

The violence of their last encounter was etched into her mind like it had happened yesterday. She'd finally had enough and told him she was no longer going to allow him to use her, manipulate her, and ride her hard work to advance his career. Everything had gone wrong from that point forward. After slamming her against the wall and choking her, he'd sworn that they weren't over until he said they were. Her hand fluttered against her neck, the memory as vivid as ever.

Pulling into the driveway, Nick turned off the truck and shook his head. "I know blaming Derek would make things easier, but it just doesn't make sense, Kat. Why don't you call out to San Francisco tomorrow and see where they are in the investigation there—if there's any new information?"

"What good will that do?" She dragged a hand through her hair. "I'm completely at His mercy, peering around every corner and constantly looking over my shoulder." She slid out of the truck but paused with her hand on the door. "And I don't know if I can take another conversation that ends with the police unable to do anything. I just can't."

Without another word, Katie shut the door and trudged into the house, swiping at the angry tears she couldn't fight.

———

"Hey, Parker. How's Whipson Mill coming? Got anything to show me yet?" Ben perched on the edge of her desk and crossed his arms.

"As a matter of fact, I do." He had asked her to create a full marketing plan for a local organic farm with a small budget, worlds away from the accounts she'd worked on at Barnaby, but she'd put a lot of effort into this client and was proud of her work.

She clicked around on her desktop and pulled up a few files. "So, Whipson is small but local, which works in their favor. The demand for organic produce and milled, non-processed flour is booming. Here's what I have so far."

A design in greens and browns filled her screen, the main

image a stylized wheat sheaf next to the name of the farm. "I wanted to stay with the small-town feel for the logo. The colors are understated and earthy and will look equally great on print collateral and their digital presence."

Ben shifted and leaned over her shoulder, one hand braced on the desk. Katie waited for him to say something, but when he didn't, she moved on to the website design.

"I didn't build it all the way out, but this is the basic format that will work best for them." He seemed so engrossed in her screen she sat up straighter, confident that he would love this as much as she did. "The homepage will highlight their weekly newsletter and any other announcements or articles they want to share. We can set up static widgets along the side for their address, hours, contact information. The menu along the top will navigate to their 'about' page, their online store, their archive of stories. I'd also like to help them build an email list so they can keep in touch with customers through a monthly email blast."

Examining the screen, Ben rubbed his chin, and Katie waited. With every passing minute that he said nothing, her confidence ebbed. The silence hung between them, raising her anxiety until she couldn't take it any longer.

"Well? What do you think?"

He frowned at the screen, his arms crossed. "I think the site's too busy, and the logo is boring. The client will hate this."

Katie was too stunned to speak at first, her cheeks heating up.

Then a small fire built in her chest, and she rose from her chair to look Ben in the eye. "I disagree. Customers looking for pure, homegrown products won't trust anything flashy or corporate-looking. Earthy and understated gives off a small-town feeling, a sense of trustworthiness, as though Whipson was the neighbor the customer has known all their life."

He narrowed his eyes. "You don't think it would be better to show them something that will jump off the page?"

"Absolutely not. If we were promoting a Vegas show, maybe, but not a family-run farm. People want to feel like they know where their food is coming from without putting in the work to grow it themselves."

With a grunt, Ben leaned toward the screen again. "Why would they do a weekly newsletter? Who will read that? I can't think of anyone who would sign up for a farm's email list, either. What would they even put in it?"

She took a deep breath and counted to three. What the hell was he playing at?

"Sales on products, what crops are in or will be in soon, the benefits of organic, details of their milling process, whatever." Katie waved her hands as she spoke. "We can leave that up to them since they're the experts. Our job is to equip them with the tools to communicate their goods and services."

He scratched at his beard but didn't reply, only continued to scrutinize her website design. Katie knew the work was good. She knew the client would understand what she was presenting. What she didn't know was what was going on in Ben's head.

"Why are you fighting me on this? You asked me to come up with a design and a plan. I am giving you a damn good one, and you know it. So why the pushback?"

The corner of Ben's mouth twitched, and he turned to face her. There was a glint in his eye that Katie hadn't noticed before, and seeing it now sent the fire in her chest into a full-on inferno.

"Are you serious? You were just messing with me?" Her hands squeezed into fists at her sides, and she was overcome with the urge to punch him.

"Come on, Parker, don't get upset. The design is brilliant, and the website is exactly what they need." He turned his back and returned to his own desk. "I was making sure you were confident about your work, that you could back it up in case the client wants clarification. You are, and you did. Great job."

Narrowing her eyes, she dropped into her chair. "I *am* confident about my work, and I don't need you to validate that I know what I'm doing."

"Okay," he answered without looking up from his desk. "But you sure seemed to need my approval, judging by the way you jumped down my throat to get it."

"I did not jump down your throat."

"If you say so." He shrugged, then crossed to her desk and leaned in close while she fumed. "But you really get worked up *not* fighting for validation. It's kind of hot."

Katie gaped as Ben strolled away, her brain scrambling for a withering reply. Before she could come up with anything, he was gone.

SEVEN

In an attempt at normalcy, Wednesday night Happy Hour at Maxie's had become a ritual for Katie and Patsy. With Nick busy running his business and their parents still traveling, it was a welcome distraction. It allowed Katie the luxury of letting down her guard, even if only a tiny bit, and only for one night.

She was trying so hard to relax but there was nowhere for her to stand that didn't leave her feeling exposed. Even if she stood with one of the wide wooden pillars behind her, she couldn't stop craning her neck to look around the room. It didn't seem like Patsy had noticed her fidgety hands or her inability to stand still, and Katie was relieved. While she liked Patsy and enjoyed spending time with her, she didn't feel close enough to talk to her about the situation.

A glass shattered behind the bar and Katie nearly jumped out of her skin. Crossing her arms tight over her stomach, she blew out several slow breaths. Everyone else was laughing and cheering, shouting things like, "Way to go, butterfingers!" Katie, on the other hand, was trying not to throw up.

It had been far too long since the last contact with her stalker. Instead of easing her mind, though, it only amped up her fear exponentially. Every face obscured by a baseball cap, every shadow darting by in the corner of her eye threatened to send her into a full-on panic. The other shoe was going to drop soon: she was sure of it. And that dread kept her in a constant state of fight or flight.

No one should have to live like that.

Patsy was preaching about the lack of musical intelligence in Enderlin, while Katie laughed and chalked her pool cue. Suddenly the skin on the back of her neck prickled, that innate warning of danger. Moving around the table, she whipped her head over each shoulder. She scanned the room, looking for anything that seemed out of place, but it all looked exactly the same as it did just a minute ago. That didn't dissipate the icy chill that had settled in her bones and kept her on alert.

"It's your shot." Patsy smiled with eyebrows raised. "Dragging it out isn't going to help you win, you know."

Katie rubbed at the goosebumps, trying to dispel the premonition of danger shrouding her, and shook her head. He would find her, might already be here, in this room. She couldn't breathe, her thoughts swirling a hundred miles an hour. Could she run? Fight him off? He was going to hurt her, here and now. In the middle of a crowded bar, He was finally going to make His move, and no one would be able to save her.

Although fear ruled her thoughts in that moment, she kept it hidden, giving no outward appearance of discomfort. Instead, she smiled and rolled her eyes at her friend.

"Yeah, yeah. Don't get ahead of yourself." She bent over the table, lining up the perfect shot to bring Patsy down a peg or two.

Before she could pull it off, a deep voice right next to her made her jump. "Did you miss me?"

All the blood in her body was suddenly replaced by ice water.

Spinning around, brandishing the cue to defend her life,

she found herself looking into a pair of familiar green eyes. "Ben?"

"Whoa, Parker." With one hand, he eased her weapon to the side, so it was no longer pointing at his face. "Go easy with that thing. You almost took out my eye."

"Jesus," she exhaled, her hand on her racing heart. "You can't just sneak up on people like that. What the hell are you doing here?"

Ben waved at Patsy, who was watching the exchange with great interest. "Free country. Public place." He held up his half-full glass with a flourish. "Beer."

When she gaped at him, he cleared his throat and shifted his weight. "Look, I'm sorry about the other day. I shouldn't have given you such a hard time. Truce?"

Raising her eyebrows without responding, she waited. He was squirming, and she had to admit it was quite satisfying.

"Come on, Parker, let me at least buy you a drink to make up for it."

He seemed sincere enough, and Katie was drawn in by his playful smirk. "Fine." She crossed her arms. "But you better open a tab because one won't cut it."

Patsy pulled Ben into the pool rotation, challenging him to a new game when he returned with a fresh round. Katie hung back, watching him. Every few minutes, a different woman would stop by the table to talk to Ben. Each one had a different move, but each one was very clearly flirting with him. A hand on the arm, a hair flip, batting eyelashes, and suggestive winks were all part of the parade of admirers. While he returned some of the flirtatious banter, his gaze sought Katie's every time he looked up. The thrill that ran through her when their eyes met wasn't unwelcome, and she couldn't stop staring.

"Come on, Parker. You're up. It's your turn to lose to me."

Katie drained her glass and scoffed. "Ben Collins, you just signed your own death warrant. Stand back and let me show you how it's done."

With a bow, he stepped away, and she set up the table. Pulling the triangle off the wall, she spun it around her finger and cocked her hip. "Still want to show me the trick to a perfect break?"

"Well, well," he drawled. "This is an interesting new version of you, Parker." He leaned his elbow on the high-top table, and she felt her cheeks redden at the heat in his eyes.

"What do you mean?"

He tilted his head as he moved closer. "You know—relaxed, funny, a little less uptight. I like it."

Before she could answer, Patsy interrupted. "Katie, it's your turn for drinks."

"I know, I know. I'm on it." Turning toward the bar, she stopped and pointed at Ben. "I'm getting our next round—you want something?"

Ben narrowed his eyes. "You're buying me a drink?"

"Yes? Is there something wrong with that?"

"Nope. But women like you rarely have to pay for drinks."

Katie frowned as Ben followed her toward the bar. "What do you mean, 'women like me'?"

"Oh, come off it, Parker." Ben sighed. "In every bar, in every city, beautiful women don't have to pay for their own drinks, let alone buy a round for anyone else."

Waiting for her turn to order, Katie's face split into a broad smile. "Did you just call me beautiful?"

"What? No."

She laughed at his immediate discomfort. "Yes. You did." Ben blushed as he helped her carry the drinks back to the table, and Katie had to fight not to wrap her arms around him. He seemed so sweet, and she suddenly wanted him to hold her hand and walk her home.

"I want to make a toast," shouted Patsy, holding her glass high above the table. "To the things that really matter—making friends, falling in love—that happen when we aren't even looking. May we never miss out on them."

"Hear, hear." Ben smiled at Katie, making her heart thump out of rhythm. Then he turned a bright smile to Patsy and clinked glasses with her. "To the moments that matter."

After another close match, Patsy suddenly downed her whole beer in one gulp, wiping her mouth with the back of her hand. She locked her eyes on a target across the bar and fluffed her hair. "Oh shit. I think I see my destiny over at the dartboards." She wiggled her eyebrows at Katie and smirked. "Don't wait up, darlin'."

Panic rumbled in Katie's gut, and she contemplated stopping her friend, begging her not to leave. The two usually shared a cab home, and Katie was terrified at the idea of going alone. It was late, and she knew Nick would already be asleep, so she hesitated to call him to come get her. Quickly scanning the faces around the bar, she searched for someone, *anyone* she'd feel comfortable asking for a ride.

Her gaze landed on Ben. Maybe she could ask him? She chewed her bottom lip, trying to determine the possible fallout from this. There were a lot of people from work here, and there would definitely be gossip tomorrow if anyone saw them leave together. Would she be giving Ben the wrong idea if she asked him to take her home?

In the moment, she almost didn't care.

Katie pressed her lips together and took a deep breath; she had a decision to make. Should she leave herself open to Him, her unidentified stalker, by taking a cab alone? Or could she find another way?

She looked at Ben again, finishing his beer on the other side of the table. They'd had a lot of fun tonight and worked well together all week. Rubbing the back of her neck where she still felt the weight of invisible eyes she nudged him. "Still up for that round of pool, just you and me? I owe you an ass-whoopin' from the night we met."

Ben lifted his bottle and peered at her with curious eyes. His mouth opened like he wanted to say something, and Katie felt a glimmer of hope. But then he looked at his watch and frowned. "Sorry, Parker, I can't. I'd better get going."

"Oh, sure." The butterflies in her stomach went into overdrive, panic surging through her veins. She had to do something, had to *say* something or she'd lose her chance. "So— want to share a cab home?"

Ben's head whipped in her direction, then he took a step closer, placing his hand on her arm. "Parker, I—"

"Ben." A dignified redhead with an elegant straight bob and bright ruby lipstick called his name across the room. She stood out from the rest of the patrons in a designer business suit and sky-high stilettos, manicured nails drumming an impatient rhythm on the bar.

Ben waved at her, flashing a quick smile. "I'll be right there."

With a jolt of disappointment she hadn't been expecting, Katie backed away, nearly knocking over the table behind her when she turned.

"Parker, wait a second." Ben reached for Katie's arm as she hustled around, putting away chalk and pool cues, deftly avoiding his touch.

"No, no, it's all right. You have other plans. Go have fun. Don't worry about me." Katie knew she was talking way too fast, but she was ashamed for hoping Ben was interested in her. And she'd melt into the floor from embarrassment if he knew how much it hurt that he wasn't.

"Parker." Ben blocked her path, forcing her to stop moving. Reluctantly, she tilted her head to meet his eyes.

Katie smiled and waved him away. "It's fine. I'll be fine."

Ben stared at her for a moment, glancing at the woman waiting for him at the bar. He looked like he wanted to say something more, but instead, he raked his fingers through his dark hair and shook his head. "Thanks for the beer."

"No problem. Anytime."

He gave her one last, long glance over his shoulder. "I just might hold you to that, Parker."

Once he was out of sight, her shoulders slumped. All night he'd been turning down propositions from the women in the bar, and Katie thought it had something to do with her. Instead, he was just wasting time until his date arrived. How had she misread the situation so completely? She looked down at her jeans and flannel shirt and laughed. At least now she knew what attracted him—and it wasn't her.

EIGHT

The next morning, Ben yanked up his jeans then dropped onto the edge of the bed. This was all wrong.

"Are you even listening to me?" Elizabeth shrugged on the jacket of her suit and smoothed her sleek red bob. Reluctantly, Ben looked up. "Darling, I really don't know where your head is these days. I was telling you my parents will be in Iowa next weekend for some charity or other, and they've invited us to have dinner with them."

Stalking across the room, he shook his head. "That will be a hard pass, thanks. Don't they realize that we've been broken up for nearly two years?"

"Oh, we have, have we?" She slid her arms around his waist from behind, pressing a kiss to his neck. "It seems that last night would contradict that statement."

"Stop it." Ben shrugged out of her embrace and stared at his face in the mirror. What the hell was he doing? "This ends. Now."

Elizabeth's haughty laugh filled the room. "Yes, so you said the last time I was here. And the time before that, and the time before that. But somehow, we always seem to fall back into each other's arms, don't we?"

Ben shook his head as he watched her glide around the room, checking her phone. He sipped his coffee and wondered why he was still letting her into his life. He and Elizabeth had a long history, and she was beautiful, he couldn't deny that. But her type of beauty was only skin-deep. She was cold and manipulative, only thinking about what she wanted without caring who she hurt in the process. Over time he'd learned that old habits die hard, and he couldn't shake her. Every time she flew in from Boston and showed up at his door, he let himself think she'd miraculously changed. Inevitably, every morning after, he remembered who she really was, and the destructive cycle of self-loathing started all over again.

"You should be going."

"Really, Ben, is that any way to treat your fiancée?"

"Ex-fiancée," he snarled. "Just because we sleep together sometimes, it doesn't mean there is anything more than sex between us. Not anymore." Ben stared at her, and a bone-deep exhaustion washed over him. He sighed. "Why are you here, Elizabeth? I mean, besides the obvious. Why do you keep flying into this little town where there is nothing for you?"

"Did it ever occur to you that I miss you?"

"No." The answer popped out of his mouth without a thought.

Narrowing her eyes, she sighed. "Will you just come back to Boston with me? You've been fooling around out here in the sticks for far too long, and I despise flying out here just to see you. And I do miss you, for what it's worth. We were good together."

Ben frowned at her gaslighting. She shouldn't be here. If there was a visual representation of 'toxic relationship,' it would look like Elizabeth Schweiger.

Snapping her compact closed with a flourish, Elizabeth slipped her purse over her arm and cocked her hip. "Fine. I'll go. My car is here anyway." Laying a hand on Ben's chest, she pressed her lips to his cheek, branding him with her bright red lipstick. "Thank you for last night. As always, you were delightful."

The door closed behind her, and Ben dropped his head into his hands. How was she able to make him feel two inches tall after all this time? And why was he letting her? He dumped out his mug and headed to the shower. No one knew about his past with Elizabeth or how he let her continue to use him, and he wanted it to stay that way. He couldn't stand the idea of his past coming out to his friends and coworkers, especially Parker.

He hadn't been able to get her out of his head since he walked into the bar the night before. With her hair loose and wild and her eyes bright, he loved watching the way she moved around the pool table; confident, unassuming, and sexy as hell. He wished with every fiber of his being that he had left with her instead of Elizabeth. Walking away from Parker last night had been harder than he expected and harder than he wanted it to be.

As her blue eyes popped into his mind, he was filled with shame. God, what would she think of him? If she knew how weak he was, knew the strength of the hold Elizabeth had on him, she'd never look at him the same again.

He slammed out the door for work, cursing Parker for getting under his skin—and cursing himself for wanting her there.

———

Walking into the office after lunch, Katie had trouble calming her churning stomach. She'd felt a real connection with Ben last night, one she'd wanted to explore, and so, it seemed, had he. Until his date had shown up, at least. In the bright light of day, Katie felt like a fool. She had completely misread the situation. Judging from the sophisticated redhead he'd left with, Katie could tell she was definitely not his type.

Her plan for the day was to play it cool, as though she hadn't entertained taking him home. The morning flew by, one or both of them busy with phone calls and meetings, no opportunity for idle conversation. But the afternoon was wide open, and the time had come to put her plan in action.

He was staring at the papers on the corkboard with his arms crossed when she walked in after lunch. He didn't acknowledge her, even when she said hello, and she worried that she'd come on too strong at the bar. But she was going to stick to the plan. So she mimicked his stance, crossing her arms and frowning, and waited for him to notice.

"Yes?"

She offered him a broad smile. "What are you contemplating so deeply? Are the answers to the meaning of life hidden on this wall somewhere?"

Laughter tugged the corner of his mouth at her glib comment, but he was all business as soon as she saw it. Ben resumed his scowl and turned his attention back to the wall in front of them.

"No. But the farmers' market season is starting, and Harvest Farms wants us to help them spread the word about their produce. I'm trying to come up with some ideas."

"Great." Katie rubbed her hands together. "Then let's brainstorm."

She grabbed a dry erase board leaning against one of the empty cubicles and pulled a marker from her drawer. "What do you have so far?"

Katie could see his lips twitching, as though he wanted to grin at her commanding behavior but wasn't ready to allow her that win.

"What do you know about Harvest Farms, city girl?"

She narrowed her eyes even as she rose to his challenge. "They're a hydroponic farm, raising tilapia and using the nutrient-rich water to feed their crops. Some of their specialties include free-range chicken and grass-fed beef, and they also sell the products of a couple of smaller dairy farms. What else do you want to know?"

Ben was motionless for several seconds, and Katie feared he was going to walk out and refuse to work with her. But then she saw the spark in his eyes before he sighed. "Fine. Let's brainstorm."

Once they got into it, the ideas flowed. Katie proposed a tagline, and Ben suggested a slight improvement. Then he came up with an idea, and she fleshed it out further. As the creativity coursed between them, Ben's sour demeanor softened, and he laughed and made jokes. She quickly forgot the misunderstanding of the night before, allowing her to enjoy the creative process.

She sat back and watched while he explained his plan. He waved his arms over the board, demonstrating the connections between different ideas. Pacing, he spoke passionately, and Katie found it hard not to get carried away by his enthusiasm.

"I love this plan." She popped out of her seat. "But there are one or two changes I'd like to make before we move forward."

He frowned at the board. "What changes? It's perfect. Maybe you don't understand the plan. Or you weren't quite listening."

"No. I heard everything you said." Katie bristled at his tone. "I just think there's a better way to do the search engine optimization."

It was Ben's turn to get his hackles up. He crossed his arms. "Oh, yeah? What's wrong with my SEO plan? It's worked for others in the past, and it'll work for this client, too."

The tension that had abated an hour ago attached itself to Katie's spine at his stubbornness. "You can't use an identical plan for a farming operation that you would use for a hair salon or a manufacturing plant. They have different target audiences with different needs and different ways of getting their information. You'll run into trouble trying to fit a square peg in a round hole just because it fit in the five other square holes before."

Ben snorted and looked over the notes once more before he pursed his lips and turned a tight expression back to Katie.

"I suppose we can try it your way, Parker," he announced. "If you screw it up, it won't cause any irreversible damage to the overall campaign." Ben looked at his watch, then strolled to his desk and started tucking papers into his briefcase. "We're done for the day. Work out your plan, and we'll talk about it tomorrow."

Katie stuck her tongue out at Ben's back as soon as he turned around. She ran her hands through her hair, attempting to throw off the irritation that had settled on her shoulders. No matter how playful and engaging he could be, his dismissive attitude was getting under her skin.

Her phone rang while she was gathering her things, and when she saw who was calling, all that tension melted away.

"Charlotte." Katie's vision blurred with tears as her best friend's smile filled the screen.

"Hello, beautiful, I miss you." Charlotte's southern drawl was more pronounced than usual in her excitement, and Katie grinned from ear to ear. "How are you, darlin'?" She stopped abruptly, her eyebrows shooting up as she focused on something over Katie's shoulder. "Aaand hello. Who do we have here?"

Whipping around, Katie found Ben straining his head over the top of her cubicle, trying to see her phone's screen. He flashed his most disarming smile, a mischievous gleam in his eye. "Hello, yourself. I'm Ben. And you are…?"

To Katie's horror, Charlotte actually giggled. "I'm Charlotte, Katie's best friend. Very nice to meet you, Ben."

Katie glared at him and turned her screen away, so he and Charlotte couldn't see each other. "Oh, hell no, stop it right now," she scolded, pointing Ben toward the door. "You need to go away."

After making sure he was gone, Katie frowned at her screen. "And you. Have you no shame? Ben is the worst."

"Oh, Katie, your face!" Charlotte dissolved into laughter. "Don't worry, that was all for your benefit—he wasn't flirting with me."

"What are you talking about?"

"Seriously? He is totally into you and was testing the waters to see what you'd do. It's a little middle school for my taste, but still kind of adorable."

"Bite your tongue." Katie rolled her eyes, but her stomach fluttered anyway. She couldn't help smiling and shook her head at the screen before she settled back in her chair. "I don't want to talk about my annoying coworker. How are you?"

Charlotte cleared her throat and wrinkled her nose. "Work is going great, but oh my god, summer break is looming on the horizon, and I can't wait. I love these tiny kindergarten monsters, but the last quarter is the worst. What about you? How are you settling in? Do you miss San Fran?"

Katie shrugged. "Yes and no. I miss you and the ocean and all the people-watching, but I love it here. Everything is so green, I've made some friends, and I get to spend time with my brother." She lowered her voice and held the phone closer. "To be honest, I love working here, and it's nowhere near as bad as it was at Barnaby. But working with Ben makes getting through each day without committing murder a challenge."

"You don't say." Charlotte smirked. "You are great at your job, Katie. I hope you're standing up for yourself."

"Oh, I am." She chuckled. "Ben pushes me to fight for what I want, and it's very satisfying when I win. Which is most of the time."

Just then, Katie's work email dinged with a new incoming message. She didn't recognize the sender's email address, but the reference line said 'PROPOSAL,' and she'd been waiting to hear back from a new client, so she clicked it open to skim the first sentence.

Run away with me. Leave everything else behind—your job, your family, that piece of trash you work with—and let's start our lives together. Once you're in my arms, you'll see how right we are for each other. But don't worry if you're still a little nervous: I'll come for you soon enough.

She felt the blood drain from her face, and her phone slipped out of her numb fingers, clattering on the desk.

"Katie? What's going on?"

But Katie couldn't make her voice work to respond. She lifted the cell and, trembling, flipped the camera toward her computer screen.

"What am I looking at?" Charlotte gasped. "No. Oh my god."

Do you know that every second I'm awake, I'm thinking of you? Hell, even when I'm not awake. You fill my dreams, too. I imagine your creamy skin under my hands, your lips against mine, and hear you uttering words of love and devotion over and over again. Knowing that it will happen—and that it will happen soon—is all that sustains me in these dark days. Stay strong, my love. I'm coming to rescue you, and then we'll never be apart again.

Silence hung in the air, and Katie realized she was holding her breath. For what, she wasn't sure, but her shaky exhale seemed as loud as a jet engine in the quiet. She was trying to make sense of the words, but her brain was buzzing with terror.

Clamping a hand over her mouth, she held back the scream that was building in her chest. She knew that if she surrendered to the fear, she'd never be able to claw her way back out of it.

"Okay, sweetie, listen to me. Call the police. They can trace the email and find out who sent it. Then call your brother and have him come wait with you. You are not to be alone right now; do you hear me?"

Smiling gratefully at her friend, Katie nodded. Then she used the office phone to call the police and her brother while Charlotte stayed on the line and kept her engaged in conversation. But Katie was only half listening.

On the surface, she smiled and replied as though her world hadn't crashed around her, but inside she was drowning. Despair settled in her chest like a lead weight, pulling her down into the truth she'd been denying since she arrived home:

Nowhere on Earth would be safe until He was dead—or she was.

NINE

Katie stared at the list in one hand and rubbed her forehead with the other. It had been a long week, and it wasn't over yet. The police were trying to track the origin of the email but hadn't had any luck yet. All day she'd been on edge, afraid to answer the phone or open any emails from addresses she didn't recognize. Throw in Ben's constant presence, popping up out of nowhere to ask a question or share an idea, and her nerves were shot.

Nick had the brilliant idea to make her go grocery shopping with him to get out of the house and pretend as though she was living a normal life.

"Oh, come on, can't we just have them delivered instead?" Katie burrowed further into the couch. "I don't really think being out in public is the best idea right now."

He took her hands and pulled her gently to her feet. "I'll be with you the whole time, you'll be safe. Just come keep your big brother company for half an hour. Forty-five minutes, tops."

She chewed her lip and tried to come up with another excuse—any excuse—not to go with him, but she came up empty. Rolling her eyes, she groaned. "Fine, I'll come. But only because you are shit at picking the good grapes."

Once inside the crowded store, Katie was torn about being there: on one hand, there were people everywhere, Nick right beside her. Her stalker wouldn't try anything with so many witnesses, would He? On the other hand, there were so many people here and faces she didn't know, she'd never see Him coming before it was too late.

"Shit, I forgot to grab the potatoes and onions and—" Nick looked around them at the steady stream of carts moving up and down the aisle. "Just stay here for a second, I'll be right back."

"Wait, Nick. I'll go with you." She tried to turn the cart to follow him but could barely move it.

Shaking his head, he was already at the end of the aisle. "With this crowd? It'll take me ten seconds, I promise."

Her brother slipped out of sight and the hair on the back of her neck stood up. She peered over her shoulder; most of these faces belonged to complete strangers. Was He there, watching her? She swallowed the hysteria trying to climb up her throat and turned back to the task at hand. Nick would be right back and the sooner they finished shopping and got home with the doors locked and the alarm set, the sooner she could breathe easy.

Caught in the flow of the grocery store traffic, she trudged along and tried to stay out of everyone's way. She rounded the corner at the end of the aisle and immediately crashed into another cart. "Shit, I'm so sorry." She looked up to see who she'd just assaulted and sighed in relief.

"Hey, Katie. You okay?" Cael Green was sliding around the carts with a sheepish expression on his face. "I wasn't looking where I was going at all."

She smiled at her former classmate and raked her fingers through her hair. "No, it's fine. I'm fine. No harm done."

"Oh, good. So, how've you been? Settling in okay? I think

you had just gotten to Enderlin the last time I saw you." He pulled his cart back and turned until he was facing the same direction she was.

"That's right, I ran into you my first night back." She pushed her cart into the next aisle and Cael strolled alongside. "You know, things are actually going well. It feels good to be back. Don't get me wrong, I loved San Francisco, but there's no place like home, right?"

"Right. Home is where the heart is."

"And will be 'til the cows come home."

"Besides, a man's home is his castle."

Katie stopped her cart and smirked at Cael. "Are we just going to trade idioms, now?"

"Nah." He leaned in and lowered his voice. "But only because I don't know any more."

Glancing at his watch, Cael let out a low whistle. "Oops, I'd better get going. But it was great running into you—literally."

"Ha, ha. Yeah, it was good to see you again."

He gave a little wave as he continued toward the checkout lanes. But before Katie could turn her attention back to her list, he called her name.

"Katie Parker. I'm at Max's for darts every Wednesday. Why don't you come by, and I can buy you a drink? We can catch up."

She shrugged, her cheeks burning at the attention from the other shoppers. "Sure, why not."

Cael's face split into a smile, and with a final wave, he disappeared around the corner and out of sight.

Katie only had a fleeting memory of spending time with him in high school. To be fair, they had graduated seven years ago. A lot happened in the time she was gone. Cael was nice and funny, and a slightly familiar face was better than none. Maybe she'd take him up on his offer.

Slipping off her shoes, Katie pulled two beers from the refrigerator while Nick grabbed the mail. She had to admit she loved the new ritual they'd set up for Friday nights. Her brother picked up a pizza, and the two shared a beer over dinner, talking about their days. It was cathartic and relaxing, and Katie felt closer to Nick than ever.

"Big something from San Francisco for you, sis." He tossed a fat, padded envelope onto the counter in front of her.

"What? I'm not expecting anything." She saw Charlotte's name and address in the corner, and Katie grabbed it. "She's such a sneak. I just talked to Char the other day, and she didn't say she sent me anything."

Katie pulled the strip on the envelope and slid out a thick stack of photographs. It seemed that Charlotte had sent her some images from their college roommate days, probably to keep her from feeling homesick. The imagery was familiar, but she was having trouble making sense of what she was seeing. Was that her on the steps of her dorm? The next few were taken on the quad when she and Charlotte were out sunbathing, but why were they so grainy and far away? Her mind cast around for an explanation; were these from the yearbook or the campus paper? No, they would have gotten permission first. With each photo her nausea built until she felt the bile scorching her throat. She flipped through them one after another, shaking her head in denial. The room started to spin. Nick must have noticed the change in her because he sprinted across the room.

"Hey, what's wrong?"

Unable to make her mouth work, she could only stare at him, pinpricks of numbness spreading across her face. She tried to show him the pictures, but they spilled out of her hands and scattered across the floor. Nick helped her sit, then started scooping them up. When he saw what they were, he gasped. "Oh my god."

There were at least a hundred of them. Images burned into Katie's brain, making it hard for her to breathe. They were snapshots of her in San Francisco: running by the beach, boarding a trolley, dancing at a club. There were dark, grainy images of her in various forms of undress taken from the street outside her dorm room, photos taken as she walked across campus or rode a ferry. Some were so close she couldn't understand how she hadn't noticed the cameraman.

But what chilled her blood were the ones taken more recently, in very familiar places. In one, she was shooting pool with Nick at Maxie's, in another getting the mail outside her house.

Clutching her stomach, she ran for the bathroom, barely making it in time.

"Oh...oh god," she sobbed. A roar filled Katie's ears, blocking out anything else even as she felt the acid rising in her throat again. Fear, anger, and humiliation threatened to overtake her.

Taking a deep breath, Katie tried to get control. Falling apart now wouldn't help her, and if she were a blubbering mess on the floor, she'd be no good to anyone. Splashing cold water on her face, she stared at the woman in the mirror. No, he *wanted* her to come apart. He wanted her vulnerable and scared and convinced she had to do his bidding to be safe. Well, she'd be damned if she'd give him the satisfaction.

Once she calmed down and set her resolve, she returned to the kitchen where Nick was picking up the photos.

"This sick bastard," he grumbled. "I knew things were serious, but this is fucking disgusting."

Katie dug in her purse until she found the business card she'd been looking for and dialed Sheriff Jacobson's number with steady fingers. She explained the situation then turned to Nick as she ended the call.

"He's on his way. He said to try not to touch them too much. He's doubtful he'll get any usable prints or anything off them, but he'd rather be safe than sorry."

Leaning against the counter, she rubbed her forehead and stared at the floor, trying to organize her thoughts. "Putting Charlotte's return address was smart. He knew I wouldn't think twice about opening it. Jesus, he could have sent a bomb, and I would have opened it with a smile on my face." Saying it out loud made the possibility very real, and she shuddered.

Nick gathered his sister against his chest and rubbed her back. "Hey, you're okay. He isn't trying to kill you—just remind you he's the one in charge." When she wriggled out of his embrace and paced the kitchen, he frowned. "*Are* you okay?"

Katie's mind was racing under a black cloud of anger and confusion. She rounded on him, her face a mask of fury. "What good are these self-defense classes, Nick? How are they protecting me—protecting us?"

Before he could answer, the doorbell rang, making them both jump. Nick ushered the sheriff into the kitchen, where he gathered evidence and took their statements, offering what assurances he could.

The sheriff left with another report to add to Katie's growing file, but she was finding it hard to sit still. Dragging Nick with her through the house, she tested the locks on each window and door, checked the bulbs in all the outside lights, and made a list of items to purchase: blackout curtains, motion detectors, door chains.

Satisfied that she had done everything she could for the time being, Katie kissed her brother's cheek and retreated to her bedroom, where she curled into a ball and cried herself to sleep.

———

Ben tapped his fingers on the desk, staring at his computer without seeing the screen. He examined his watch for what felt like the hundredth time that morning, but the clock wasn't lying to him. It was almost 9:30, and Parker wasn't in the office yet. He was worried. Ben had tried casually to pry information out of Patsy, asking without asking, if Parker had called in sick, but she didn't seem to know anything more than he did.

In the short time they'd been working together, Ben had begun to look forward to coming to the office. He'd always enjoyed the work he did, but Parker had become a bonus to the daily grind. Before she showed up, he had been spending all his time at the office to build the department and to avoid going home to his empty house. Now he spent all his time at the office just to be around her. What did she have that fascinated him so much?

He smiled as he pictured her, standing with her hands on her hips and her chin lifted, shaking his head at the absurdity of it. She was brilliant and talented and never let him get away with anything. He loved making her laugh and, even more than that, watching her blue eyes light up when she could see a new idea forming in front of her. More and more, he was thinking about her smile before work and replaying their conversations in his head well after the end of the day. There were times he caught her looking at him, the hint of a smile playing around her lips, lost in her thoughts. Could she be feeling the same attraction to him?

Ben frowned. What was he thinking? The last thing he needed was any kind of office romance, not with Elizabeth sniffing around. Butting heads with Parker made him crazy—and he hadn't felt this alive in years, filled with a longing he'd all but forgotten. She was an enticing challenge that made him want to tear his hair out most days, but a challenge was all she could be to him.

Now it was after 9:30, and no one had heard from her.

Ben checked the clock and his watch one more time, then dug his phone out of his pocket with a huff. He had been trying to avoid calling her himself, but his concern was growing with every passing minute. Before he could fire off a text or make a call, though, she came barreling into the room.

"Nice of you to show up, Parker." Ben worked to keep his tone teasing so she couldn't tell how relieved he was that she was finally there.

"Yeah, sure. Everything's fine. I overslept, that's all. I'm fine." Katie ducked into her cubicle without looking at him.

Something about her tone didn't sit right, so Ben followed and leaned against her wall. She looked up at him with dark circles under her eyes and tried on a weak smile, but all he saw was her messy ponytail, the makeup she hadn't washed off from yesterday, her mismatched shoes. He cocked an eyebrow and pointed. Katie followed his gaze, only just realizing her mistake. Covering her face with her hands, she slouched in her chair.

"What the hell happened, Parker? Did you knock out a few too many last night?"

"No. I just... I didn't get much sleep this weekend. I got some bad news and—" Katie looked up at Ben and groaned. "I didn't hear my alarm and bolted out of bed about half an hour ago."

Her eyes told him there was more to her story, but he could tell she didn't need an interrogation. Ben offered her his hand. "Come on, Parker. Let's get you some coffee. Take a deep breath and start this day over."

Katie slipped her hand in his and stood with a grateful smile. "Thanks."

Ben smirked over his shoulder, pulling her behind him. "And you can re-button your blouse. Looks like you got dressed in the dark."

Katie stopped to inspect her clothing, and he saw a flush

creep into her cheeks. Her blouse was askew, the buttons lined up wrong, gaping in the middle and exposing her bra underneath. "Jesus Christ," she muttered, diving back behind the safety of her cubicle wall to fix the buttons.

Ben waited patiently, his back turned, but he couldn't help chuckling at her string of expletives. Listening to her irritation, he felt a sense of relief. If she was still herself enough to paint that tapestry of curses, then things must not be too bad.

When Katie rejoined him, she had twisted her hair into a loose bun on the back of her head. Her clothes were straightened, and she seemed much more in control. She flashed a small, grateful smile.

"I think you said something about coffee?"

———

Leaning against the counter in the break room, a warm mug between her palms, Katie was feeling more like herself. The night before had been rough. She had gone to bed, exhausted both physically and emotionally, but then her mind wouldn't stop spinning. How long had He been following her? Why had no one noticed Him lurking outside her San Francisco apartment? It all made her feel dirty and paranoid.

She'd been on edge well into the early morning hours. The customary creaks and pops of her old house kept her from closing her eyes for long. She was too hot, so she threw her covers off, but then she felt too exposed, so she burrowed under them again. Even though she was on the second floor, she was convinced there was someone peering in her window. Irrational fear took control, and it paralyzed her under the comforter, eyes wide and fixed on the dark panes of glass she could see through the crack in the curtains. Around five am, her eyelids finally drooped, and she melted into the mattress.

Now she was struggling to pull herself together in front of Ben, the last person she wanted to see her fall apart.

"Feeling better?" Ben regarded her from a few steps away. "You had me worried, Parker. Almost sent out a search and rescue."

She kept her eyes down and studied the depths of her cup. "Yeah, sorry. I, uh, just overslept. It won't happen again."

"Hmph." Ben grunted. "Parker, you don't have to report to me. I'm not your boss." He was quiet as he watched her. "Is everything okay?"

"Everything's fine."

Ben chewed his bottom lip. "You said you got bad news—do you have malaria or something?"

"Uh, no. Not that I'm aware of." Trying to lighten the dark mood, she gasped with a hand on her chest. "Why? What have you heard?"

"Ha, ha, very funny." He ran a hand through his hair and scratched at his beard, avoiding eye contact. "Look, I know I come off as a dick sometimes, but you can always talk to me. I'll help if I can, or just listen if you want to bitch about something."

Their eyes met, and Katie felt an electric charge pass between them.

"I can be a good listener and a sympathetic shoulder from time to time." Ben offered a lopsided grin. "Despite prior evidence to the contrary."

She returned his smile and felt the weight she'd been carrying loosen its stranglehold. "I'll keep that in mind."

His phone chimed, and when he read the message, his face darkened. He shoved the phone back in his pocket and started cleaning up the counter space, slamming things back into the cupboard and muttering under his breath.

Clearing her throat, she brushed her bangs to the side. "You know, that offer extends both ways."

"What?"

She shrugged. "If you ever want to talk, I can be a good listener."

"What would I need to talk about?"

"Well, that message sure pissed you off. It might help to talk about it." Watching his features, it seemed he was fighting some internal struggle, pursing his lips and blinking. Then suddenly, it was over, and his face became an unreadable mask.

"Mind your own business, Parker."

His words struck like shards of glass. "Are you kidding me right now?"

Without replying, he turned away.

"Oh, so, it's okay for you to dig into my personal life because I didn't put makeup on today, but I'm out of line by offering to be a friend?" Katie barked out a laugh. "Boy, that's rich."

"Well, I somehow manage to dress myself and show up to work on time, don't I? Drop it, Parker."

Katie dumped the rest of her coffee. "You are something else, Ben Collins." She stomped past him without looking back.

———

After a day of icy silence, Ben poked his head over the top of her cubicle. "Hey."

Katie stopped typing but kept her back to him. He cleared his throat.

"Uh, look, I'm sorry for being an ass earlier. You were being nice and didn't deserve it."

She turned in her seat to face him and was surprised by the sincerity of his sheepish expression. "Thank you."

With a relieved sigh, he strolled into her workspace. "What are you working on?"

"The Whipson Mill proposal. You're presenting it in a few days."

Ben shook his head. "No, I'm not. You are."

Katie's jaw dropped, and she stared at him. "What?"

"Are you having a stroke, Parker?" He laughed. "Which word didn't you understand?"

Katie rolled her eyes and snapped back, "Don't be a jerk. I understand all the words." She scrutinized Ben's face, trying to read behind his amused expression. "You...want me to present? Why?"

"Why not? You came up with the plan, wrote the commercial treatment—this is all you. You should present the proposal." He laughed. "You act like you've never done this before."

Her voice barely audible, she stared at her desk. "I haven't."

The shock on his face was genuine, but suspicion quickly replaced it. "Wait a minute—what about all this great marketing experience in the big city that you've been throwing in my face? Was that all bullshit?"

"You don't understand what it was like there." Katie rubbed her hands over her face and sighed. "There were exactly zero female senior representatives, in marketing or sales or anywhere else. My official title was Art Director, which put me in charge of ordering supplies, of drawing the images I was told to draw, of creating the graphics the reps needed."

Ben's expression darkened. "So, you aren't the genius marketer you made yourself out to be? You don't have any experience?"

"Oh, I have the experience, but I didn't get the credit for it." She drummed her nails on the desk as she ordered her thoughts. "I got paired with a rep to help him develop the artistic branding for a client. We worked well together. He bounced ideas off me, and I helped improve his rough concept. Soon he requested my help on all his projects, and we became...*partners*."

Katie frowned, trying to decide how much to explain. What would Ben think if she told him the truth about her relationship with Derek? There was no way to explain it, and Katie didn't think she could stomach his judgment.

"We worked on a lot of projects together. He would meet with the client and fill me in on their end goals. I would build the plan, create the visuals and write the copy. Then he would put on the show and sell it to the bigwigs. But without mentioning me."

Ben scoffed. "Your partner sounds like a real piece of work. Is that why you left?"

Katie hesitated before responding, "Yes, and no. There were multiple reasons." Condescending board members, Barnaby's smug face, Derek's anger and threats—all flashed through her mind. "My partner was only one piece. After he abruptly left, they reassigned all the projects we built together." The still-raw resentment bubbled in her chest. "I had put up with two years of head pats, indulgent looks, and backhanded compliments about how I looked rather than what I contributed. Then, when I was on my own and thought I'd be able to show what I could do, they promoted this moron that I had trained, Liam Callahan, over me. They made it clear that it was because he was a man, and I was not. That was the final straw."

"Jesus, Parker, that's shit." Ben shook his head. "You put all that trust in a partner who was only using you."

"He wasn't using me." She felt anger and humiliation creeping up her spine. What he said was true, to be honest, but knowing she hadn't seen it for so long was embarrassing.

"Come off it, Parker. Don't defend him. He took your hard work and passed it off as his. Then, when he got a better offer, he dropped you like a bad habit and rode off into the sunset on a career you built for him. That is the very definition of using someone."

Katie turned her back. "Please leave, Ben." She could hear

the ice dripping from her words, but she didn't care. "If I am presenting this, I need to be ready. And I need you to go away."

After a moment's pause, he mumbled, "Fine." Then he spun on his heel, leaving Katie to her work.

———

Her irritation spurred her on through the rest of the workday. She was aware of Ben peeking into her cubicle at one point, but she refused to look at him. When he left without saying anything, it was just fine with her.

Keeping her head down and focusing on the presentation helped Katie cool down. After all, Ben didn't know anything more about the situation than she'd told him, so she couldn't fault him for misunderstanding her relationship with Derek.

Or was she the one not seeing it for what it was?

She frowned and poked her head out into the office to tell Ben she was leaving, but he wasn't at his desk. In fact, all his files and papers were stacked neatly, his computer dark, his chair pushed in. How long had she been in here working? One glance at the clock told her all she needed to know, and she quickly packed up her things.

Katie walked through the building, checking for any other late employees, shutting off lights as she went. She felt good about the presentation she'd put together and was ready to show Whipson Mill—and Ben—what she could do. The corners of her mouth curled up and she hooked her bag on her shoulder. It was going to feel amazing to see the look on his face after the accusations he'd thrown at her earlier. Every detail was in place, each step of the plan spelled out, and Katie had never felt so confident. At the moment, however, all she wanted was to lounge on her couch with a good book. Stifling a yawn with the back of her hand, she shuffled into the parking lot, thinking about how great it was going to feel to slip out of her shoes.

The streetlight above her head started to flicker and her steps faltered. Whipping her head around she looked up. It was only then she realized how dark the parking lot actually was; at least one other light was burned out and the rest weren't very bright. She turned toward her car, every muscle urging her to sprint, and her keys slipped out of her hand. "Son of a bitch." Katie retrieved them and kept moving, keeping her eyes glued to her singular destination and refuge. Her heart was pounding in her ears and her scalp tingled. This didn't feel right. Something was off. Each breath became more of a gasp, making her feel lightheaded, her surroundings otherworldly. Then she was at her car, safety in sight, and she released a calming breath. She'd made it. Shaking her head, she wondered why she always tended to overreact.

Without warning, Katie was slammed up against her door, knocking the air from her lungs. A rough hand clamped over her mouth, another gripped her throat, and the weight of the body pressing against her from behind trapped her arms, leaving her helpless.

"At last, we meet."

She whimpered as terror coursed through her veins at the gravelly, distorted voice. He'd found her. Jesus, He'd finally caught up to her. How had she left herself so vulnerable? Katie tried not to panic, tried to remember anything she'd learned in her classes, but his hot breath on her cheek made her unable to order her thoughts.

"I can feel your heart racing, just as mine does every time I see you." He buried His face in her hair, inhaling with a groan. "Oh Katherine, my Katherine. I've wanted this, wanted you for so long. And now you're here."

Grunting with effort, Katie flailed from side to side, scrambling to get her feet under her so she could throw Him off balance. But His weight kept her immobilized. She tried to scream in the hopes that someone passing by on the sidewalk would hear her, but all that came out was a strangled sob.

"Shh, now none of that. There's nothing for you to be afraid of. I only want to make you happy. That's all I've ever wanted. You know that, don't you?"

Katie could only moan in response, tears spilling onto her cheeks. No one would hear her, even if she could scream; no one would see what was happening to her, because the parking lot was hidden from the street. She'd let her guard down, and for what? To prove a point to Ben? To get his approval and feed her ego? It would be hours before anyone realized she was missing. Nick would never know what had happened to her. Katie's mind ran wild with the horrors that likely lay ahead for her, and she thrashed against her captor.

He tightened his grip and sighed heavily in her ear. "Well. Perhaps you aren't quite ready yet. I've waited a long, lonely time to finally be with you, but I hoped you'd come to me willingly, your love guiding you. I didn't want it to be like this."

Her keys. She still had the key fob in her hand if she could only turn it just right. Passing her thumb over the buttons, she tried to gain enough control of her fear to remember which one it was. With a silent prayer, she pressed the button and waited.

The car's lights started blinking, the horn piercing the silent darkness, and both she and her captor jumped. "Oh, very clever, Katherine. I admire your quick thinking. But that was a grave mistake, indeed." Uncovering her mouth, He wrapped both hands around her throat and squeezed, pressing His mouth to her cheek.

She struggled and gasped, but His grip was solid. She was going to die right here, just yards from the street and the promise of rescue. She'd lost.

"Hey, what's going on back there?"

Lights flashed over her face, and she heard shouts and running footsteps.

Suddenly His grip was gone from her throat, and the weight on her back disappeared. Coughing and sucking in air, she tried to run, but He shoved her forward with a low growl, and she smacked her head on the car hard enough to make her knees buckle.

Katie crumpled to the ground, stars bursting in front of her eyes, and He was gone.

TEN

What was he doing wrong? Ben had no idea how he kept setting her off. He thought he was being supportive, backing her up when she told him about the shit she dealt with at her last job. Pointing out her unfair treatment, how she deserved more, should have drawn Parker closer to him, not jam a wedge between them.

He walked through the front doors of Dixie Printing, shaking his head. Maybe today would be better. Parker had done a fantastic job of ignoring him all day, and it had kept him tossing and turning most of the night. The bright, fresh morning would hopefully have her in a forgiving frame of mind, and she'd let him try to make it up to her.

Looking up to greet Jocelyn at the front desk, Ben was surprised to see her desk unattended. He strolled into the office, frowning at Parker's empty desk, and slumped in his chair. Damn. Where was everyone? In the back of his mind, he hoped to be met with one of Parker's bright smiles—or at least some indication of whether he'd been forgiven. With a shake of his head, he resigned himself to the fact that he'd have to sweat it out a little longer.

He fired up his computer and glanced around the room.

There was Jocelyn, her red curls bouncing in conversation with Brandon and the other customer service reps. Some juicy bit of gossip, no doubt, that he had no interest in hearing. It was odd to see them huddled like that, their heads close together, whispering. And if they were just gossiping, why were they doing it here instead of in the breakroom? He needed to get some work done, and their little gaggle was distracting.

No big deal. He'd give them some more time to break it up before he dropped the hammer and asked them to go away. After a quick trip to freshen up his coffee, he sat down to wait for Parker and started scrolling through his emails. Right away, one with a reference line in all caps made him freeze.

ATTENTION: ALL DIXIE PRINTING EMPLOYEES

RE: URGENT! PARKING LOT SAFETY

Last night, there was a physical attack in the parking lot behind Dixie Printing. The victim suffered only minor injuries, but the attacker has not been apprehended and remains at large. Each and every employee is urged to use extreme caution when coming to and leaving work. We will be adding several more lights to the rear of the building and installing a security camera to cover the entire parking lot. Walk to your cars in pairs, stay vigilant to your surroundings, and look out for each other.

Cold tendrils of dread wound their way around Ben's chest as he stared at Parker's empty chair. Nothing on the desk had been touched and it was obvious she hadn't been in yet. It was early, still, but she was almost always at work before he was. Had she overslept again? No fucking way. She'd been mortified by the one time she'd been late, and he knew it wouldn't happen again, come hell or high water.

Ben read through the email two more times, looking for

any kind of clue as to who was attacked. It didn't say it was an employee. It also didn't say it wasn't. Had he seen Parker leave yesterday? No, he was pretty sure she was still working when he went home. He remembered because he tried to tell her goodnight, but she refused to look up when he stopped by her cubicle.

Chewing his lip, he picked up his cell phone, wondering if he should call her. He didn't want her to think he was a creep, but the longer he sat there and looked at her empty desk, the more his skin prickled with fear. Dialing her number quickly, his stomach tightened with every unanswered ring. Until he swore under his breath, grabbed his keys, and dashed out to his car.

———

Pulling up to the Parker house minutes later, Ben ran up to the door with his heart in his throat, chanting silently, *please let her be okay*. Despite the repetition of this little prayer, his heart beat his ribs relentlessly as he drew closer.

The door cracked open, and Nick Parker slipped out before Ben could ring the bell. "What are you doing here, Collins?"

"Hey, Nick. Is she okay? What happened?"

Folding his arms over his chest, Nick narrowed his eyes. "What do you mean?"

"Look, I know you're being protective, but I also know something happened to her last night." Nick's eyes flitted toward the door, confirming his suspicions, and Ben's heart jumped. "Someone was attacked in the parking lot—she isn't at work or answering her phone—it doesn't take a genius to figure it out."

It was almost as if Nick deflated when faced with Ben's logic, and he rubbed his hands down his face. "Okay, yeah. Someone jumped her as she was leaving last night."

Swallowing the panic bubbling into his throat, he knew

Nick was holding back details, and he needed to know more. "Jesus. Was she hurt? Did she get mugged or something? What the hell, man?"

Nick regarded him without saying anything for several minutes, and it was all Ben could do not to grab him and shake some answers out of him. When he thought his patience had run out, Nick gave a little nod.

"She'll be okay. Pretty upset, of course, and a little banged up, but nothing too serious." A shadow passed behind his eyes. "I should have been there to pick her up or something. Katie should never have been out there alone."

Nick just said exactly what Ben had been feeling since he learned about the attack. If not for his wounded pride, he would have stayed late at work with her, and none of this would have happened. He shoved his hands in his pockets and shifted his weight from one foot to the other. "Can I see her?"

Smiling sadly, Nick clapped him on the shoulder. "Nah, man. Not today. Like I said, she's shaken up and needs some time to process what happened. I promise you, she's okay. Just has a bump on her head and some bruises. But I'll tell her you stopped by." He started to go inside but stopped with one foot in the door, looking back over his shoulder. "I know it'll mean a lot to her that you were here."

Then the door closed, and Ben scratched his beard. Finally, he retreated to his car and headed back to work, only because he didn't know what else he could do.

———

Walking into Maxie's with Rick, the production floor lead, Ben was ready to get out some frustrations in a Wednesday night dart tournament. He'd been avoiding the bar since the last time Elizabeth had been in town, afraid she'd show up and make a scene since he wouldn't return any of her calls. All he wanted tonight was to get to the boards without incident so he could go home. Alone.

A subdued but familiar laugh caught his attention, and his stomach flipped when he caught sight of Parker at the pool table. After the attack, she took some time to recuperate, and it had been nearly a week since he'd seen or talked to her. Even from across the room he could see the shadows under her eyes And when she laughed at Patsy's antics, the smile shaping her lips was half-hearted. But damn, she was still breathtaking. Watching her from the other side of the bar, he realized how much he missed her, missed their sparring and their conversation. Her hair was loose, she was dressed down in jeans and a T-shirt, and he could see the sadness behind the smile she wore for everyone else. In that instant, Ben was painfully aware of his desperation to take her in his arms, to hold her and offer her some kind of comfort.

While Ben was daydreaming about his coworker, Rick had been shepherded away by a short, soft woman with big chestnut hair and a friendly smile. Since he couldn't get into the tournament with no partner, he meandered toward the bar and buried himself in a crowd of patrons, trying to disappear.

"Hey."

Ben didn't see Katie approach and jumped when she sat next to him. Despite the thrill he felt at hearing her voice, he eased his expression into a casually friendly smile and turned. Jesus, those eyes drew him in every time, and it took him a moment to catch his breath. Up close, her haunted expression was even more obvious, but he didn't want to chase her away by forcing a conversation she wasn't ready to have yet. At least, not with him.

Instead, he opted for a playful tone. "Hey, Parker. What are you doing over here? You lose a bet?"

"No, but I am on a mission of mercy." His heart thumped at the way she grinned with her lower lip between her teeth. "Come join us."

"Why?" He narrowed his eyes. "Is this some kind of sick, prom queen and pig's blood joke?"

"Damn, you caught me." They both laughed. "No, jerk, it's a legitimate invitation to hang out with your much cooler coworkers."

Just then, Ben's phone buzzed, and he frowned at the incoming message from Elizabeth.

I can be there in an hour. I want to see you—tonight. I miss you.

He studied Parker's face for a second, taking in her genuine, welcoming smile, and he had no doubt who he wanted to spend his time with tonight. "Okay, I'll bite." He deleted the message from his phone. "But you better not be part of a cult looking to use me for a ritual sacrifice. I'll be pissed."

———

Life in Enderlin fell into a comfortable pattern for Katie. Monday night was self-defense class; Wednesday was Happy Hour at Max's with Patsy; Friday was pizza and a movie with Nick.

And every night was sleepless and fraught with nightmares.

When she closed her eyes, Katie saw faceless, dark shapes, snarling as they reached for her. More than once, she woke up coughing, feeling the imaginary fingers of her attacker wrapped around her neck, and she had to turn on all the lights to fall back to sleep.

The terrifying encounter in the parking lot was always hovering just below the surface of her mind, leaking through at random times. It had taken her a couple minutes to get her bearings after He'd rammed her head into the car, leaving her in a heap on the ground. The two strangers who had interrupted the attack sat her in the front of her car and called the sheriff, then stayed with her until he arrived. After he took her report and had the EMTs check her out, he followed her home to make sure she got there without further incident. Katie wondered if he would have let her drive if he had seen the violent tremors racking her body. She told Nick about what happened, and they held each other while he added his helpless tears to hers. It took a few days for the bump on her head and the finger-shaped bruises on her neck to fade, so she used up her only sick days and stayed in the house. The last thing she needed—or wanted—was to face an interrogation by her coworkers. Especially Ben.

She was touched that he had come to the house to check on her. It was unexpected, to be sure, but the fact that he cared enough to visit meant a lot. More than she wanted to examine, if she was being honest. Workplace romance was always a bad idea, and, besides, he already had a girlfriend. Best not to read anything into his concern.

The day after the pictures showed up, Nick had a local security company at the house, installing a top-of-the-line system with cameras at every entrance, alarms on all the windows and doors, and motion detectors in every hallway. The attack in the parking lot reminded her that none of that mattered, that she wasn't safe anywhere, and Katie's fear became a constant weight that kept her on edge, waiting for the other shoe to drop.

Work was her only release most days. When she could put her head down and dive into planning and creating, everything else fell away. Her job at Dixie Printing was different in nearly every way from Barnaby Marketing, and she had a strong suspicion Ben was the reason she was enjoying it so much. It was a relief that he didn't treat her any differently when she returned to the office. She didn't think she could have handled that on top of everything else. The way he challenged her gave her strength and confidence in her ideas, even when he teased her about the bad ones. He also seemed to know when she needed a little space, never pushing her to talk or looking at her with pity and she was grateful for it.

After putting the finishing touches on a proposal, Katie looked up, and her stomach dropped. The surrounding office was dark and silent. She groaned. When had everyone left, and how had she missed it? Again?

Fingers of fear tracked up her spine as she gathered her things. The idea that she was in danger became a very real weight on her shoulders and her eyes filled with tears. How could she have been so careless? She knew Nick was right outside to pick her up, just like every day since she was attacked. But as she grabbed her phone to shove it into her bag, she noticed several missed texts from her brother over the past hour.

NICK:

Hey Kat, I'm running late be there asap

Still caught up at the shop I'm sorry

Don't go anywhere

OMG KAT I'M SO SORRY I'M SO LATE I PROMISE I'LL BE THERE SOON!!!

She shrank into the depths of her cubicle and took a deep breath. Okay, he was on his way. The office doors were on an automatic lock at five pm every weeknight, and she knew no one could get into the building this late.

So why was she hearing shuffling steps in the main office?

Katie dropped low to tuck herself under her desk, but she rammed her chair into the wall and banged her head against the corner. "Ouch! Son of a bitch." She clapped a hand over her mouth, but she was too late. The sounds of movement cut off, and her heart leapt into her throat.

"Who's there?" She tucked her keys firmly between her

fingers to create a makeshift weapon and poked her head around the corner of her cubicle.

Ben stepped out of the shadows, holding his hands up in surrender. "Keep your shirt on, Parker. It's not the bogeyman."

He turned on his desk light, and equal measures of relief and irritation washed over her. "No, it's worse."

"Ha, ha." Ben rummaged through some papers, humming in the silence. "What are you doing here so late?"

Katie rubbed her eyes. "Just polishing up the presentation for Thursday. I lost track of time, and my ride is running late." She thought she caught a frown as he glanced her way, but it was gone as quickly as it appeared.

More rustling papers. "Don't you have a life, Parker? Shouldn't you be out on dates, breaking hearts or something?"

"I have a life," she retorted.

"Hmph."

Katie sorted her notes and art mockups into neat piles on her desk. She leaned forward to push her drawer shut, and something whizzed by, an inch from her nose.

She pressed herself back against the wall of her cubicle. "What the hell was that?"

"A rubber band."

Katie heard a *ping* on the monitor behind her and a chuckle from the shadowy figure across the room.

"So was that."

"Oh. My. God. What are you—twelve?" Another rubber band flew past her face, so close she felt her hair move in the breeze of it. "What is wrong with you?"

Ben's lips twitched in the dim light. "You're wound too tight, Parker. Learn to have some fun."

"I'm so sorry." Katie bristled at the insult, sarcasm dripping from every syllable. "I must have missed the memo that says you get to tell me what to do."

"Must have," Ben deadpanned, letting another rubber

band fly. "Come on, you could be a lot of fun if you'd only loosen up a little."

With her hand on her hip, Katie glared. "I'm plenty loose."

She regretted her choice of words even before she registered his raised eyebrows.

"That's not what I... I didn't mean..." she spluttered. Shaking her head, she lifted her chin and brushed her bangs from her forehead. "You are such a child."

"And you are such an old lady."

Ben smiled and shot another rubber band in Katie's direction. It hit her in the middle of the chest, and she gasped. His eyes flew open wide, and he clapped a hand over his mouth. But not before a chuckle escaped.

Katie narrowed her eyes. "Oh, it's on."

They simultaneously dropped to the floor, taking refuge behind cubicle walls. Katie scrambled to gather the errant rubber bands that had flown her way, then listened for movement. Hearing nothing, she peeked around the side of the desk, weapon at the ready, and barely missed taking a direct hit in the face. She fired in Ben's direction and giggled when she heard a muffled, "Ow."

With a satisfied smile, she inched her head above her protective barrier and fired another missile across the room.

"Not even close, Parker." Ben's voice sounded on her left, and Katie stood up just in time to get a rubber band in the ribs.

"Shit!" She ducked behind another stall. The two traded rapid volleys amid shouts and laughter as they maneuvered from one safe space to another, trying to avoid the sting of a hit while gathering ammo along the way.

"Holy crap, Parker," Ben yelled from under a desk. "You almost took out my eye."

"Don't be such a baby," she called and dashed through the doorway.

When there was a lull in the battle, Ben shouted, "Hey, want to call a truce? I'm out of rubber bands over here."

Katie crawled on her hands and knees, scouting the floor, hoping to get the upper hand on her adversary.

"Too bad for you." Spotting a lone rubber band in the middle of the room, she sprinted for it—at the same time as Ben.

"Oh, hell, no." Ben growled and dove to the floor. But Katie was faster, snatching the projectile out of his reach triumphantly.

"Aha! Looks like I won."

With a crooked grin, Ben rose slowly, and the glint in his eye caught her breath. His voice came out as a growl. "You better run, Parker. You have something I want, and I'm a sore loser."

Katie took a couple of unsure steps backward.

"What—what are you going to do?" She wasn't sure if she should laugh, stand her ground, or run for the door. But the mischievous smile on his face told her he wasn't about to let her get away. Squealing, Katie sprinted down the hallway, realizing too late the door ahead of her was locked, and there was no other way out.

She whipped around to find Ben creeping toward her, suddenly only a few feet away. Frantically, she looked for an escape or defense and, finding none, reverted to playground tactics. Squeezing the rubber band in her fist, she clasped her hands behind her back.

He stared at her for a moment before throwing his head back and laughing. Closing the distance between them, he stopped so close Katie could feel the heat radiating from his body. Her smug smile faded when their eyes locked. Ben stood in front of her with his arms crossed and a wolfish smile curving his lips.

"Well, well, well," he whispered. "Looks like you're in a bit of a situation, huh, Parker?"

"You can have the rubber band." She thrust her open hand out in front of her. "I don't want to play anymore."

Ben glanced at the rubber band then recaptured Katie's gaze. Deliberately, gently, he took her hand in his, the projectile falling forgotten to the floor. He rubbed his thumb in small circles over her palm, moving closer without ever breaking eye contact. Something deep and fiery that made it hard for her to catch her breath had replaced the playfulness of a moment ago.

His closeness made her uncomfortable in an enjoyable way, like the thrill at the top of the rollercoaster, and she shivered when he brushed her hair out of her eyes.

"I don't think the rubber band is what I want." His voice was thick, and he inched even closer, wrapping her arm around his waist.

Katie knew she should pull away—nothing good could come of this—but she really didn't want to. A swirling ball of heat formed in the center of her chest, and the longer she looked into Ben's eyes, the farther that heat spread through her body.

This is a bad idea, a horrifically bad idea. Katie closed her eyes, lifting her face toward his. When he brushed his lips lightly against hers, she gasped, unprepared for the electricity his touch generated. His fingers traced an excruciatingly slow line over the sensitive skin stretching from just behind her ear all the way to her collarbone, and she had to fight to keep from trembling.

Without thinking, she leaned into him, craving more. His kisses left a trail of fire, burning away all rational thought. Every graze of his skin against hers was soft, featherlight, and made her blood race in a way she'd never felt. And she wanted to drown in the feeling.

Suddenly, the overhead lights fired up, making Katie jump, her heart in her throat. The familiar icy fear climbed up her spine and she froze, Ben's shirt bunched in her fist, unable to take a breath. It wasn't until she heard the whir of a vacuum that she realized it was only the cleaning crew arriving with no idea that anyone else was in the building. Silently, she thanked them with a rush of relief for showing up when they did—and stopping her from making what was sure to be a huge mistake.

Ben released a long, low sigh, biting his lip and watching her with hunger in his eyes while she tried to smooth her hair and straighten her clothing.

"Jesus." She exhaled and shoved past him, trying to regain her composure. "What the hell was *that*?"

Ben called after her as she tried to walk away on wobbly knees. "That, Parker, was a hell of a lot of fun."

ELEVEN

W hen Katie and Nick arrived at the restaurant, Cael had already gotten a table. He slid out of the booth as they approached, shaking Nick's hand and clapping him on the back.

"Hey, man. Glad you could make it." Cael turned his attention to Katie, and his eyebrows shot up. "Wow. You look fantastic."

She rolled her eyes, glancing at her t-shirt and patting her messy bun. "Hardly. But thanks for letting me tag along."

"You're always welcome to hang out with us. Adds some class that would be severely diminished without you." He chuckled at Nick, who had already sat down and was in the process of shoving a chip with salsa into his mouth. He froze when Cael flicked him on the back of the head, making Katie laugh. "See what I mean?"

Katie had recently learned that Nick and Cael had been meeting up regularly for years to have drinks and watch whatever sports were in season. They'd all gone to high school together, and after Katie graduated and left town, Cael had kept in touch with Nick. He seemed to know how close she and her brother had been, and that Nick would be lonely without her. Seeing their banter now, she was happy that they'd stayed friends,

Once they'd ordered a round of margaritas and a handful of appetizers, Katie relaxed in her seat. Nick and Cael were engaged in a friendly argument about last year's fast-pitch softball tournament, allowing her the chance to just enjoy her drink and relax in the company of an old friend.

"You should have seen this guy." Nick motioned at Cael with a chip. "Bottom of the ninth, bases are loaded, and he's out in deep centerfield. Alone."

Cael groaned. "Jesus, man, don't tell this story. She'll lose all respect for me."

"That's assuming I had any to begin with."

Cael waggled his eyebrows at her comically. "Oh, come on. You know you're powerless against my raw animal magnetism."

Shoving Cael's shoulder, Nick guffawed and motioned for another round of drinks. "Come on. It's a great story. You two can flirt later."

"If you insist." Cael winked and shot finger guns at Katie, who wrinkled her nose and giggled at his blatant cheesiness.

"Anyway—bottom of the ninth, two outs, bases loaded. Our pitcher's arm was a limp noodle, and the last batter was a big hitter."

Cael leaned across the table, holding up one hand. "Don't forget it was also about a million and five degrees out, and we'd been drinking beer between innings."

"Of course you were." Katie shook her head. "Idiots."

Her companions looked at each other and shrugged before draining the last of their margaritas.

"So, the pitch flies, there's the crack of the bat, and all the rest of us could do was stare stupidly as the ball sailed straight toward centerfield. Cael's out there by himself, suddenly wide awake and shuffling in a backward, serpentine pattern to get underneath the ball. It looks like it's just gonna drop into his glove—"

"Until there was a gust of wind that, I swear to you, held it in the air and carried it over my head."

Waving a hand, Nick scoffed. "Pssh. Whatever, man. So, he's backpedaling, backpedaling, trying to keep his eye on that damn ball, and he turns to put on some speed to catch up to it. The problem is that he didn't realize how close to the fence he was."

Katie's mouth dropped open. "Oh, no."

"Oh, yes." Nick was almost in tears, laughing at the memory. Katie cast a glance at Cael to see if he was truly mortified or if he was laughing, too.

But he was watching her as she listened to the story, a glint in his eye and a playful smile on his face. "Just wait. It gets better."

Everyone turned their attention back to Nick. "He turns to run, his arm outstretched, expecting that ball to just fall into his hand, and sees the fence a split-second too late. Our friend here rams into it at full speed. It's not real tall, so it catches him in the hips, and there's nothing to stop the forward momentum of his upper half. His legs stop, his shoulders keep going, and he flips over the top, smashing his face into the chain link. The top of the fence snags his pants, and…" He stopped to take a swig of his drink, raising his eyebrows.

With her hand over her mouth, Katie turned to Cael. His face was fully aflame now, but he was laughing nearly as hard as Nick.

"Yep. The full moon came out right then and there, in front of god and everybody." He shook his head. "Not only that, but it was front page of the next day's sports section. Naked parts blurred tastefully, of course."

Katie shook her head. "Oh, god, I wish I'd seen that."

"I'm happy to recreate it for you." Cael's smile broadened, and he winked at her playfully. "But I think that's enough embarrassing stories about me for tonight. Now I'm completely off my game."

"I wouldn't be too sure." Katie inclined her head toward the bar behind him. "That sassy brunette has been eyeing you for the last ten minutes. She seems to have something she wants to, uh, talk to you about."

He peered over his shoulder, and his admirer flashed a brilliant smile, raising her glass to him. Raising his glass in return, he slid from his seat with a chuckle. "Ah, yes. That's Brenda. We've been on a few dates. I'd better go say hello."

Once he was gone, Nick leaned close. "None of them are ever serious."

"None of what?" She glanced at her brother before returning to the animated show across the restaurant. Brenda was laughing at something Cael said, laying a hand on his arm, while he smiled and stepped closer to whisper in her ear.

"I'm saying that he never goes out with anyone more than a couple times. If you're interested, that is."

"In Cael?" She tried to look at her friend objectively, taking in his boyish features and kind smile. Sure, he was good-looking, and she liked hanging out with him. But there was no spark when she looked at him, no fluttering in her stomach or heat rising under her skin. "I'm not, but thanks."

While Cael was chatting with Brenda, another woman strolled by and caught his eye, pulling his gaze for more than a couple of seconds. He smiled at her as she passed before turning back to Brenda, and Katie rolled her eyes.

"Good lord. Are all the men in this town players?" She thought about the redhead she'd seen Ben leave Maxie's with and the giggly blonde who'd been draped on him the first night they met. The image definitely had a visceral impact on her, dampening her palms and making her heart beat faster. Good grief, was she jealous? Afraid of losing the attention of a man who wasn't hers in the first place? She felt the blood rising in her cheeks and shook her head. Well, it was a good thing she wasn't interested in dating anytime soon. Her life was a mess, and the last thing she needed was a distraction. No matter how charming.

Cael caught her gaze, and his eyebrow lifted. Excusing himself from Brenda, he strolled back to the table, eyes locked on Katie the whole way.

"Hey." He wriggled his eyebrows as he slid back into the booth, making her laugh.

"Not a chance."

They all chuckled, then settled into pleasant conversation as they ate, sharing stories of their lives since high school.

"What about you, Katie? You must have had San Francisco eating out of the palm of your hand." Leaning back in his seat, Cael cocked his head and regarded her. "I imagine anyone who came in contact with your quick wit and those gorgeous eyes must have become a puddle of goo at your feet." His lips curved into a roguish grin. "You'd be hard to resist."

"Don't be ridiculous. I most certainly didn't liquefy anyone."

"If you say so." He shrugged. "How are things going at your new job? Are you settling in, getting comfortable?"

Memories of her recent late night at work flashed through her mind, and Katie had to push down the butterflies that were trying to steal her breath. She could still feel the fire of Ben's lips and the electric touch of his hands on her, and a shiver coursed through her. "Yep. Yes. I am definitely getting comfortable."

Nick's head snapped up and he narrowed his eyes. "Kat, tell me you aren't getting involved with Ben Collins."

"What does that even mean, 'involved'? We work together. That's all."

Dropping his head back against the seat, Nick groaned. "What was the one thing I told you when you met him? Steer clear of that guy. You don't know anything about him."

Katie glared at her brother. "I can't steer clear of him, not entirely. We are partners in the marketing department, I spend every day working with him. Besides, who I do or don't get involved with is really none of your business."

"Well, if he's potentially dangerous, it is Nick's business." Cael tried to reach for her hand, but she snatched it out of his reach. "He's just trying to look out for you, that's all, and he knows Ben better than you do."

She rounded on her brother with her eyes wide. "The hell, Nick? Are you telling everyone my business?"

Cael held up his hands. "Hey, he's just worried about you. We both are. I saw him the day after your...encounter in the parking lot, and he was freaked out. All he's trying to say is to be extra careful who you get close to. Not everyone has your best interests at heart the way that we do."

She wanted to yell and scream and tell them how far they'd overstepped, but Nick looked more distressed than angry, and Katie immediately softened. "Look, I know you both mean well. But I promise you that I am being careful and I'm not looking to jump into anything anytime soon." She slid out of the booth and held out a hand to her brother. "Come on. Let's go home."

———

Katie hadn't said more than a handful of words to Ben in the last few days and he was worried he'd screwed everything up. Honestly, he could see how stressed and tense she was, and he'd only wanted to lighten things up a little, to see her smile again. But the whole thing had quickly run off the rails and out of his control. A thrill ran through him every time he thought about how close he had come to kissing her senseless the other night. The little bit of contact they'd had, the tentative kisses, her skin under his hands, had nearly consumed him ever since. And now he didn't know what to say to her. It seemed she felt awkward around him, too, barely making eye contact and turning a delicious shade of pink if they were too close. He typed up long, narrative texts ten times a day, telling her how he felt and that he wanted to see where things could go between them, but could never make himself press send.

Now he was leaning against a rental car in the office parking lot, waiting for Parker to arrive. When he scheduled this little video shoot for a client, he hadn't given much thought to the fact that he'd be confined to a small space with her for a couple hours. His palms started to sweat knowing he was going to have to come up with things to talk about that didn't include his growing feelings for her.

Things had gotten completely out of hand where Parker was concerned. Pathetic as it was, he wanted to be around her all the time. He was a grown man losing a battle against the worst crush he'd ever experienced. Whenever she was near, he turned into an awkward preteen, and he hated it. But he also loved it. He hadn't felt this alive in years. She was amazing for so much more than her stunning blue eyes, her thick, brown curls he ached to bury his face in, or the most genuine smile he'd ever seen. No, it was her fire, her insatiable drive to learn, to grow, to excel—and it was contagious. Anything was possible to her, and she made Ben believe it was possible for him, too. That was a new, exhilarating drug, keeping him on a high whenever Parker was around. Ben wanted to feel like that all the time.

That's why he was planning on telling her how he felt.

He didn't know what he would say or when, and he had no idea how she would react. But the way she had trembled when he touched her, the way she closed her eyes and sighed when he had kissed her, gave him hope.

He hadn't seen or heard from Elizabeth in a couple weeks, which was a good sign that she was finally getting the hint. It had taken far too long, but at last, he felt like he was out from under her spell and ready to start something new.

The headlights of Parker's car swept over him as she

finally pulled into the parking lot. His stomach flipped at the possibilities of the drive ahead of them. This expedition could bring a marked uptick in their relationship if she felt the same about him. Or, if she didn't, the drive home could become a tomb on wheels, suffocating him.

"Morning."

Katie looked at him sideways and yawned as they slid into their seats and Ben started the car. "Remind me why I have to be here for this video shoot."

"I need another set of hands to hold bounce cards, set up shots, things like that." The withering look she gave him left no doubt that she was not amused. "Come on, Parker, where's your 'go-get-em' spirit? This'll be fun."

Katie relaxed in her seat. "Fine. You'd better deliver on that 'fun' part, or you'll have a strike on your hands."

He couldn't be sure, but Ben thought he saw the start of a smile before she turned her gaze out the window.

———

The miles sped by, and Katie was soon dozing, lulled by the sound of the tires. Ben hummed along with the radio, acting as though everything was normal. Butterflies danced in her stomach, thinking about how close she had been to him and how badly she had wanted to... Katie sighed. In the past couple of days, she had wondered if there could be more than a working relationship between them. He was infuriating: childish, cocky, a bit of a playboy, and inconsistent in his behavior toward her. All exceptionally good reasons to stay far away from him.

But every now and then, she caught glimpses of his sweet and vulnerable side. Katie couldn't deny a physical attraction —a very strong one—but it was more than that. Ben was kind and silly, even thoughtful at times. That combination was very alluring to Katie, and she found it harder and harder to resist the draw. But she swore to herself she wouldn't do anything stupid. Not today, at least.

Stopping in the parking lot of a long, low, concrete building, Ben turned a crooked smile her way. "Are you ready to be my grip?"

The twinkle in his eye and the curve of his lips sent a rush of warmth through her chest. It was obvious that he was trying to embarrass her, and she was not about to let him get away with that again. Time for a little taste of his own medicine.

Leaning over the console, she raised an eyebrow and spoke in a breathy voice. "What, exactly, will I be gripping, Ben?"

His eyes opened a little wider and he licked his lips, the question hanging in the air for a few seconds. "Did you have something in mind, Parker?"

The response caught her off guard. Here she was, trying to unnerve him, and it was backfiring. Suddenly, it occurred to Katie that their mouths were tantalizingly close and, judging by Ben's quickening breath, he'd noticed it too.

One of his fingers began lazy circles on her forearm, making goosebumps run up her spine. Was she really contemplating kissing her coworker in this rental car at roughly nine o'clock in the morning outside a client's building?

Lord, help her, she was.

"Relax, Parker. I'm kidding." He laughed and unbuckled his seatbelt. "All a grip does is carry shit around and help the cameraman set up shots. Nothing untoward required."

Heat flooded her cheeks. "I know what a grip does, Ben." Not only had he turned her attempt at teasing around on her, now she couldn't get her seatbelt unbuckled. "It was a stupid joke."

Her door opened and Ben leaned into the car, his mouth so close that it tickled her ear. "I liked it." With one click the belt came loose and Ben was gone.

Trying to catch her breath, Katie sat for a moment with a

hand on her chest. "Son of a bitch." She heard the trunk pop open, and Ben called from the back of the car.

"Let's go, Parker. Time's wasting."

She sighed. This was going to be a long day.

This was not going to work at all.

Ben sighed and stopped recording, scratching his beard and tilting his head. His video subject was about as lively as wet cardboard, and he had no idea how to get him to engage.

"What's up? Are we done here?" Parker approached with her hands in her back pockets. "I can tell that Bill here is ready to get back to work."

Leaning toward her slightly, Ben clenched his teeth. "No, we are not done. Everything out of his mouth sounds forced, and he moves like a mannequin come to life. Somehow, he manages to do exactly the opposite of everything I ask him to do. How the hell do I get him to relax?"

He'd never had so much trouble with an interview before. Bill could be the best damn Plant Manager in the world, but he was not good on camera. He was forgetting lines and kept looking at his feet to make sure he was hitting his mark. All the other items for the day were done: shots of the lathes and their operators, the CNC machined parts they had in stock, and Kelly, the new general manager. Bill was the last thing on the list and Ben wanted to wrap things up and get back in the car with Parker. Their little exchange in the parking lot had made it hard for him to concentrate on the job at hand and he wanted to be alone with her again. Soon.

Chewing her bottom lip, Parker seemed lost in thought for a moment. Then she lifted her eyebrows and smiled. "I'll be right back. Just turn on the camera and keep rolling."

Bill looked up, his brow furrowed, looking confused as Parker approached. Ben gave him a smile and pretended to be fiddling with something on the camera waiting to see what she was going to do. After a pointed look from Parker, Ben started recording and pulled his headphones in place.

"Hey, Bill. You're doing great, and we're almost done here. Just another question or two." She reached out and repositioned his lapel microphone, smiling broadly. "Do you have big plans for the weekend? I think there's a lake nearby; do you fish?"

To Ben's surprise, Bill's shoulders relaxed a little and he shifted his weight. "Yeah, yeah, I do. I go out to Mopinla Lake every chance I get."

Parker straightened Bill's collar, managing to maneuver him slightly so he was standing exactly where he needed to be. Then she took a step back, just out of the shot, and nodded encouragingly.

"There's something just so peaceful and centering about getting out on the lake early in the morning, isn't there?"

At her question, the tightness around Bill's eyes melted away into something like relief. "Exactly. It's just me and the water and the sounds of the surrounding woods. Sometimes my wife, Esther, comes with me. We don't talk much, but I like having her there."

The man in the video was not the same one Ben had been filming just a minute ago. Somehow Parker had gotten him to loosen up and speak naturally.

"When did you and Esther move to the area? Did you come for this position or for the fishing?"

Bill chuckled then answered, "Esther and I moved here about six years ago from southern Missouri. I'd been working as night shift manager for an aerospace engineering manufacturer down there for the past five years. We decided I was getting too old for overnights and, with the kids gone, Esther hated being home alone. She was the one who found this job for me and encouraged me to apply."

Holy shit. She was interviewing him, and he had no idea.

Without thinking about the camera or the questions, Bill was at ease and seemed to be just having a conversation with a pleasant young woman who'd taken an interest in his career.

It was hard not to smile like an idiot while he watched her work. This Parker was very different from the one who had started working with him a couple of months ago. She had been quiet and a little timid. Not anymore.

Ben was spellbound. Her posture was casual, and her questions sounded organic, like they'd popped into her head just that moment. When she laughed at Bill's answers, it was low and throaty and stirred something in Ben's chest. Every move, every laugh, every facial expression was full of life and passion, and it drew him in. He could only see one side of her face, but he couldn't tear his gaze away and had almost forgotten that they were there to do a job. As far as he was concerned, there was nothing but Parker.

He was so mesmerized that when she turned and gave him a thumbs up, it took him a minute to figure out that she was asking him if they were finished.

"Ben? Do you think you got what you need?"

Jerking out of his stupor, he pulled off his headphones and smiled. "Oh, yeah. Bill, you were great. Thank you so much for your time. We'll send Kelly a link to the final video when it's ready if you want to see it. Suppose we should get out of here, Parker?"

Once they were all packed up and headed back to Enderlin, Ben nudged her. "Hey. You were damn good today."

"I was?"

"Hell yeah, you were. You don't think so?"

Parker smiled and cocked her head. "Oh no, I know I was good today. I just like hearing *you* say it."

"Well, I can give credit where credit is due. I have no idea what you did to old Bill, but whatever it was, it sure worked."

Her laughter filled the car, making Ben's skin prickle with excitement. "Well, old Bill is a pretty all-right guy. I saw a photo of him holding an enormous fish and grinning like a crazy person—and no other pictures of his kids or his wife—and I figured that was something he loved."

"Good catch."

"That's what he said." She scrunched up her face even as Ben groaned, then they burst into laughter. "God, that was weak. I couldn't help myself. But he also told me about a place we have to stop for lunch on the way home. Best burgers in the state for three years running."

"I don't know if we should stop." All Ben really wanted to do *was* stop and look into those eyes, run his hands over her soft skin. "I want to get this all downloaded and indexed before we go home for the weekend."

"Best. Burgers." She stared at him until he started laughing. "We're stopping."

TWELVE

After putting in their orders, Katie leaned back in her chair. "Okay, I'm curious about something."

With a raised eyebrow, Ben rested his elbows on the table. "Oh yeah? What would that be?"

"I grew up in Enderlin. My family still lives here. I know this town, and I know the people."

He narrowed his eyes. "Okay."

"Enderlin is not a mecca of business by any stretch of the imagination. Most people don't know where Iowa is, let alone a town of fifteen thousand people *in* Iowa."

"Is there a question lurking somewhere in there?"

She threw her hands in the air. "How did you end up in Enderlin?"

The corner of his mouth twitched, and Ben regarded Katie for a moment. "I'm not sure I want to tell you. You either won't believe me, or you'll laugh."

"Well, I can't promise that won't happen, but I will try my best to keep it together. What brought you to Enderlin?"

"A dart."

Katie's eyes widened. "A dart?"

"Yeah, a dart thrown at a map on a wall." Ben paused like

he was waiting for the teasing, the laughter, some kind of reaction. "Come on, say something. I know you're secretly judging me."

"No, I'm not judging you. But I have questions."

"I expected as much. Shoot."

"What made you leave Boston in the first place, and why on earth would you trust your future to a dart thrown at a map? I'm not sure if I buy this."

"It's true. After I graduated from college, my father convinced me to work for him—great salary, unreal benefits package, and the opportunity to learn more about corporate finance." He leaned toward Katie and whispered, "Never mind that my degree is in marketing and business, not finance."

"Okay, so daddy wanted you to follow in his footsteps. Then what?"

Ben laughed. "You can't possibly want to hear this bullshit story. Unless it's for the obvious entertainment factor, of course."

She shrugged. "I don't know. I want to know more about you. I have a sneaking suspicion there's a heart of gold beating in there somewhere."

There was a sudden intensity behind Ben's green eyes as he peered across the table. "Careful, Parker," he murmured, "Or I'm gonna think you're starting to like me."

His searching gaze made her heart ricochet against her ribs, and when he reached across the table to lace his fingers through hers, she didn't even think about pulling away.

The door to the little restaurant opened and Katie glanced up at the sudden light spilling in. Filling the doorway was a figure half hidden in shadow and a chill washed over her. She yanked her hand out of Ben's and tried to order her frantic thoughts. How was He here? Was there no escape from this man? Her legs began to tremble, and she was halfway out of her seat casting her eyes around for a way out, somewhere to run.

"Parker?"

Snapping out of her near panic, she looked at Ben then back at the door. It swung shut and revealed the figure to be an old man in overalls, greeting everyone he passed. Lowering back to her seat, she pressed her lips together. It had been nothing, just a local patron. This time.

"You okay? You look like you saw a ghost."

She shook her head and chuckled. "I'm fine. That just surprised me, that's all." Clasping her hands in her lap to hide the way they were quaking, she took a deep breath to calm her racing pulse. Then she smiled. "I'm fine. Keep going; you were telling me your father wanted you to work with him, right?"

He didn't look convinced at first, but Katie just waited with eyebrows raised. After a beat, he seemed to decide she wasn't going to tell him anything more, so he launched into his story. "He insisted that I take it, to be honest. So I did, and it was fine for a while. Then one day, I ran into Elizabeth, an ex-girlfriend I'd dated off-and-on through college. We broke up years before when she got paranoid and controlling, convinced I was cheating on her, telling me who I could hang out with. But when I saw her again, she seemed like a different person, and it didn't take long for us to fall back into a relationship. It also didn't take long for her to revert to her old ways. She used people. She lied to me and manipulated me. Looking back now, I can't believe I ever considered building a life with her."

Derek's scowling face immediately popped into her mind, and she shuddered. "Hindsight is twenty-twenty, right?"

Ben gave her hand a light squeeze, and then didn't let go. She watched his thumb drift slowly over her knuckles and was surprised by how the contact felt completely natural and comforting.

"Wanna talk about it?"

She shook her head. There was no way she wanted to open up that wound, not today and not with Ben. "No, we're talking about you. Tell me more about what happened in Boston."

"Working with my dad was all right, but I never felt comfortable managing the amounts of money people entrusted to me. My heart was in marketing, so I applied for a dream job in the Pacific Northwest—about as far away from Boston as I could get. I waited and waited to hear back, and Elizabeth just kept telling me to be patient while she made plans and looked at properties. Every time I called, the hiring manager was busy or away, and her secretary promised she'd call me back. Then I got a scathing email, telling me they were only interested in candidates with strong moral character, and they would not be offering me the position." He sighed and picked at his napkin. "Turns out, they had called to offer me the job a couple weeks earlier. But I never got that message."

Katie groaned. "Oh, no. Elizabeth?"

He nodded. "Yep. I forgot my phone at home one day, and she said she'd bring it to me on her lunch break. Instead, when the company called to offer me the job, she put on this whole performance. Let's see—what all did she say?" Everything about his demeanor tightened, his lips pressed into a thin line. "She cried, told them how she hoped that job would help me kick my cocaine habit, and speculated that maybe once we left Boston, I'd finally acknowledge the three illegitimate children we had together. There was more, but that's the highlight reel."

"You're joking."

He glowered. "I wish. Seems Elizabeth was not interested in moving, but she wasn't interested in letting me go, either. So, she pretended to be excited about the opportunity and made plans with me, looked at houses, the whole thing. But she never was going to let me leave."

Katie's jaw dropped. "Wow. I'm so sorry. What did you do?"

Leaning back in his seat, Ben laced his fingers together behind his head. "It wasn't pretty. I threw what one might call a tantrum, made a scene, yelled, threw things. I vowed I was leaving, and she'd never see me again. I had no idea where I wanted to go, didn't have anything else lined up, but I knew I couldn't stay there."

Ben smiled sheepishly. "The day came that I had to do something, so I threw caution to the wind—or, more precisely, threw a dart at a map. It landed in the middle of nowhere, Iowa, so I hit the road and headed west. I stopped in a couple cities and towns along the way, but when I got to Enderlin, I knew it was where I wanted to be."

Katie leaned forward, incredulous. "Really? You just knew?"

Ben shrugged. "Yeah, it sounds ridiculous, but I felt fate had guided me there. I'm sure you think I'm being superstitious, but it was as good a place as any, and I liked the people. I bought a house with the money I'd saved and put down roots. That was two years ago, and Enderlin is my home more than Boston ever was."

The honest affection in his green eyes turned her insides to molten lava. That dart had been pretty lucky for her, bringing Ben into her life. "Well, I'm glad you're here."

Their gaze locked and he reached for her hand, pulling her into his orbit across the table. "So am I."

"Can I get you two anything else?" The waitress appeared out of nowhere, making Katie and Ben both jump back as she slid the check onto the table between them.

Ben pursed his lips and looked up, brows pulled down and eyes cold as he glared at her. "No. No, thank you, I think we're fine."

Covering her mouth to hide her laughter, Katie shook her head. "We'd better get back, anyway. You have all that indexing to get to."

After searching her face long enough to make Katie's

cheeks heat up, Ben scrubbed his hands down his face and heaved a sigh.

"Right. Indexing."

Walking out to the car, Katie couldn't stop smiling. Spending the day with Ben had been nicer than she would have expected, especially his little displays of affection in the restaurant. They were both stalling in the lot behind the building, standing on either side of the car and smiling at each other over the roof. Ben fiddled with the keys, his bottom lip trapped between his teeth.

"Something on your mind, Collins?" Katie raised an eyebrow, her heart hammering against her ribs.

The corner of his mouth twitched before he cocked his head. "Oh, yes. Lots of things."

She ducked her head to hide the heat blooming in her cheeks, and her eyes landed on the cell phone that she'd apparently dropped on the car's floor. The screen was lit up with multiple notifications of missed calls, text messages, and voicemails. Her stomach dropped; had something happened to Nick? Or her parents, or Charlotte?

"Ben, unlock the car. Quick. Something's wrong."

Snatching up the phone, she didn't recognize any of the numbers calling and was immediately convinced it was the hospital or highway patrol trying to reach her with bad news. She opened up the first voicemail and her blood froze.

"You shouldn't have run away, Katherine." There was a pause and then a long low sigh. The voice was muffled, electronically altered and it sent a chill through her. She knew that voice. "But I'll forgive you. It seems sometimes that you are so close to discovering me, so close to just falling into my arms. I can hardly wait for that day. Come to me, my love."

Her knees buckled and suddenly Ben was at her side, supporting her by the elbow. "Parker? What's wrong? Here, sit down before you fall."

The next message was already playing. "I saw you. I

watched you get into the car with that asshole. I try to be patient—really, I do—but you're not making this easy on me. You know that no one else can have you, right? Believe me when I tell you that I will soon make that fact very clear."

There was a harder edge to the voice, a seething rage that made the hair on the back of her neck stand up. A tremor traveled up her arm, shaking it so violently that the phone slipped out of her fingers. Ben caught it and guided her to the car seat, but she barely noticed.

Because the next voice message had started.

"How could you do this to me? I have done nothing but love you since the moment I first laid eyes on you, and you repay my loyalty by whoring yourself out with any man who looks at you twice?"

The message continued to play, the caller's voice rising in rage to a volume that Katie could hear even though the phone was no longer in her own hand. Quaking from her head to her toes, Katie covered her ears in an attempt to block out the violence being spewed at her.

"I will find you, and I'll show you what happens when you betray me. When I'm done, you will never forget that you belong to ME and only me, and no one will ever dare to try to take you from me again. Do you hear me? No one else will ever have you!"

The tirade finally stopped when Ben turned off the phone, and the sudden silence was unnerving. Folding in on herself, Katie pressed her forehead into her hands and tried to calm her shuddering. That voice. It had haunted her nightmares since the attack in the parking lot. And now she'd hear it replay every minute of every day for the rest of her life.

"Who the hell was that?" Ben lowered himself in front of her, taking her hands in his. "Jesus, your hands are like ice. What's going on?"

She shook her head. "I don't even know where to start."

"The beginning is a good place." He squeezed her hands, his voice warm and soothing. "I'm not going anywhere."

She rubbed her forehead and frowned as she tried to decide how to put it all into words. "I couldn't wait to get out of Enderlin for City College of San Francisco right after graduation. You know, a small-town girl destined for bigger and better things. I hadn't been at school more than a couple of months when I started getting anonymous love letters. I thought it was funny and sweet at first, just compliments about my hair and my smile. A secret admirer, you know? But then it started to include specific, personal information, like which classes I was taking and what I was wearing. He'd write shit like, 'I loved that brown sweater you wore to Western Civ. You looked so full of life, and your eyes sparkled in the cool air.' Creepy things like that. The letters were always written on a particular yellow stationery, so I started just throwing them away as soon as I got them. He sent them all four years, but I stopped reading them pretty early on. They made me uncomfortable, and I didn't want to think about them.

"Right after graduation, Charlotte and I moved off campus. It seemed logical to think he worked for the school or was another student, right? I'd never gotten the letters before I went to college, and they never got sent to my home in Enderlin. So, I ignored them, started my life, and figured that would be the end of it."

"Obviously, it wasn't."

She shook her head. "No. They stopped for a little while. Then I got the job at Barnaby Marketing, where I met Derek."

Ben frowned. "Your partner, who stole your work?"

"Yes." Pressing her lips together, she paused. "I didn't tell you this before, but Derek and I were more than just business partners. We got involved shortly after we started working together, and that's when the letters appeared again. But they were different now: they were darker, more desperate." She pushed herself out of the car, pacing as she talked. "Whoever was writing the letters thought I was playing hard to get, that I wanted Him to work harder to earn my affection. When Derek found the letters, he accused me of cheating on him."

"Seriously?"

Katie paused in her orbit and took a deep breath. She hadn't spoken about all of this to anyone but the police and her closest circle—ever—and dredging up the memories was harder than she expected. "Derek wasn't a great guy. He was flashy and exciting, but behind closed doors, he was mean. My secret admirer seemed to take personal offense that I would date someone like him. The letters started blaming me for everything wrong in His life. It was my fault He was alone, that He couldn't work, that He couldn't eat or sleep. He insisted that we were soulmates, and if I would only recognize that, we could be happy. Before long, He seemed convinced that Derek was holding me hostage because how could I ever love Derek when He was my destiny? His words would change from loving and protective to abusive and threatening in just a few lines. How I was too stuck up and ignorant to see that He was my one true love and that He'd find a way to get to me and teach me a lesson." A shiver ran through her, and she had to swallow the lump in her throat before she could continue. "And that's when I filed a report with the San Francisco police."

Ben laid a hand on her shoulder. "God, Parker, that had to be terrifying."

Stepping out of his reach with a quick nod, she found it hard to meet his gaze. "At about the same time, I confronted Derek about stealing my work, and I broke things off with him. He wasn't happy about that. He attacked me in my apartment, threatened me, and tried to choke me. He might have succeeded, too, if the guy delivering flowers from my stalker hadn't knocked on the door at that moment. Derek ran out, and that was the last I saw of him. That anyone saw of him."

"What does that mean? Where did he go?"

"I don't know, Ben." Katie leaned back against the car and stared at her feet. "He stopped coming to work. He stopped calling me, stopped seeing his friends. His folks got text messages for a couple of months, saying that he was taking some time to examine his life and repent." She looked up at Ben and raised her eyebrows. "That is definitely not something Derek would do. Nothing he did was ever wrong, as far as he was concerned. But no one had proof of anything else."

"Do you think he's the one who's harassing you now?"

Katie could only shrug. It didn't make a lot of sense, but she already knew it was a possibility. "Maybe? I started getting letters long before I met Derek, but they didn't become ugly and threatening until after we were together, so…" She retrieved the worn, folded letter from her purse, her hands shaking as she held it out to Ben.

"What's that?"

"Just one of the letters I kept. I made copies of everything else and gave the originals to the police. I don't really know why I held onto this one."

Ben unfolded the page, his scowl deepening with every word he read. When he looked up at her, his eyes were sad. "Jesus, Parker. Is this why you left San Francisco?"

"Yes, and no. The stress was getting to me: looking over my shoulder all the time, every noise in my apartment sending me into panic mode. Nick and I thought moving home might throw Derek—or whoever it is—off my scent, get him to let me go."

Ben leaned against the car next to her and Katie buried her face in her hands. She drew in a trembling breath. "He followed me. I don't know how, but I hadn't been in town a day when He left yellow roses wrapped in black ribbon on the front porch of my parents' house."

Ben wrapped a warm hand around hers. "Parker—"

She jumped up and resumed pacing as she blurted out the

rest. "He sent me pictures, Ben. Pictures of me. Most were from San Francisco, but some of them were in Enderlin. How did He get so close? No one saw Him, thought it was odd He was taking pictures of me without my knowledge? How did He get pictures of me shopping, or riding the trolley, or eating —close pictures—without me noticing? If this guy can get that close, unnoticed, who's to say He couldn't get close enough to hurt Nick? Or hurt my parents? He could take everything from me, and there's nothing I can do to stop Him." Closing her eyes, she pressed her fingertips against her lips, trying to calm the mounting hysteria.

When Ben's hand grazed her arm, she jumped. He didn't say anything, but so much kindness and concern shone from his eyes that Katie fell into his arms. The warmth of his chest was comforting, and she felt some of her tension ease. As he rubbed her back and kissed the top of her head, her body melted into his.

Her phone vibrated in the silence, and they both jumped. It was another San Francisco number, and she groaned.

"Why can't He just leave me alone?"

Ben took the phone from her and answered it in a hard, dark voice that she'd never heard from him before. "Stop calling, you psychopath. She doesn't want to talk to you, and you're done terrorizing her, do you hear me? When I find out who you are—"

Katie held her breath, watching Ben as he listened to the voice on the other end of the call. His face turned red, and he held the phone out to her, his voice barely above a whisper. "It's the San Francisco Police, Parker. They have an update for you."

Her stomach tied itself in knots, and she grasped the phone so hard her knuckles ached. "Hello? This is Katherine Parker."

"Ms. Parker, this is Detective Henry Ballesteros from the San Francisco Police Department."

"Yes, of course, Detective." She furrowed her brow. "Do you have an update on my stalking case?"

There was a beat of silence from the detective then he cleared his throat. "I'm not calling about that, Ms. Parker. I'm calling because we found Derek Franklin."

Katie's face split into a smile, and she grasped Ben's arm. "Oh, my god. Does that mean this is over? Did he admit to the letters, to the flowers, to attacking me the other day?"

"Hold on—you think he attacked you? Recently?"

"I don't know who it was, but the same person who attacked me in Enderlin called me several times today and left threatening voicemails. It just happened, so I didn't have a chance to file a report with you. Sorry." The detective was silent again, and Katie's smile faded.

"We found Mr. Franklin, but he couldn't be the one stalking you. Ms. Parker, his body washed up under the Oakland Bay Bridge yesterday. We're still waiting on the coroner's report, but judging by the condition of the body, I'd say he's been dead for several months."

Everything around her went dark and she felt like she was floating outside of herself. Derek was dead? When she finally found her voice, she croaked, "No. No, you've made a mistake. It isn't Derek."

"I assure you it is. We matched dental records already, Ms. Parker. There is no mistake. Mr. Franklin did not simply run off, and he is not the one who is stalking you. Unfortunately, that also means we're no closer to finding out who is."

THIRTEEN

With Parker settled safely inside the car, Ben pressed the phone to his ear. He explained to the detective who he was and tried to get the details on what had upset her so badly.

"So, Derek has been dead for months, maybe even since right after he attacked her in her apartment. Do you have any other clues as to who's been threatening her?"

"Not at the moment. The Franklin angle was our best bet, but it seems that was a false lead," Detective Ballesteros muttered. "Do you know what the caller said in the most recent phone calls? We need Ms. Parker to file a report, to send us the recordings; there may be a clue in his words or his voice. Something."

Ben took in her slumped shoulders and vacant, tear-filled stare. "Yeah, I don't think she can do that right now. This was a lot to drop on her."

With the events of the last hour replaying in his mind, Ben wasn't about to let Parker drive home alone. It was clear this threat was very close by, watching her and following her every move, so he drove her straight to her house.

Pulling into her driveway, he looked her over again. Her

eyes were glassy, her skin pale. It was as though this new information had sucked every ounce of life from her. Taking the key from her unsteady hand, he walked her inside and sat on the couch next to her, wondering what he was supposed to do next.

"Hey." He brushed a tear from her cheek when she turned toward his voice. "Should I call Nick? The sheriff? What can I do?"

Those deep blue eyes searched his, threatening to drown him in the hopelessness he saw. It was all so unfair. She didn't deserve this, to have her already terrifying world turned on end.

Staring at their joined hands, she shrugged. "I... I don't know how to feel right now, Ben. There's this storm of emotions swirling inside me, and I don't know if I can sort them out."

The defeat in her voice clutched his heart. He knew he couldn't make this better for her, but he also knew he had to try. "Anything you need Parker, say the word."

Her eyes were round and full of fear when she met his gaze again. "Can you just..." Laying her head on his chest, she leaned into him. "Can you just... hold me? I don't want to think about this anymore tonight."

Stomach fluttering, Ben pulled her close, wrapping her in his arms. But she gently pushed him back onto the couch, lying on her side in front of him. There was only a moment's hesitation before he gathered her in, where she nestled against him like she was built to be there. Clutching his arm where it draped across her, she sighed when he stroked her hair. He whispered soothing words and listened to her quiet tears until her breathing evened out, and they both drifted off to sleep.

———

When Monday rolled around, Ben didn't know how he was going to convince Parker to let him help her, but he was ready to take on the challenge. After learning about her ex-boyfriend's death, they'd slept in each other's arms until Nick came home. At first, he wasn't too happy to see Ben there and threatened several creative, painful ways he could get him away from his sister. But once he heard what had happened, he thanked Ben and told him to go home. He didn't want to leave, but Nick had been insistent. Parker was never far from his thoughts, though, and he had to fight the urge to call and check on her.

Early Monday morning, he strolled into the office and found Parker already at her desk. She didn't look up when he came in, so he called out, "Good morning."

Without taking her eyes off the notes she was poring over, Katie mumbled, "Good morning, Ben."

He frowned at her tepid response. Was she still reeling from learning about Derek? Or hadn't she felt the same connection between them that he had? She'd had an exciting reaction each time the electricity between them caught her off guard, and he hoped that meant there was more between them than just as coworkers.

After setting his bag at his desk, he peered over the top of her cubicle, resting his chin on his hands. Her shoulders were tense, riding up around her ears, and it hurt Ben to see it. All he wanted was to ease her worry a little, but he knew he couldn't approach her with pity and concern. His lips curved.

"You're here early. What's the matter, Parker—were you starting to miss me?"

She snorted. "Hardly."

Damn it. She was so absorbed by what she was reading, she wouldn't even glance his way. Well, he'd take that challenge. "Really? Because I missed you. Couldn't stop thinking about you if I'm honest."

Her head shot up, mouth open and eyes wide, making Ben laugh.

"There you are. Wondered if I'd get to see you today. I kinda like your face, Parker. Actually, I kinda like a lot of things about you."

Before she could respond, he retreated to his own cubicle, eager to see where the rest of the day might go.

———

Katie blinked rapidly, willing her heart to calm the fuck down, thank you very much. If she wasn't careful, she would end up having a coronary right there in the marketing department of Dixie Printing. And god damned Ben Collins would have to perform CPR. On second thought, she mused, maybe that wasn't a bad idea. An emergency like that would require Ben to put his mouth on hers—then she could quit lying awake at night, thinking about how much she wanted that.

The attraction she'd been fighting for months was only growing stronger. That physical spark was lit the first time she met Ben, and the fact that it had hung on for so long was mildly annoying. But after learning so much about him, seeing his softer side and opening up to him about her situation, Katie just wanted to be with Ben. And that, to her, was a big problem.

Once she was back home, she'd reached out to Detective Ballesteros and to Sheriff Jacobson, updating both of them on the most recent phone calls. It wasn't hard to hear the frustration in their voices as they came to realize all their leads were dead ends. But Katie wasn't just disappointed and sad by the discovery of Derek's body—the threat level jumped to DEFCON 1, and it was clear her stalker really could be anyone, anywhere. How was she supposed to protect herself now?

Pressing the heels of her hands against her forehead, she

tried to banish the wild thoughts she was having. She came with a unique set of baggage that Ben didn't need to carry for her, and the idea that Derek might have died because of her was an added warning that chilled her blood. It was bad enough she'd dragged Ben in as far as she had, but she refused to risk his life. No, she needed to squash those feelings and focus on the work.

She was doing fine with that plan of action until she actually saw him. And then he had to get all cute and flirty at seven-thirty in the morning, before she'd even finished her coffee. His words were not at all what she was expecting, and she was mortified that she had let Ben see how much it affected her.

Pathetic.

The next day Katie became even more flustered by Ben's behavior as events of the day unfolded.

The morning kicked off with the two of them huddled in Katie's cubicle, rehashing some notes on a potential new client. For over two hours, Ben hovered next to Katie's shoulder, his arm laying casually across the back of her chair. His seat was so close to hers that their thighs were in almost constant contact. Every now and then, he would lean across her to point at or pick up something on the opposite side of her desk, his face coming excruciatingly close to hers. In these moments, Katie would hold her breath to keep from sighing. God, he smelled amazing. She caught him staring at her when he sat back, a lazy smile teasing his mouth; probably because he could read on her face exactly what he was doing to her.

An exercise in extreme self-discipline, the morning had Katie feeling like she was running a marathon. Her heart pounded, and she couldn't catch her breath. Nearing afternoon, she was organizing their notes but realized she didn't have enough folders, binders, or plastic sleeves to compile it the way she wanted.

Oh, thank god.

"Do you want anything from the supply closet?" Standing up, she pressed herself as far into the corner as she could, until Ben rolled his chair backward and she could maneuver around him. When he shook his head, she bolted from the room. The short trip down the hall would afford her a reprieve to get her shit together.

Gripping the shelf in front of her, Katie closed her eyes and tried to catch her breath. Ben was playing games; she was sure of it. And god damn, if he wasn't winning. She breathed deeply through her nose and blew it out slowly, commanding the butterflies in her stomach to keep still.

She jumped at the sound of the door, swearing under her breath when Ben slid into the small space. He leaned back to push the door closed behind him but didn't move any closer.

"Hi?" Katie's hands planted on her hips. "Why are you here?"

Ben held her gaze for a moment, then let his eyes roam over the shelves, taking deliberate, languid steps farther into the narrow closet. "Oh, I realized there was something in here I wanted, after all." He fixed her with a penetrating stare, rooting her in place.

Shit. Shit, shit, shit.

Katie froze and watched his relaxed progress toward her, the intensity in his eyes rendering her immobile. The supply closet was exactly that—a narrow closet. She could have pushed past him and didn't for a second imagine he would restrain her. But she didn't have the same faith that she'd keep her hands to herself if they touched.

"What, uh, what are you doing?" She heard the tremble in her voice and nearly melted into the floor at the twitch of Ben's lips when he heard it, too.

"Nothing, yet."

He continued to draw steadily closer, the unhurried movement causing excitement to batter Katie's chest.

He stopped, tantalizingly close without actually touching

her. The heat in his gaze at such close proximity hinted that the tightness of the space was having as much of an effect on him as it was having on her, but that only made the moment more enticing.

Katie stood her ground and lifted her chin. He was trying to fluster her, there was no doubt, but she refused to let him get the best of her. If she were being honest, she was curious to see how far he would take this little game. She'd stop it before it went too far—but how far was she willing to let him go? "You could have asked me from the door to get whatever you wanted."

"Mm-hmm," he murmured, reaching past her to grab something on a shelf above her head. The movement caused his body to brush against her, and she gasped. He locked his eyes on hers. "But where's the fun in that?"

She didn't know what to do with her hands, and they fluttered at her sides until the moment Ben's body connected with hers. Then she found herself gripping his belt loops for dear life. Her chest was heaving, like some ridiculous damsel in one of the cheesy romance novels she grew up reading. And was she pushing at his hips or, god forbid, pulling him tighter against her?

Katie could feel the increasing rhythm of Ben's heart beating through his shirt, and his own breathing was becoming erratic. She couldn't take her eyes off his slightly parted lips, and when the tip of his tongue darted out to wet them, her knees threatened to buckle under the weight of her desire. Lifting one hand to drift his fingertips over her cheek, Ben leaned in. "Jesus, Parker."

At last, his mouth was on hers, soft and testing. She slid her arms around him, and he cupped the back of her neck, holding her against him as his tongue slipped past her lips. A groan vibrated through his chest, and she knotted her fingers in his hair. Closer. God, she needed him closer. The drive to kiss him was consuming her from the inside, and the way his hands burned against her skin was pushing her over a line she had promised herself she'd never cross again. But at that moment, there was nothing more important to her than feeling his lips on hers and stoking the fire that was about to burn out of control.

Voices sounded in the hallway outside the door, and they froze as they waited for the voices to pass. Then Ben cleared his throat and stared at the box of paper clips in his hand as though he had no recollection of grabbing them. Katie pressed against the back shelves, flushed and clutching some three-ring binders to her chest like a shield.

She watched him compose himself, a wide smile spreading across his face. "Thanks, Parker." Then he flung the door open, and Katie was left trying to remember how to make her body move.

FOURTEEN

The next couple of days were a frustrating nightmare. Katie put most of her energy into avoiding being alone with Ben. Not because she feared what he might do; she was avoiding him because she couldn't trust *herself* not to do something stupid.

For the life of her, she couldn't figure out how he could keep her on edge while simultaneously starring in her most vivid daydreams. She caught herself thinking about his piercing green eyes, his crooked grin, and how those inviting lips felt against hers.

Things had gotten well beyond complicated, and Katie needed to keep things under control. If—who was she kidding —*when* their attraction tipped over the event horizon, it would be on her terms, when she was ready. It seemed that Ben had his own thoughts on that matter, so it was more important than ever for her to keep temptation at bay.

For now.

Ben was already seated at his desk, his back to the room, when Katie arrived Wednesday morning. Squaring her shoulders, she vowed he would not fluster her. She had steeled herself to battle any nonsense he might throw her way but was disappointed when he didn't even look up at her entrance.

She had plenty to keep her busy without Ben distracting her, so she sat at her desk and buckled down. The morning flew by until Patsy was at Katie's elbow, asking if she wanted to grab lunch. With a sideways glance at Ben, who had hardly moved and responded to her questions with one-syllable answers, Katie realized he wouldn't notice her absence. The pang in her chest at that knowledge was unexpected.

In the local Mexican restaurant, Katie twisted a strand of hair around her finger, staring at the bowl of salsa as though it held the answers to the universe.

"Hello? Earth to Katie." Patsy waved a hand in front of her, snapping her out of her trance. "You were a million miles away."

With a grimace, Katie focused her attention. "Sorry. I'm a little spacey today, aren't I?"

Patsy shrugged and shoved a chip into her mouth. "I usually don't mind the quiet, but I can tell you've got something on your mind. Wanna talk about it?"

"Yes. No. I don't know if I can or if I should or..." Katie groaned.

"So, don't be specific. Let's deal in generalities and 'I have this friend' scenarios."

Katie gave Patsy's hand a grateful squeeze.

"Okay, so I have this *friend*." They giggled like middle schoolers and continued to shovel salsa-loaded tortilla chips into their mouths. "My friend is attracted to this guy—I have no idea what she sees in him: he's irritating and conceited and thinks he's so damn smart—and she can't stop thinking about him and how much she wants to, um, hm, put her hands on him."

Patsy's eyebrows lifted. "Go on."

"This guy has recently made it clear that he would like my friend to go ahead and *put* her hands on him. But now, all of a sudden, he hasn't even acknowledged my—her—existence. Is it only fun if he thinks I'm—she's—not interested? The thrill of the chase bullshit? Or was it all in my head?" She covered her mouth with both hands, pleading eyes peeking out over her fingertips.

Patsy cleared her throat. "Well, I don't know how good I am at relationship advice, but I'd tell your friend to bite the bullet and tell him what she wants. Being unsure is the worst, and I, personally, think you would feel a lot better if you came right out and asked Ben to go to bed with you."

Shocked by what she was hearing, Katie's mouth dropped open. Was Patsy telling her to put up or shut up? She narrowed her eyes. "I never said it was Ben."

Patsy nearly choked on her drink. "Jesus, Katie, you'd have to be blind not to see the way you two are together. Do you know how he looks at you when you're not looking?"

"How could I, if I'm not looking?"

"You know what I mean." Patsy laughed. "Makes me want to throw up a little, but it's sweet. Almost the whole office is talking about how you two need to just get on with it."

Katie grimaced. "God. Is it that obvious that I like him?"

"Not you. Him. Ben isn't very good at hiding how he feels about you."

Her mind replayed the confrontation in the supply closet, and her face immediately caught fire. "Tell me about it."

Patsy perked up at the comment and leaned forward. "Oh damn. What happened? Did you kiss him? Is he a good kisser? I bet he's amazing. Did it go farther than kissing? Did you—"

"Good god, Patsy, calm down." Katie cast a furtive look around them. "I can't, I mean, it wouldn't be a good idea to... Oh, to hell with it."

She told Patsy everything that happened, going into detail when describing the supply closet because, well, she wanted to relive it herself. She told about the snub he'd doled out that day and then slumped in the booth with a frown.

Patsy twiddled with her earring, spinning it around while she processed what she'd heard. After a long pause, she straightened her spine and smiled wickedly. "I stand by my previous statement. He's toying with you. I don't know if it's only to torture you for some pervy little fetish or if he's into you and is trying to guess how you feel. Either way, you need to suck it up and take that man to bed. Immediately. *You* seal the deal. Don't wait for him."

"Are you sure?"

Patsy rolled her eyes and snorted. "One hundred percent. If this is something you want, do not let the opportunity pass you by."

———

Ben stared in disbelief at his phone. This had to be an alternate reality that he'd slipped into by accident. It couldn't be his real life.

On the one hand, there was Parker. Smart, gorgeous, and funny, she made him feel good about himself and his work. He was drawn to her and never felt like he was selling his soul just to be near her.

But every time it seemed they were getting closer, something came up to drive a wedge between them. The way she'd reacted to him in the tight quarters of the supply closet told him she was feeling something strong, too. It hadn't taken much of a push to knock her walls down and set her free to do what they both were waiting for. Even being interrupted hadn't quenched the fire he'd seen in her eyes. She'd been avoiding him, but that only made it more obvious.

He never should have answered that phone call.

The day was supposed to go in a very different direction. Parker's resolve was cracking, even though she'd been ignoring him all week. He was going to turn on the charm and get her laughing and smiling. Then he'd ask her out on a proper date. There was a good chance she'd say yes without any further convincing—well, maybe a seventy percent chance —but he was falling for her much harder and much faster than he expected. He couldn't wait much longer.

Whistling as he drove to work, he was riding a high of anticipation that he hadn't felt in a decade. His phone rang, and he answered it without looking at the caller I.D. That was his first mistake.

"Good morning."

There was a brief pause, and then Elizabeth's voice filled the car. "Well, good morning to you, too, darling. Someone's in a good mood."

Ben's sunny disposition blew out the window, and his shoulders tightened. Why hadn't he blocked her yet? "Elizabeth. What do you want?"

"Tsk. I don't know why you feel the need to be so rude. Can't I call just to hear your voice and tell you I'm thinking about you?"

"No." His knuckles had turned white from gripping the steering wheel, and he had to consciously relax his hands. "Again, what do you want?"

She didn't answer right away, and Ben got a sinking feeling in the pit of his stomach. The office came into view, and he was anxious to end this call as soon as possible. He needed to get his head right before Parker came in, so he could warm her up before winning her heart.

"Well, this has been a delight. I'm at work now, so I have to let you go. Don't call me again, Elizabeth. This is over."

There was a sharp intake of air on the other end of the line, and then she blurted out, "I'm pregnant."

It was a good thing Ben's car was already parked, or he might have crashed into oncoming traffic. His head was swimming. "What? What did you say?"

"I said, I'm pregnant, Ben. *We* are pregnant. I just found out and couldn't wait to give you the good news."

He could hear her shifting the phone around, but he couldn't get his brain to process what she'd said. Pregnant? He scrubbed a hand down his face. This couldn't be happening. "Are you sure? Jesus, Elizabeth. How the hell did this happen?"

Her laughter made his blood boil. "I think you know how this happened, darling. It was a shock to me at first, too, but I'm already in love with the little peanut. Yes, I am going to keep this baby and yes, you can run a paternity test whenever you want." A heavy sigh resonated around him in the small space. "We'll find a way to manage on our own. Maybe my parents will take me in for a while, or I can pick up a second job to make ends meet. We'll be fine, don't worry."

Ben ground the heel of his hand against the steering wheel, and his head dropped back against the seat. He was going to worry, and she knew that. If the baby was truly his, there was no question in his mind that he would do everything he could to take care of them. Fatherhood was always something he'd wanted for himself, and part of him was thrilled at this unexpected turn of events.

Another part of him knew it tied him to Elizabeth for the next twenty years, whether he wanted to be or not. It also meant the dream he'd built around Katie Parker could never be his.

"Elizabeth, I'm not sure what to say. This is a conversation that needs to wait until later. I can't deal with this right now."

Suddenly her voice became low and menacing. "You are not going to make me feel guilty about this pregnancy, Ben Collins. This is your responsibility, too, and I will not be pushed into doing anything I don't agree with."

"Whoa, hold on just a damn minute." He grabbed the phone, taking it off hands-free, and snapped at her. "Don't go putting words in my mouth. All I said was that I couldn't talk about this now, but we *will* talk later."

"I know what that means." Her voice broke, and she let out

a sob. "You just want to 'take care' of this, right? Make it all go away? I won't have an abortion, and you can't make me."

"Jesus Christ, Elizabeth." He rubbed at his forehead. A dull ache was already setting up residence there, and the day hadn't officially started. "I didn't suggest any such thing, so knock it off. Look, I can't talk about this right now. Come to Enderlin tomorrow, and we will talk, face-to-face, and figure out what comes next."

There was a pause. "Fine. Tomorrow." Then the call ended.

Burying his face in his hands at his desk, Ben tried to wrap his brain around how he'd ended up in this situation. Was he in love with Elizabeth? Hell no, not even close. Her behavior years ago had destroyed those feelings. But she kept coming around, reminding him of the good times and gaslighting him about the shit she'd done, and playing on his loneliness. She'd managed to worm her way back into his life, and he'd allowed it to happen. Now, it seemed like it was for good.

"Hey Ben, are you ready to dive back in this afternoon?"

Parker breezed into the office after lunch, fresh and cheerful, and his heart wilted. Here was everything he wanted, right in front of him: a woman with heart and strength of character, beautiful and smart, challenging, and exhilarating. But he was so ashamed he couldn't even look her in the eye. Without saying a word, he grabbed his things and pushed past her. If he hadn't already been filled with self-loathing, the look on her face as he left would have done the trick.

FIFTEEN

"I just can't figure him out." Katie and Patsy had relinquished the pool table and were nursing beers as they talked about the day. "He blows hot and cold. He flirts with me one second, then acts like I don't exist the next. After you and I talked at lunch today, I came back to the office ready to see where things might go, but he wouldn't even look at me. I'm going to end up with whiplash trying to follow along."

Patsy shook her head. "Try not to take it to heart. Maybe he hasn't reached your level of enlightenment yet and isn't ready to give in to his primal urges." She waved at someone over Katie's shoulder and slid off her stool, adding, "Like I'm about to. Will you be okay if I go?"

Katie waved her off. "Oh yeah, I'm good. I was thinking of leaving soon, anyway. Been a weird day. Have fun and be safe." After planting a kiss on Katie's cheek, Patsy danced away.

Glancing around the room as she finished her drink, Katie's eyes fell on a lone figure at the bar, staring morosely into his drink.

While it was no surprise to see Ben in Maxie's—he had become as much a fixture of Happy Hour as the rest of them—

it was unexpected to see him alone. It would be a challenge to find someone in that bar who didn't know and like Ben Collins, especially the ladies, so he could have blended with anyone. She gathered the empty bottles from her table and took them up to the bar.

"Hey."

Ben looked up with bleary eyes. "Oh, heeeey, Parker. Want a drink?" He waggled his empty glass at her.

"Sure, but not whatever that is." She ordered a new bottle of beer, and Ben got a fresh gin and tonic. He took a swig and resumed contemplation of his coaster as though she wasn't there. Judging by his disheveled appearance, it seemed obvious something was bothering him. She hated to see him upset so she settled on the stool next to him and nudged him with her shoulder.

"Are you okay?"

He didn't reply at first, just swirled the liquid in his glass between sips. With a sigh, he shook his head and shifted in his seat.

"I don't know what happened, Parker," Ben mumbled after a long pause. He drained his glass and ordered another. "I liked my life here. A nice house, some decent friends, a good job. It was simple. I was happy. Or something like happy, at least." With the new drink in hand, he turned to glare at Katie. "And then you had to show up."

Eyes wide, Katie scoffed. "Me? What the hell did I do?"

"You rolled into town and ruined everything. Why d'you have to make things so hard?" Katie's heart broke at the sadness on his face. "God, Parker, I wish I'd never met you."

Even though she knew Ben had been drinking and wasn't really himself, embarrassment and hurt bubbled up in her chest. She couldn't quite convince herself that he didn't mean what he said; the truth usually came out when alcohol broke down the walls of polite behavior. Intentional or not, his words still stung.

"Oh, the feeling's mutual. You can be a real asshole, some-times." She swallowed half her beer, trying not to let on that his words had cut her deep.

Finishing the last of his drink, Ben passed a hand over his face and groaned. "I'm sorry, Katie. It's good that you're here; I'm glad you're here. Work is a lot more fun with you around. And your work is really good, Katie, you know that?"

She wrinkled her nose and frowned. "That sounds so weird."

He blinked, looking like he was having trouble keeping her in focus. "What sounds weird? Thashuregood?"

"You just called me Katie. Twice."

"So? That's your name, right? Do you want me to call you *Kaaatherine?*" He drew out her full name in a nasally tone.

"God, no. But you've never called me Katie. You have only ever called me Parker. I was beginning to think you didn't know my first name."

He stared at her for several seconds, as though waiting for that observation to sink into his muddled brain, then he cleared his throat. "Sorry."

"I mean, I don't mind. But can I ask why you only call me Parker?"

Ben heaved a sigh and looked up at the ceiling. "I don' wanna say."

The way he avoided answering piqued her curiosity further. She laid a hand on his arm and leaned in close. "Come on, Ben. Why don't you call me by my first name?"

The corner of his mouth twitched, and Ben's resistance seemed to melt away at her touch. He stared at the spot where she was touching him and shrugged. "I didn't wanna like you. I wanted to hate you. You weren't supposed to stick around more than a week. I thought I could push you out, and then I could go back to my regular life." Shaking his head, he sighed. "But then you had to be smart and funny and beautiful and just…" He waved his hands at her. "Calling you Parker should have made it easier to not care about you. To distance myself from you like you were any other coworker." Ben twisted his mouth and sniffled. "It didn't work."

"Ben..."

Katie searched his eyes, trying to read his true feelings. She was having a hard time reconciling his words with his past actions. Blowing hot and cold, playing games: how could she trust him now, saying he cared about her?

"Wow." Ben's whisper was full of childlike wonder. "Your eyes—"

"What about them?" Drunk Ben was fascinating, and, she had to admit, adorable, no matter how frustrating he was. Katie wanted to see what other secrets his addled mind would reveal.

He leaned in closer and gaped. "They're like sapphires. I think they might be mazhic."

With a chuckle, Katie pushed a little further. "Magic, huh? How do you mean?"

Behind his dreamy expression, Katie watched a sudden moment of clarity push to the surface, his voice low and thick with emotion.

"I get sucked in and, like, hypnotized. I feel like I could do anything. They make me feel safe. *You* make me feel safe."

Her heart thudded painfully against her ribs, his romantic, sincere declaration catching her off guard.

The alcohol won out once again, and his words became mushier as he stared more intently. "It's like—if I could always look atchyur eyes, nothing else would matter. All the other bullshit in my life would go away. I feel... I don't know." He shrugged. "Better? Like a better man? I could look in your eyes f'rever, even though it's hard to breathe when you're lookin' back at me."

Katie couldn't have foreseen this turn of events. Ben's intoxicated candor was more than she was expecting and sweeter than she thought he was capable of. He continued to examine the depths of her eyes with a sort of reverence, and Katie was at a loss for words. She placed her hand on his cheek and felt a charge chase up her arm when he leaned into her touch. He wore a contented smile for a long moment while Katie tried to figure out what to say—or how to feel. She cleared her throat, breaking contact, and Ben's eyes opened wide.

"That is one of the loveliest things that has ever been said to me." She released a shaky breath. "And don't stop calling me Parker. I like the way you say it."

Ben gave up a tipsy grin and patted Katie on the top of her head as if she were a child. "You're welcome," he murmured.

With a roll of her eyes, she took hold of his arm. "Come on, lush. Let's get you home."

Ben tossed a few bills on the bar and staggered. He tried to waggle his eyebrows at Katie but only managed to blink both eyes at her. "Ms. Parker, I believe you're trying to seduce me." He laughed at his own cleverness but didn't resist when Katie tossed his arm around her shoulder.

"You wish. If I were trying to seduce you, you sure as shit would know it."

She helped Ben stumble out the door and folded him into the back of an Uber. After he mumbled his address to the driver, he laid his head back on the seat, dozing immediately. Katie hesitated for a fraction of a second, then ducked inside next to him.

Ben jumped when she shut the door, and he squinted at her. "Parker?"

"Don't say a word. I don't trust you to make it inside your house instead of passing out in the hedges. I promise your virtue will be intact in the morning."

"Heh." Ben relaxed again and sighed with closed eyes. "That's too bad."

It wasn't a long ride from Maxie's to Ben's house, but it gave Katie a few minutes to gather her thoughts. His revelations had been surprising, to say the least. Over the last few weeks, her feelings for him had grown, but she could never quite get a read on how he felt. Hearing him talk about her that way only confused her further.

The car pulled up to a red brick, ranch-style house. "Hey." Katie nudged him. "You're home. Let's get you inside."

Ben startled and looked around groggily but relaxed when he saw Katie. "Oh, hi."

She guided him up the sidewalk and managed to get her inebriated charge over the threshold. "Which way?"

Without a word, Ben disentangled himself and tottered down the hallway. She followed and watched with amusement as he stood at the foot of his bed and fell face first on top of the covers. He rolled over with a contented sigh. "Mmmmm. I love my bed."

"I'm sure your bed loves you, too." Katie laughed and tugged at Ben's shoes. "You get settled then I'll go home so you can sleep it off."

She walked around the side of the bed to pull a blanket up over him. But as she turned to leave, he grabbed her wrist.

Looking up with sorrowful eyes, he whispered, "Please stay."

"Ben..." A flush of affection swept through her despite knowing he was drunk and not thinking clearly. She knew it didn't mean anything, that he wouldn't ask her to stay otherwise. But oh, how she wanted it to be real.

He shook his head, loosening his hold and running his thumb over the sensitive skin of her palm. "Not like that. Just...it was a shit day, and I don't want to be alone. Stay for a little while." Ben turned pleading eyes her way. "Please."

This sudden vulnerability tugged at her heart and was more than Katie could fight. And just like that, her resolve didn't crumble–it disintegrated. She nodded. "Sure. Yeah, I'll stay for a little while."

With a long, satisfied exhale, Ben settled back to sleep,

keeping her hand tucked in his. She stood by the bed for a moment, watching him drift out of consciousness, heartache still plain in his features. When she traced the worry lines on his forehead, his features relaxed, and he curled her hand against his chest with a contented sigh.

Her heart lurched. "Damn it, Collins."

Settling on the edge of the bed, she watched the rise and fall of his chest. This had been the damnedest night. What the hell was she supposed to make of it all? One minute he ignored her, then he made her melt into the floor with sultry looks and seductive words before turning around and making her think she had imagined all of it. She didn't know how much more she could take.

He snored loudly and rolled over, throwing his arm across her lap and pulling her closer, a satisfied smile on his face. Afraid of waking him, she didn't immediately extract herself. He looked so serene, she couldn't stop herself from stroking his hair. The temptation to kiss him like her very own Sleeping Beauty was strong, and she nearly gave in to it.

Instead, she sighed, dismissing her ridiculous romantic notions, and pulled out her phone to text her brother.

Hey. Staying at a friend's tonight. I'll be home in the morning.

Nick responded almost immediately.

Everything okay? Are you safe?

With a rueful smile, she typed back:

Yes. Everything's good. Weird, but good. I'll fill you in later.

When Katie felt herself dozing, she slid out of Ben's grasp, pausing in the doorway for one last look at what had become, despite her best intentions, a welcome complication. Then she laid down on the couch and replayed the night's events.

The man sleeping in the other room didn't seem like the Ben she knew. There was a darkness hiding behind his eyes that he had allowed her to see tonight. What could have hurt him so badly? His heartbroken expression danced in her mind as she drifted off to sleep.

———

"Parker?"

Katie jolted awake at the sound of her name, unsure where she was for a moment. Trying not to panic, she scanned the room, stopping short when her eyes landed on Ben standing in the hall, dripping wet in only a towel.

He was rubbing his hair, standing practically naked in the doorway. With a catch in her throat, Katie took it all in, letting her eyes roam over his exposed skin, finally coming to rest on the amused sparkle in his deep green eyes. She gulped and looked away, but she could already feel the heat creeping into her cheeks. And she knew Ben had seen it, too.

"So...why are you on my couch?" His teasing tone only flustered Katie further. "Not that I'm not happy to see you. I'm just confused."

She ran her hands through her hair, trying to smooth out the crazy knots that always appeared overnight. Jumping to her feet, she started folding the blanket to distract herself. Keeping her eyes from feasting on Ben's naked skin was a lot harder than she wanted to admit.

Her mind suddenly went blank, every word she'd ever known just gone. *Come on, Katie, pull yourself together. You'd think this was the first half-naked man you've seen.* "It, uh, seemed like you needed some help to get home from the bar last night, so I made sure you didn't die in your yard somewhere. Then you asked me to stay, so...I stayed." Katie placed her hands on her hips and held eye contact with Ben with some difficulty. Her gaze kept trying to wander and get another peek.

In that moment all she could think about was Patsy's advice: *"You seal the deal. Don't wait for him."* It was a tantalizing thought that made her heart jump. Could she do it? Could she make that move and see where it carried them? The idea was beyond tempting, but it was quite a leap to make.

145

"So, you carried me to my bedroom, huh? Undressed me and tucked me in?"

Rolling her eyes, Katie busied herself with fluffing the throw pillows. "Don't be a child. Nothing happened."

"Good to know my honor is unscathed. I applaud your restraint."

She crossed her arms and laughed. "I should leave. It's getting crowded in here with you and your ego."

Ben took a few steps into the living room, causing Katie to take a few startled steps backward. He glanced down at his towel before giving Katie a roguish lift of his eyebrows. "Let me get dressed, and I'll cook us breakfast."

"You don't need to do that—cook me breakfast, I mean. You should get dressed. But only if you want to." Jesus. Why did she let him fluster her so badly? "I need to go home and get ready for work."

Ben waved his hand to dismiss her argument. "Nobody will miss us. And I insist. It's the least I can do to repay your kindness." As he sauntered down the hallway toward his room, he tossed a crooked smile over his shoulder. "And they say chivalry is dead."

"Fuck," she muttered. Left standing alone, she suddenly felt exposed. "Hey—where's the bathroom?"

"First door on the left."

Katie shut the door and leaned her fevered forehead against the cool wood. What was she doing? This was all kinds of wrong. Glancing in the mirror, she did a horrified double-take at her own reflection. Her hair was wild and knotted, her makeup smeared under her eyes. Mortification spread over her like a wet blanket. Dear god, how could Ben have even looked at her with a straight face? If she decided to make a move, this was not that moment. She hurried to remove the dark smudges and drag her fingers through the raging mess perched on her head.

"Get your shit together, Katie. Nothing happened—nothing is going to happen—it's only breakfast."

Then why was her heart racing?

Ben's face lit up when he saw her. "There you are. I thought you'd bolted on me." His eyes were bright and clear, and he looked happy she hadn't disappeared. "What's your pleasure?"

Katie froze, a thousand racy images dancing in her vision. "Um. What?"

He raised an eyebrow. "Breakfast? You do eat breakfast, don't you?"

"Oh, yeah, sure."

"What did you think I meant?" He leaned in close, the corner of his mouth lifting.

Intelligent thought escaped her, and her heart thumped hard against her ribcage.

He chuckled and pivoted to the refrigerator. "I'll surprise you then. How about you start the coffee?"

"Yes. Good. Right." Katie jumped at the request, thankful to have something to do. Once she was in the small kitchen space, she stopped and turned to Ben. "Where is the coffee, exactly?"

With his eyes trained on hers, he crept forward. Katie stumbled back, unable to evade his laser focus. Backed against the counter, she searched for an escape, but there was nowhere to go. Ben leaned in so close that the clean, male scent of him almost overwhelmed her senses. She couldn't tear her eyes away, his direct gaze making it impossible to think.

"Here you go." He magically produced the bag of grounds from somewhere behind her, and she resumed breathing. Ben chuckled. "Damn, Parker, it's far too easy to ruffle your feathers." He turned back to the stove and continued his preparations.

Her cheeks on fire, Katie frowned. "You could have just told me, you know."

"Where's the fun in that?" He hummed, moving deftly from stove to refrigerator to counter and back.

"You're awfully chipper for someone who was in your condition last night."

"I don't know." Ben shrugged and turned the bacon. "I wasn't that bad off, was I?"

She narrowed her eyes. "What do you remember?"

"Hmm. Well, I guess," he frowned in concentration, "not much. I remember gin. Lots of gin. Too much gin."

"Do you remember talking to me at the bar?"

"I remember seeing you." He peeked at Katie from the corner of his eye and smiled. "I like watching you when you stop worrying about what other people think."

"What? I don't worry about that."

"You do. All the time. You always worry about what people see when they look at you. You're afraid to say or do the wrong thing." He flipped the hash browns in one pan and stirred the eggs in another, then turned to Katie. "Like right now. You're nervous. I can't say I don't like it because I do. But only because there's something damn exciting about knowing that I have that effect on you. Watching you last night, it was almost like you were someone else."

"You don't make me nervous." She pouted. "And what do you mean? Did I do something stupid last night?"

"There you go, worrying again. Relax, Parker. You didn't do anything wrong, you just carried yourself differently. You were more open." When he turned to look at her this time, his expression was serious and probing. He stepped toward her, the tip of his tongue touching the corner of his mouth, and Katie's knees turned to jelly. "It was sexy as hell." He tucked a stray curl behind her ear, his fingers lingering on her neck, and she closed her eyes.

His voice was soft and low, and so close she felt his breath on her cheek. "You moved like a woman who knows who she is and what she wants. I couldn't keep my eyes off you."

She wasn't able to make herself move, not even when Ben stroked a hand over her shoulder and down the length of her arm. "Every man was looking at you, wanting to know you, to be with you." He lifted her hand and pressed his lips to the soft, sensitive skin on the inside of her wrist. Her eyes fluttered open to find him studying her, a glow in his gaze that made her dizzy. With a lopsided grin, he brushed his mouth over her skin again. "Mmmm. Can't say I blame them. You are a fascinating creature, Parker."

Transfixed by his eyes, his touch, his voice, Katie leaned into him, aching for further contact. He slid her hand to the small of his back and tangled his fingers in her unruly hair.

"Ben..." What was happening to her? Why wouldn't her body listen to her, push him away, remove herself from his embrace?

Because she wanted this, wanted *him*, more than anything.

He brushed his lips against her throat, tightening his grip at the soft moan that escaped her when he did.

"God, you are magic," he murmured against her lips.

Every move of his hands drove her crazy. No one had ever drawn this kind of reaction from her, and she was drowning in the sensation of his lips on hers. He nibbled his way along her jaw, and she trembled under his touch. "Ben—"

"God yes, Parker." He groaned against her cheek, pulling her against him.

Katie somehow found the presence of mind to get her hands between them, pushing at him. "No, Ben—I think something's burning!"

With a start, he spun around to the hash browns smoking and the bacon curling and turning black. "Oh, shit!"

He scrambled to turn off burners and salvage what he could, while Katie put some much-needed space between them, her legs shaking. Her heart was still beating out of control, and everywhere his lips had been was on fire. If he touched her like that again, she could not be held responsible for what might happen next.

"Well, that was almost a disaster." Ben surveyed the aftermath, his hands on his hips and looking amused.

"In more ways than one." Katie fought to calm the flopping in her stomach.

"It's still salvageable if you don't mind crispy bacon." Ben held out a plate of black potatoes and almost unrecognizable charcoal strips. They both stared at the plate, then at each other, until laughter overtook them. "Yeah, that's not even close to edible. Come on. I'll buy you breakfast instead."

Katie shook her head and backed into the living room. "No, you don't have to. I told you, you don't owe me anything."

Ben rolled his eyes. "Jesus, Parker, stop doing that. I know I don't owe you anything. Did it ever occur to you that I don't want you to leave? That I just like being around you?"

"You do?" The genuine interest in his eyes stirred something deep in her belly. She knew he liked to push her buttons and catch her off guard, but that admission left her speechless.

"Yes. Now stop gawking at me and let's find some food that's not burned to ashes."

SIXTEEN

B reakfast with Ben wasn't what Katie expected. He was charming and funny and seemed genuinely curious about her life. He told her stories about the shenanigans he got up to in college, lamenting that he had lost touch with most of the guys he had known. Katie leaned in, enthralled by his voice and his humor. It was a simple thing to answer his questions, sitting in a corner of Back Alley Café, sharing a plate of perfectly cooked bacon and pancakes. This morning, in this place, he had a casual way about him that put her at ease, and the rest of the world melted away. There was only the café, and Ben, and the delicious food between them.

When they both had their fill, Katie studied him as he sipped his coffee.

"What?"

"I don't know." She shook her head. "Nothing."

Ben narrowed his eyes. "Lies. It's obviously something. What are you thinking?"

She fidgeted with her coffee cup, rearranged the silverware, and smoothed her napkin. "I was just thinking that this is nice."

His eyes sparked over the rim of his cup. "I agree. But I

think we both know that if you hadn't distracted me, the breakfast I was preparing would have put this one to shame."

"Excuse me? I distracted you? Oh, no, no, no. I think the gin you were trying to drown yourself in last night burned out a few too many brain cells. It's obviously affected your short-term memory. What happened in that kitchen rests firmly on your shoulders."

A throaty voice interrupted them. "Ooh, what happened in the kitchen, Benjamin?"

Standing next to the table looking impeccable and elegant was the beautiful redhead Katie had seen Ben with a few weeks ago.

"What are you doing here?" Ben's voice was low and tight, and the venom in it surprised Katie.

The woman leaned in to kiss Ben's cheek, but he ducked out of her reach.

"Oh come, now, darling, don't be like that," she cooed. She examined Katie with a sneer. "And who might you be?"

Katie smiled, offering her hand. "I'm Katie."

The woman stared at her and raised an eyebrow. "Of course you are." Turning her back to Katie, she focused on Ben. "You told me to come visit you today. So, here I am."

"You should have called first, Elizabeth."

The name caught Katie's attention, and she jumped out of the booth, glaring at Ben. "Wait a minute—this is Elizabeth? Your fiancée, Elizabeth?"

"Oh, Benjamin, you told her about me." She tried to slip her hand into the crook of Ben's elbow when he stood up. "That's so sweet."

Ben pushed her hand away and stepped toward Katie. "Ex-fiancée, Parker. I told you that."

"Well, we can agree to disagree on that for now." Elizabeth pressed herself against Ben's back, sliding one arm around his waist and resting her chin on his shoulder.

Katie's stomach twisted, and the blood rushed to her

cheeks. Feeling like a fool, she refused to look at Ben and give him the satisfaction of seeing how upset she was. She dropped some cash on the table and turned to the exit. "Yeah, I'm just going to go. Thanks for breakfast."

Grabbing at her before she could slip past, Ben tried to disentangle himself from Elizabeth's arms. "Parker, wait! Just let me explain. Please."

She glared at his hand on her skin. "How you live your life is none of my business, Ben. I'm your coworker, nothing more. I'll see you at work." Wrenching her arm out of his grasp, she dashed from the diner before he could say anything more.

How could she have been so stupid? Katie slid around the corner at the end of the block and leaned against the brick wall, trying not to cry. What in the world made her think she was anything more than a distraction to Ben? It seemed her initial impression of him as a womanizer was correct, after all. He'd been playing with her, plain and simple.

She pressed the heels of her hands against her eyes, trying to banish the sight of Elizabeth's mocking smile. Taking a deep breath, she resolved to walk the few blocks to Maxie's to retrieve her car and go home for a shower before heading to the office. Or maybe she'd call in and just crawl under the covers, where she could wallow and lick her wounds. No, work would be the best thing for her right now. She was sure Ben would be otherwise occupied with Elizabeth, so that would allow her to focus on work instead of thinking about him. At least she hoped it would.

Pushing off the wall, Katie wrapped her arms around herself and trudged along the sidewalk. She caught sight of her reflection in a shop window as she passed and was stunned at the image staring back at her.

Her hair waved around her face, the curls unkempt and untamed. She thought she'd wiped off the makeup from the night before, but it was still smeared under her eyes, giving her a hollow, haunted look. Great. Elizabeth probably had a field day with that. Katie rubbed at her face in an attempt to make herself look less frantic.

Over her shoulder she noticed a figure standing motionless across the street behind her, and the hair on the back of her neck stood up.

From this angle, his face was completely obscured by the hood of his sweatshirt. He was hunched forward, partially hidden behind a light pole, but his hood was definitely trained in her direction. Something about his posture reflected in the window felt sinister and violent, sending pinpricks of fear down her spine. She knew in an instant it was Him.

Katie ducked into the convenience store on the corner and tried to disappear between the shelves while watching the traffic pass by outside. She could see Him still watching, hands hanging loose at His sides, adding to the ominous air surrounding Him.

There was a loud crash in the store behind her, and she whirled toward the noise. It was nothing more than a stack of cups being pulled down by someone's errant toddler, so she pivoted back to her surveillance.

He was gone.

Katie scanned the shop, frozen with fear and certain He had slipped inside while she was distracted. Her eyes darted from face to face in a matter of seconds, but He wasn't among the patrons wandering the aisles.

She hurried to the front door and paused on the threshold, peering up and down the sidewalk.

Oh my god, where did He go? Panic rose in her chest, and she willed herself to keep it together, just get to her car and get the hell home. She raced down the pavement, trying not to look over her shoulder, convinced with every breath that He was only steps behind. The morning sun did nothing to dispel the frantic chill that was seeping into her bones, and only the ragged breath of exertion kept her from screaming. Scanning each face that she rushed past, she realized that everyone was a threat. She didn't have any idea what He looked like and that gave Him a dangerous advantage.

Maxie's came into view, drawing closer with each step, thank god. From the corner of her eye, she caught sight of the hooded figure on the other side of the road, keeping pace with her but staying a few steps behind. Was this it? Would He take her here, now, in the open? If she screamed, would anyone even realize what was happening in time to save her?

She stuck her hand in her purse, feeling around for her cell but it was nowhere to be found. Her brain scrambled to remember what she'd learned in her self-defense classes. He wouldn't win, not today.

Keeping Him in sight as she quickened her pace, she put her head down and pushed on toward her car. She fished her keys out as she walked, almost dropping them in her fear. The car was coming closer and closer, but so was the figure. Unwilling to wait, knowing it could mean the difference between life and death, Katie ran across the street against the light, earning herself some squealing brakes and angry horns. Fumbling with her key at the car door, her hands trembled so badly she couldn't fit it in the lock. Once the door was opened, she threw herself inside, scrambling to lock all the doors.

When she looked up again, the hooded man was stopped at the edge of the parking lot, hands jammed in His pockets, watching. She still couldn't see any features—how the hell was He able to find just the right angle to stay hidden? His stance was so casual, without a worry in the world. Of course, He was in no hurry. He had her right where He wanted her.

Her heart was racing, and her breaths were coming in ragged gasps, but the key wouldn't go into the ignition. Katie was on the verge of coming undone, her own sobs choking her. But the engine wouldn't catch. It turned over but wouldn't start, and He stood there, motionless and patient.

She cranked the key, slamming the gas pedal to the floor, as the tears spilled over and blurred her vision. Trapped. She was trapped in her car, He had finally caught up to her, and she was powerless. If she got out and tried to run, He'd be on her in a second. If she stayed in her finicky vehicle, He just had to wait her out.

Eyes wide, she peered through the window, expecting to see a monster's face leering at her. But the figure was gone. The place He'd been just seconds ago was empty, and she craned her neck to scan all around her. The parking lot was completely vacant.

In her relief, Katie let a sob escape. Laying her head against the steering wheel, her adrenaline began to ebb, and she was finally able to breathe again.

A loud rap on the window made her jump and slam her elbow into the horn. Ben was frowning at her through the glass. Wiping at her wet cheeks, she rolled down the window. "What do you want, Ben?"

"You left your phone." After handing it to her, he hesitated, his scowl deepening. "Are you okay? Can we talk?"

"Now is not a good time, Ben." Suddenly exhausted, she laid her head back against the seat and closed her eyes. "Go back to your fiancée, please, and leave me alone."

"I told you, she's my ex-fiancée. Things are complicated with her right now, but she's not the one I want to be with. Talk to me, Parker."

This had been the most unhinged morning Katie had ever had. The emotional rollercoaster just kept going, and she didn't think she could handle any more. Opening her eyes, she took in Ben's earnest expression, and her chest tightened. Heaving a sigh, she leaned across to unlock the passenger door. "Fine. You have five minutes."

Jumping at the invitation, he rushed around and climbed in, twisting to see her face. "I'm sorry she showed up like that, but I swear that we are not together." He rubbed at his forehead with his eyes closed. "I haven't seen her in weeks, but she and I have some things to talk about, and we were supposed to meet later today. Then I drank too much last night, and you were there this morning so flawless and beautiful, and I forgot about everything but you. You're the one I care about, Parker, not her."

Watching hope ignite in his pleading green eyes, she wanted more than anything to believe that what he said was true. But her mind was so chaotic, racing with the fear of the shadowy figure pursuing her in broad daylight and the humiliation of Elizabeth's sneer, that she couldn't think straight.

He wound his fingers through hers, his eyes never leaving her face. "Don't shut me out, Parker. Not now. I want to see what we can be together. But you have to let me in and believe me when I say that it's only you if you're willing to take a chance."

Staring at their joined hands, Katie sighed. Her chest ached at his words. Saying yes, diving in with him, was what she wanted deep inside, with all her heart. There was so much baggage between them, she was afraid it could shatter them both, and she didn't know if she would survive another heartbreak. Especially if it was Ben's.

Sliding her hand out of his, she trained her eyes through the windshield, knowing she'd fall apart if she looked at him. "Let's just focus on working together, on being friends, and leave it at that."

She could sense him staring at her, barely breathing. From the corner of her eye, she watched his shoulders droop, shooting a pang of regret through her chest. Then he ran a hand through his hair and scratched his beard.

"Friends. Okay, yeah, if that's what you want." He got out of the car and hesitated before leaning back in. "I won't push, Parker, but I won't give up, either. Just know that I'm here, and I will *be* here if or when you change your mind."

He pushed the door closed and stepped back. The car started on the first try and with tears in her eyes, Katie drove toward the much-needed sanctuary of home.

Watching her drive away nearly tore Ben's heart in two. How could he explain Elizabeth to her? What could he possibly say to explain the dysfunction that somehow kept him tied to her after all these years? Shoving his hands in his pockets, he stared at his feet before turning back toward the diner. What a mess.

Elizabeth was standing on the sidewalk, tapping her stiletto and glancing at her watch. "There you are. Where on earth did you go? Let's just go back to your house where we can...talk."

"You need to go home." He was so disgusted he could barely look at her. There was no love between them, probably never had been. Learning that she was carrying his child did nothing to change the way he felt toward her.

Her heels clicked on the pavement behind him. "Ben, you're being ridiculous. Just calm down a moment, and let's talk this through."

Rounding on her, he stopped so suddenly she almost ran into him. "Talk what through, exactly? Talk through how you finally got what you wanted, and chained me to you for the rest of my life? Maybe we should talk through how you've been manipulating me since the moment we met and have never felt anything resembling love for me? Or we could always talk about how you just humiliated me in front of the one person who means something to me. Where would you like to start?"

Her lips pressed together in a tight line, and she frowned, a flush coloring her cheeks. Fuck. Now he felt like an ass for being so harsh. Neither one spoke for a moment as his words hung in the air between them. Then he took a deep breath and let his anger slip away.

"Look. This is a difficult situation for everyone, and none of us have any idea how to navigate it." Dragging both hands through his hair, Ben sighed. "We need to talk. I know that. But not today. I need a minute to process it all."

She lifted her chin and regarded him with narrowed eyes. "Fine. I can be patient—to a point. No matter what your little fantasy world looks like with her, the fact remains that this baby and I need to be your priority, and soon."

Without waiting for a reply, she walked away with her head held high. And Ben was left feeling more alone than ever.

SEVENTEEN

Pulling onto her street, Katie wasn't expecting to see the police cruiser parked in her driveway, and her heart tripped. Had something happened to Nick? Was he hurt? As she drew closer, the reason for their presence became painfully obvious, making her gasp.

Black paint covered the front of the pretty blue house she had known her whole life, spelling out ugly, hateful words. Words that were, without question, meant for her, and her alone.

WHORE
MINE
SOON

That's why He'd let her see him. He'd been at the house again, on the porch, too close for comfort. She parked the car and struggled to catch her breath, feeling like the wind had been knocked out of her. Climbing out of the driver's seat, her head swam.

"Kat!" Nick rushed toward her, relief flooding his face. "Jesus, you're okay. Where have you been?"

All she could do was shake her head and shrug. Nick

wrapped his arms around her, but she couldn't tear her eyes away from what had now become the most frightening word she'd ever seen.

SOON

He'd followed her halfway across the country and was letting her know that she wasn't safe in her own home. She wasn't safe anywhere. He would always find her.

Nick was talking, waving a hand at the sheriff who was asking her something. She struggled to focus on his words and choke out answers to his questions, but her brother did most of the talking. When Sheriff Jacobson was finished, Nick guided Katie inside and sat next to her on the couch, holding her hand.

"How are you doing?"

With a snort, she shook her head. "You wouldn't believe me if I told you. I keep waiting to wake up." Looking at her brother, the enormity of what could have happened crashed down all at once. Her voice broke when she tried to speak, but she swallowed her tears. "Nick, what if He had broken in? He could have hurt you. You could have died because of me." No longer able to fight her fear, Katie covered her face and cried.

Nick offered what comfort he could, but she knew she had to carry the guilt alone. She brought the threat here by coming home; she led Him right to Enderlin. Now the people she loved most in the world were in danger, and that knowledge broke her heart.

Would she ever be free, or would He forever be lurking around the next corner? Was her life going to be one terrifying encounter after another until He eventually killed her?

"Why don't you go upstairs and get some rest?"

Katie frowned. "I don't want to rest, Nick. And I can't just leave that there. I need to scrub it off or cover it up or—"

He propelled her toward the stairs. "Don't worry about it. I'll take care of it."

"He came here for *me*. This is my fault. It's not your problem, Nick, and I hate that I've dumped this on you."

"Stop it." He grabbed her shoulders and spun her to face him. "You're my sister, and I love you. Your problems are my problems—that's what family does. No, this sicko isn't after me, but you're wrong that this is in any way your fault. Kat, I wish I could take this off of you, make it all go away, but I can't. So, let me help where I can."

Kissing his cheek before plodding up the stairs, Katie was suddenly exhausted. She crawled under the covers, pulling them over her head. Her stomach felt like it was twisting in flaming knots, and no matter how tired she was, sleep would not come easily.

———

Katie opened her eyes and reveled in the warm blankets and the silence of her bedroom. It was so peaceful that for a moment, she forgot the events of the day.

But only for a moment.

A creak in the hallway grabbed her attention. She watched in terror as a shadow materialized in the sliver of light beneath the door and hovered for an unbearable amount of time. Her heart racing, eyes focused on the dark shape, she slid off the bed. Reaching for the bat she kept underneath, she held her breath, ready to pounce as the doorknob turned.

Nick peeked into the room. "Can I come in?"

With a shaky sigh of relief and a quick nod, Katie lowered the bat and climbed back on the bed. She smiled and took the cup of hot tea Nick offered her, sipping at it before setting it down with a trembling hand. They sat side-by-side on the edge of the bed, and Katie leaned her head on Nick's shoulder.

"Feeling a little better?"

She dragged her hands down her face. "I hate the idea that I'm putting you at risk. Maybe I should leave. Change my name, chop off my hair, dye it blonde. If I keep running, at least you won't be in danger. He'll give up eventually, right? That, or He'll catch up to me." Her voice dropped to a near whisper. "Either way, this will all be over."

"Jesus, Kat. That's a fucked-up thing to say."

Katie flopped back on the bed. "I know. I know. Sorry. I'm worn out, and it just keeps coming, keeps escalating. What else can I do? I carry mace with me, I've mastered an arsenal of self-defense moves, we installed an alarm system. But I feel like I have control over nothing. He still found a way to let me know He can get to me. He can get to the people I love. You don't deserve that."

"You don't deserve it either, Kat. I hope you know that."

Refusing to meet his gaze, she pulled a pillow over her head. "I must have pissed someone off, somewhere."

"You didn't do anything."

She felt the tears welling up again. "I wish I could believe that."

Neither of them spoke for several moments, then Nick cleared his throat, propped himself on his elbow, and faced his sister.

"So." He chuckled. "You and Ben Collins, huh?"

Katie groaned, swatting him with the pillow. "God, Nick. That's not even—I slept on the couch. Nothing happened." She could feel her cheeks blazing, recalling their encounter in the kitchen. Nothing *much* happened, she thought to herself.

"Does he know about all this?"

She nodded.

"And?" he prompted.

Jumping off the bed, Katie paced the room. "And what? He was with me when I got all those voicemails and when I got the call about Derek. I kind of had to tell him. But he's got unresolved baggage of his own, and I sure as shit don't want to drag him into the middle of this nightmare. Not right now."

"What about what he wants?" Nick strolled into the

hallway and paused at the door. "Give him a chance, Kat. I think he might surprise you."

———

It was nearing 7:00 p.m., and a simple homemade meal of lasagna with garlic bread was almost ready. Katie kept peeking through the curtains, watching for the familiar car to turn up the street. It had been months since the whole family was home at the same time, and she was eager to see her parents again. She couldn't sit still and kept pacing around the kitchen and through the living room. Nick was a little more composed.

"Good lord, Kat, will you sit down, please? You're making me dizzy. You can't make them get home any faster."

"I know. But moving around helps my nerves." She drummed her fingers on the kitchen island. "How can you be so relaxed?"

Nick shrugged. "They'll get here when they get here." He studied her from the corner of his eye. "How are you feeling? I know it's been a rough couple of days."

Katie fiddled with the napkins and silverware. "I'm…all right. Just tired, I guess. I don't know what to do, and I hate feeling so helpless."

"You are far from helpless. And you're not in this alone." He paused while setting the table. "He's smart, though. How the hell did this guy avoid all the cameras? How did He find you walking down the street? It's all crazy."

Goosebumps raced up the backs of her arms, and she rubbed at them. "Crazy is an understatement. Did you know that I actually turned my purse inside out, tearing a hole in the lining to look for a tracking device? I'm living in a horror movie."

"Are you going to tell Mom and Dad?"

"Tell us what?"

At the sound of her mother's voice, Katie squealed and darted across the kitchen, leaping into her arms. "Oof! Good heavens, Kat, be careful. I'm old—you'll break me."

Looking at Karen Parker, it was easy to see who Katie took after. Her round, rosy cheeks made her seem much younger than her sixty years, but the intelligence and affection that shined from blue eyes identical to her daughter's was unmistakable.

"Look at that—you're both here." Katie's dad shuffled in behind his wife, who had finally been released from Katie's death grip so Nick could have a chance to welcome her home. David Parker wrapped his daughter in a bear hug while she buried her face against his shoulder and fought the urge to cry.

"Oh, Dad, I'm so glad you guys are home."

He rained kisses on the top of her head and laughed. "So am I, kiddo—believe me, so am I."

Once they had brought in the luggage, Nick proudly served up their favorite lasagna, full of gooey cheese and Italian sausage, while Karen and David shared tales of their exploits. The little family delighted in all being under the same roof at last, sharing stories and gossip and laughter.

After dinner, Katie and David worked side by side, cleaning up the dishes. "Dad, I can manage this. Why don't you go up to bed?"

"Jetlag, Kat. I'm sure I'll be up for several more hours either way. Thanks for dinner, though. You and your brother didn't have to go to so much trouble."

"It was no trouble, Dad. You've been gone on the trip of a lifetime, and we figured you'd appreciate an old family staple."

Karen and Nick wandered in from the living room. "Oh, we did. What a wonderful surprise that was—after so much unfamiliar food I couldn't pronounce, it was heavenly."

During a lull in the conversation, David cleared his throat.

"So what were you two talking about when we came in? That sounded serious."

The siblings glanced at each other.

Katie grimaced. "I'm afraid it's not anything good. There's kind of a lot going on, and, unfortunately, everyone here may get caught up in it."

Nick and Katie tried to explain everything that had happened so far. From the pictures to the phone calls, the attack in the parking lot, the discovery of Derek's body, and finally to the graffiti on the house, they traded off leading the story.

"…and so, Nick painted over the words. Sheriff Jacobson and his team are working on the case, although I don't know what they can do." She twisted her fingers and stared at the floor. "Knowing He was here, at the house… it scares the shit out of me."

Her parents took it all in without saying a word. Then David pulled Katie into an embrace, and Karen dragged Nick across the room so they could join in.

"Whatever happens, your father and I will be here. Anything you need, you only have to ask."

Biting her lip, Katie leaned against the counter. "He wants me to know in no uncertain terms that He can get to me or to you, with or without an alarm system, and that changes everything. He wants me scared. And I am, make no mistake. But I'm also pissed. The police aren't making any headway, and He's just getting closer and closer to me. It's time for me to take some control and bring the fight to Him."

"I don't like the sound of that." Nick frowned. "Are you going to stalk the stalker?"

"Sort of. If the San Francisco police can't find Him with their resources and manpower, Enderlin's finest aren't going to do much better." Everyone stared at her, each with a different expression. Her mother's brow furrowed in worry,

Nick scowled at Kat with his arms crossed, while her dad stroked his chin.

Katie rubbed her forehead and sighed. "Look, I don't really have a plan, and I promise I won't do anything stupid. Something has to change, whether that means hiring a private investigator or getting a gun or—I don't know what. But this is my life, and I won't let Him chase me out of it."

EIGHTEEN

P arker had called out of work since the mess at the diner and wouldn't answer his texts or take his calls, so Ben was relieved to see her at her desk Monday morning. He knew he should talk to her—he *wanted* to talk to her—but he didn't have the foggiest idea where to start after the Elizabeth shitshow.

That was a conversation he was dreading. Never in a million years did he think he would be in this kind of situation. A year ago—shit, six months ago—he probably would have just sucked it up and married Elizabeth. For the baby, he would have sacrificed true love and found a way to make it work. But now, happiness was right in front of him in the form of Katie Parker, and he'd be damned if he walked away from her without fighting for what they could have together.

He peered over the top of Parker's cubicle wall and cleared his throat. The unexpected noise made her jump, and she cursed profusely under her breath. "Damn it, Ben, don't sneak up on me like that." She turned her chair to face him and dragged her hands down her face. "How was your weekend?"

When she looked up at him, his heart leapt with the sense that things might be okay between them, and he shrugged.

"Fine, I guess. How was yours? I heard you had some excitement at your house the other night."

Her posture tensed, and she narrowed her eyes. "Hm. I forgot what it was like to live in a small town." He watched her smooth her hair behind her ears with trembling fingers. "The things He spray-painted on the house were terrible, but they're gone now, thank god. The police took a report, but that's all they could do. He managed to keep out of sight of the cameras, so we don't know anything more about Him than we did before."

A chill ran through Ben, and he shook his head. "Whoa, whoa, whoa—what? I hadn't heard anything about that. What the hell happened?"

"Oh. Well, I guess while I was, um, asleep at your house, the stalker decided to leave me a few choice messages. He didn't break in or anything, but He was at my house. Again." Ben thought he saw a shadow pass over her face, but it disappeared so quickly, he couldn't be sure.

"Jesus, Parker. Is there anything I can do?"

"No, thanks." She tipped her head to the side and narrowed her eyes. "Wait a minute: if you didn't know about that, then what were you talking about? What excitement?"

He stood next to her desk and crossed his arms. "Didn't David and Karen get home?"

She gaped at him. "David and—How do you know my parents?"

With a chuckle, he brushed her hair off her forehead, resisting the urge to scoop her into his arms. "Like you said, Parker, it's a small town. Your parents are involved in everything. The only way I wouldn't know them is if I lived under a rock. They're fantastic and are easily my favorite people in town."

She scowled and rolled her chair a few inches away from him. "I know they're fantastic. They're *my* parents. Are you telling me you're, what? Friends with them?"

"Oh, yeah." He loved having this connection with her and rushed to prove how linked they were already. "Who could spend five minutes with them and not adore them? I should have realized you were Karen's daughter as soon as I saw you; you've both got those incredible blue eyes. And when you talk? That is David, through and through."

"Don't talk about my parents like you know them—or me."

Ouch. It was hard not to feel that like a punch in the gut. Did she really not see how crazy he was about her? Instead of sinking into the hurt, he took her words as a challenge. Ben's eyebrows lifted and his head tipped to the side. "You think I don't know you?"

"Of course, you don't." Those gorgeous blues popped wide in surprise. "How could you?"

"Fine." He grabbed the arms of her chair and leaned in close, staring into her eyes. Now. Just tell her. She'd never know how important she was to him if he didn't tell her. He took a deep breath. "You chew your lip when you're worried or nervous, like you're doing right now. You're self-conscious about your hair. Someone told you it was messy at some point, didn't they? Too bad, I like it when it's wild. You're very talented and one of the smartest people I know, but you don't see yourself that way. You're stubborn as a god damned mule, but you're also kind and funny. And you're incredibly sexy, whether you think so or not, especially when you aren't trying. You don't trust many people and think you have to face everything on your own to prove how strong you are." He took a step back and pressed his lips together. "And you're afraid of getting close to anyone again because you got burned so badly before."

For a long moment, she didn't move. Parker sat pressed against the back of her chair, her eyes unblinking, and he immediately regretted being so aggressive. Why was he always screwing up around her?

Nothing had gone the way he planned. He intended to smooth things over and, instead, made everything worse. Once upon a time, he had been suave and charming around women. But, somehow, he ended up jamming his foot in his mouth whenever Parker was around. What the hell was wrong with him?

Even as he berated himself for behaving like a caveman, her features relaxed, and the shock disappeared. With a nonchalant shrug, she turned away from him. "I'm not afraid, and certainly not of you."

"Of course not." He sighed, shaking his head.

Yep. Stubborn.

———

She couldn't move even after Ben backed away, his perception overwhelming. Now was the perfect time for a scathing reply to show him he didn't know a damned thing about her, but a petulant retort was all she could manage.

Because he did know her. Somehow, he had noticed things that no one else—not Charlotte, not Nick, certainly not Derek —had ever seen. It was unnerving.

The inside of her lower lip had been hamburger for the past few weeks, the gnawing far too frequent. So much was out of her control, she was in a constant state of anxiety and didn't even realize she was doing it. And she certainly didn't think that anyone had noticed.

Twisting a lock of her hair around her finger, she replayed every time Derek had suggested a sleek hairstyle or pushed her curls away as though they were choking him. She'd let him dictate so much; not just about her life but about who she was and who she was allowed to be. But Ben said he liked her curls, liked her hair wild, which was exactly how she preferred it, too. No one had ever told her that before.

Katie shifted in her seat so she could see his reflection in her monitor and she thought about the other things he said: he thought she was talented and smart, funny, kind, stubborn and...did he say sexy? Her cheeks burned but she also couldn't hide the thrill that curled her lips.

Until she realized the truth of his last observations. She didn't trust people, not many at least, and she worked hard to keep people at arms' length to ensure their safety, and hers. When you opened yourself up to other people, you revealed the gaps in your armor and made yourself vulnerable. She'd made that mistake before, with Derek, and it had only brought her pain and sadness.

Ben walked out of the room, smiling over his shoulder as he passed, making her heart squeeze painfully. She so badly wanted to believe that he was different. Every atom of her being was drawn to him; she craved not only the touch of his hands and lips, but his conversation, his laughter, and his infectious confidence.

But was the way he made her feel worth the risk of playing with fire, knowing that it could incinerate them both?

———

The Fourth of July dawned with a group of Dixie Printing employees meeting at the firehouse for the annual pancake breakfast and Bloody Mary bar. After they had their fill, they found an optimal spot to watch the parade, where they whistled and shouted when Dixie rode by as Grand Marshal.

Noon rolled around, and people peeled away from the group one or two at a time. Jocelyn ran off holding hands with one of the account reps, Brandon, to treat Dixie to lunch. Patsy had taken a liking to one of the new guys at MetalWorks and decided he needed to see what the fuss over Enderlin's festival was all about. That left Ben and Katie standing in the carnival midway, shuffling their feet and avoiding eye contact.

"So." She was desperately hoping he wouldn't walk away

and floundered for something to talk about. "What was the Fourth of July like for you growing up?"

"Oh god, it was horrendous. I didn't have any friends who lived close by, and my parents made me sit through a very tasteful dinner party with all of their friends. The only fireworks I saw were from the houses around us or on tv. That was it."

Katie gaped. "Ben, that is...the saddest thing I've ever heard. You never gorged yourself on cotton candy and corn dogs and funnel cakes until you puked and spent all your allowance on rigged games for a cheesy prize worth less than a dollar?"

"Uh, no." Ben laughed. "And until hearing your description, I had no idea I'd missed out on anything."

She grabbed his hand. "In that case, I insist on showing you the ropes."

"All right, maestro, I am yours to command. Where to first?"

Katie smiled as she walked backward and towed him with her. "Well, we're already on the midway—let's start here. I'll show you how to game the system to get the best prizes."

Ben raised his eyebrows. "Parker, I never took you for a grifter. Gotta say, I'm impressed. And a little turned on."

She nestled her hand in the crook of his elbow and steered him toward the games. The conversation was fun and easy, and Katie soon found herself relaxed and laughing, having more fun than she had in the last year. She introduced him to a big pillow of cotton candy that they shared as they walked. Stopping in front of one game, Ben puffed out his chest and pointed behind the carnival barker.

"See that giant dog, there? I'm going to win that for you, Parker."

"That's very gallant of you, but what am I going to do with a giant dog?"

Several games and even more dollars later, Katie hefted an

enormous, fluffy, stuffed toy around the festival while Ben strutted next to her, looking like the cat who swallowed the canary.

At the bingo stand, Katie spotted her parents sharing a slice of peach cobbler and comparing their cards. Karen and David looked up and beamed.

"Ben." Katie's dad stood up to shake his hand after Ben had planted a kiss on Karen's cheek.

"Hey! What am I, chopped liver? Again, those are *my* parents." Her dad tried to hug her around the enormous stuffed toy, and her mom only shook her head.

"Kat, what in the world are you going to do with a giant dog like that?"

"Ha!" Katie spun around and jabbed an accusing finger into Ben's chest. "That's exactly what I said."

He rolled his eyes before pressing a kiss to her cheek. "I haven't seen you put it down for one second since you got it, though."

David nodded at his wife once, then slung his arm around Ben's shoulders. "Hey, I've got some ideas I wanted to run past you about updating the city square." Katie watched the two men walk away, her chest filling with warmth. Then she sat next to her mom and took over her dad's bingo card.

"You know that dog is ridiculous, don't you?" Karen lifted its floppy ears and squeezed its nose.

Katie sighed. "I know. But you should have seen how excited Ben was to win it. He didn't do anything like this growing up. How could I tell him no?"

"I'm sure you couldn't."

"He's terrible at the games, but he was having so much fun I didn't have the heart to tell him we could have purchased this crazy thing for half what he shelled out trying to win it…" Katie trailed off at the knowing smile on her mother's face. "What? What's that look for?"

"Nothing. I just love seeing you happy. The way you and

Ben are together, the way he looks at you—I can tell you're crazy about each other."

Blushing, Katie focused on the card in front of her. "We are not," she mumbled through a grin.

"Don't deny it. It's sweet, and I'm thrilled that you found each other. We've known Ben since he moved here, and we adore him." Karen leaned toward her daughter and lowered her voice. "I was going to introduce you to him the next time you came home, anyway. After our first conversation with him, your father turned to me and said, 'That is the man Katie should marry.' And I agree."

"Oh, dear god." Katie rolled her eyes. "Don't reserve the church just yet. But, uh, how does he look at me, exactly?"

Karen nudged her daughter and inclined her head toward David and Ben. "The way he's looking at you now, like he's seeing the sun for the first time."

Katie peeked at Ben. Sure enough, he was listening to her father, but his gaze was trained on her, a dreamy, crooked smile on his face and a light in his eyes. Her heart leapt, and she couldn't stop herself from smiling back at him.

"Mom, you don't know what you're talking about."

David and Ben wandered back to the bingo table, and Katie relinquished her seat. They made small talk until Karen glanced at her watch and placed a hand on her husband's arm.

"Oh, David, we were supposed to meet up with the Welches about ten minutes ago. I'm so sorry, Kat, we have to run. Ben, as always, it has been a joy to see you. Take care of my girl."

At Katie's surprised look, Ben just gave her a wink. "It would be my pleasure." She elbowed him in the ribs then hugged both her parents goodbye.

Ben picked up the dog and reached out for Katie's hand. "Okay, Parker, what's next on the agenda? I believe someone promised me corn dogs and other food that might kill me."

It felt so natural to nest her hand in his as he pulled her

from stand to stand, sampling one of everything. This was a new and alluring Ben. Gone was the cocky attitude and condescension. Instead, he was showing her a playful, sweet side that she wanted to see all the time. Her cheeks blazed at the realization that she was falling for Ben.

Correction: *had* fallen for him. Hopelessly.

He noticed the change in her expression and cupped her chin, lifting it until she was looking into his eyes. "What? What's wrong?"

"Nothing. I'm fine."

He wound his fingers around hers, as though by instinct. "Good. I was afraid you'd have to run off, too. And I'm not quite done with you."

She hated how he could make her stomach dance like she was thirteen again. But she also secretly loved that he had that effect on her. It made her feel so alive and feminine and *sexy*.

"I'm not going anywhere."

———

"Hurry up! The fireworks are about to start."

The first big boom made them jump. They were running to find a viewing spot and weren't expecting the tremendous noise. Still holding hands, they spun around to see the display, staring up at the sky in wide-eyed awe.

All afternoon, Ben couldn't tear his eyes away from Parker and wondered at the fact that she was here, sharing this with him. The red, green, and gold lights played over her face, giving her an ethereal appearance, and a wave of longing washed through him. Everything about her was intoxicating. Overcome with emotion, he drew her close and whispered in her ear.

"Come home with me."

Lost in the fireworks, she barely looked at him. "What?"

He turned her to face him, pressing their bodies together.

"Come home with me. Tonight." Ben skimmed his lips against her temple, breathing in the scent of her. "I want you, Parker."

Holding their joined hands to his lips, he brushed a kiss over her knuckles. "Come home with me. I want to kiss you until we can't breathe, I want to lose myself in you." His need to be with her, to hold her intensified and he groaned. "You're looking at a ruined man, Parker. Come home with me and put me out of my misery."

She arched toward him, her eyes shining and a smile playing around her soft lips. Everything around them melted away, and his blood buzzed in his ears. Was this finally happening? His breath caught in his throat; every nerve alive as he leaned into the one person he wanted more than anything. Before their lips could meet, she placed a hand on his chest and stepped back.

"I—I can't, Ben."

Brushing the backs of his fingers over her cheek, he looked deep into her eyes. "What's stopping you? We're consenting adults." Her expression softened, and he leaned in to whisper against her ear. "We could be good together, Parker. Give me the chance to show you."

She pulled out of his embrace and wrapped her arms around herself. "This is a terrible idea, Ben. Things like this never end well." She smiled sadly at him. "Not for me."

He frowned, a spark of anger flaring in his chest. "I'm not Derek, you know."

Parker sighed and ran her hands through her hair. "I know, but that's not all I'm talking about. There's Elizabeth, our work together, not to mention the danger that's following me, Ben. Danger that you don't deserve, and you don't need. I can't do that to you. I won't."

"Don't I get a say in this?" Ben tried to rein in the disappointment in his gut that was quickly blazing into anger. "Does it matter that I want to shoulder that burden with you?

You don't have to face this alone, you know. We can fight it together."

She closed her eyes, and a lone tear sparkled in the light of the fireworks. "Ben—"

He didn't let her finish, his own hurt feelings overshadowing his sympathy. "So that's it, huh?" She flinched as though he'd struck her. "You're not even going to give me a chance to prove how I feel about you? God, you are so stubborn. I'm standing here, offering you everything I have, and your...what? Pride? Won't let you even consider it?"

"So now you're mad at me?" Katie folded her arms and glared right back. "Because I won't sleep with you?"

He felt like she had doused him in ice water. "What? Hold on just a second; that's not what I said. That's why you think I'm mad?"

"It doesn't take a genius to figure it out. You asked me to come home with you, and I said no, and now you're pissed. Seems pretty damn obvious. You're so used to every woman you meet falling into bed with you that you think you're entitled to anything you want. But let me tell you—"

Ben interrupted her, his voice low and deep and furious. "For an intelligent woman, you are fucking clueless sometimes, Parker. You can spout all the excuses you want, but this has nothing to do with sex or my ego or anything else." He grasped her upper arms and pulled her close, his voice thick with the turbulent emotions he was trying to keep under control. "This is about your lack of trust, about knowing what we could be and refusing to let go, to let me in." He knew he was on the verge of saying something he'd regret, so Ben released her and turned away. He wanted to crush her to him, to kiss her until her knees buckled and she was no longer afraid; to make her see she was in her own way. But he wouldn't take anything she wasn't willing to give.

The crowd around them gasped in awe at the fireworks, but Ben was too hurt to watch with them. He could feel Parker hovering behind him, and he felt like an ass. Deep inside, he knew she was afraid and that she had every right to be. So who did he think he was to demand that she put everything on the line for him?

Hanging his head, he turned to her, laying a hand on her arm. "Shit, Parker. I—"

She twisted away from his touch without meeting his eyes. "I have to go." Then she stalked off, leaving him standing alone in the flashing lights.

NINETEEN

The next morning, Katie and her family worked together in the yard and on small maintenance projects. Rocking back on her heels in the grass, she could still visualize the ugliness splashed across the house despite Nick's expert paint job. The words were burned into her memory. Her tormentor was ensuring she was fully aware that He knew where she lived, what she was doing, and who she was with.

She wanted to be brave. She wanted to take control and refuse to be terrorized, but it wasn't only her safety at risk anymore. Her throat tightened as she watched her dad and her brother inspect the picket fence. This was her world, right here, and no one was going to hurt them. Swiping a single tear from her cheek, Katie turned her attention back to the garden.

"Penny for your thoughts?" Karen kneeled next to her.

Katie tried to smile, but even she knew it was a pathetic attempt. "Just thinking. There's been a lot going on."

Her mom looked up at the house, her hands on her knees. "It isn't your fault. You know that, right?"

Busying her hands with digging in the dirt again, Katie shrugged. "Oh, yeah. I know."

Karen laid a hand on Katie's arm, commanding her full

attention. "Do you, though? I'm not so sure. What this man does is not in your control. You can't stop him from doing something any more than you made him start."

"But mom—"

"Kat, what did you do to make him contact you in the first place?"

A shadow of despair flitted over Katie's face, and she could only shake her head.

"Sweetheart, if you didn't do anything to make this start, how can you possibly do anything to make it stop? This person is broken somehow. Who knows what made him fixate on you? You can't carry that responsibility. It isn't yours."

Katie felt the weight she'd been hauling around with her lighten a little. "Are you sure? You don't think I need to try not to make Him angry?"

"How are you going to do that? I want you safe, but I also want you to be happy, to live your life without fear. You can't know what he will do, or when he'll contact you. If you let him control you, he's already won."

Her mom's words swam in her head, chasing the doubt and terror that had set up camp there. A few weeks ago, she'd thought the same thing, and it made sense. She couldn't let Him chase her out of her own life.

"What does Ben have to say about all of this?"

Katie was surprised at the question but still answered. "Nothing. Well, nothing much. I try not to talk to him about what's going on. That's one thing we've been fighting about." She sighed, pulled off her gloves, and rubbed her hands over her face. "Ben wants...well, he wants us to be more. But I'm scared, Mom. I couldn't handle it if something happened to him because of me."

Taking hold of Katie's hands, Karen looked her in the eye. "Kat. Do you have feelings for Ben?"

Reluctantly, Katie nodded.

"Have you told him that?" When Katie bit her lip, Karen

continued. "You owe it to yourself and to him to tell him how you feel. Tell him everything, Kat. Doesn't he deserve the opportunity to make that decision, to choose whether his feelings for you are worth the risk?" She smoothed Katie's hair. "Something tells me he thinks you're worth it. He cares about you, honey. Let him."

———

Katie tossed and turned in bed, her mind racing in circles with thoughts of Ben. If her mom was right, her stalker was going to do what He wanted, no matter what she did or didn't do. She knew she had to let go of that burden, but knowing that didn't make it any easier. And Patsy had been right: This wasn't the Dark Ages, for god's sake. She had every right to go after what she wanted, as much as anyone else.

And, dear god, did she want Ben Collins.

It had taken her far too long to admit it, but their time together at the carnival had sealed her fate with Ben. Katie couldn't dismiss the frantic 'what-ifs' that were keeping her awake. What if he didn't feel the same way about her? What if she was nothing more than another sexual conquest for him? What if they dove into a wild love affair, and her stalker decided Ben was in the way?

That last one gave her pause. He seemed to know what she was doing and who she was with, even here in Enderlin. Nothing had happened for a while, and that was a good thing —so why did it make her heart batter against her ribs? No news was good news, wasn't it?

She wasn't so sure.

What she *was* sure about was that Ben was on her mind. Constantly. Vacillating between desire and irritation, she was thinking about him every waking moment. Even when she wasn't awake, his lazy smile haunted her dreams, causing her to wake feeling distracted and dissatisfied. His seductive invitation was probably just a product of being caught up in the experiences of the day. It wasn't anything more than wanting to scratch an itch, and she was reading far too much into it. Wasn't she? But holy shit, the pure longing behind his words had nearly been her undoing. There was a brief second when she wanted to throw herself into his arms before that voice of reason, of fear, made her step back and ask if she could take that chance. So much was at stake if she gave in to her desire, falling in love with Ben Collins not the least of her concerns. She already felt like she was standing on the edge of that precipice, one foot poised to step into the void with no other thought than of being with him.

Katie buried her face in her pillow and groaned. She could spend weeks working out every possible scenario regarding Ben without a satisfactory answer. She rolled over and glared at the clock: 11:30 pm. Staring at the ceiling, she couldn't keep still. Her fingers drummed on the sheets, her foot wiggled, and her eyes kept popping open every time she tried to relax.

"Fuck it," she muttered and leapt out from under the covers, pulling on clothes faster than she ever had in her life.

Ben took a long pull from his beer. His eyes were trained on the television, but he had no idea what he was watching. His mind was elsewhere: specifically, with a certain curvy, chocolate-haired, fragile but stubborn woman with eyes the color of sapphires.

Thinking about Parker had become something of a nightly ritual. Picturing those eyes and the dimples that framed her delicious smile somehow helped him sleep.

He took another drink and sighed. It seemed like an impossible situation. Ever since Elizabeth had delivered her news, he'd been hard pressed to find pleasure in anything. But then yesterday had been amazing in every way—because he'd spent it with Parker. He was disappointed in himself for jumping the gun and all but begging her to sleep with him. His feelings overwhelmed him, and he didn't stop to think beyond his hunger for her. With Elizabeth in the picture, it had all gotten very complicated, and he had no right to add to her troubles. He had sworn to himself that he'd be careful—with his own heart and with hers. She'd had enough shit piled on her, and he'd be damned if he'd add to it. Especially not by pushing for something that probably hadn't crossed her mind. He'd wait, though. She was worth waiting for. He just hoped she thought *he* was.

The flash of headlights out front drew his attention, and he checked his watch, surprised that it was nearly midnight already. He switched off the television and padded to the window in the dim light. What he saw made his heart jump into his throat.

Parker's car had just pulled into his driveway, as though his pining and craving had finally conjured her out of thin air.

He let the curtain fall back in place, hoping she hadn't seen him. What the hell was she doing here? At this hour? He worried that there was an emergency, but judging by the way she sat behind the wheel with her hands glued at ten and two, he figured whatever brought her here wasn't necessarily urgent.

She stepped out of the car and turned to shut the door but stalled in her movement, chewing her bottom lip in that way that made him weak. She ran one hand through her wild hair, looking like she had just tumbled out of bed. God, he hoped she had. What an enticing image. She started to get back into the car—Ben almost banged on the window to stop her—but then her face lit up with determination, and she slammed the door.

———

One foot in front of the other, slowly, she began the short walk to Ben's front door, where she hoped Ben was home, awake— and alone.

She froze. *Shit.* What if he wasn't alone? She hadn't contemplated that possibility. Spinning until she was facing the car again, her frazzled nerves pulled her away from the house. It would be no big thing to jump in the car and haul ass back to her dark, quiet, safe bedroom. She could pretend this near humiliation never happened and go back to bed.

And lie there, thinking about Ben and how badly she wanted to see him and touch him and feel his soft lips against hers.

Fuck. She'd driven all the way here; she couldn't chicken out now. Didn't she owe it to herself to find out if there could be something real between them?

Without realizing it, her feet had carried her onto the porch, her hand poised to knock on the door. *Well, here goes nothing.* She took a deep breath in hopes of not passing out. But before her knuckles made contact, the door creaked open to reveal Ben leaning against the frame. He was wearing only a pair of faded blue jeans, with bare feet and no shirt, a beer bottle dangling from his free hand.

Yeah, that passing out thing was still a distinct possibility.

"Parker?"

This was such a monumentally bad idea, Katie almost ran. "Um. Hi, Ben."

He cocked one eyebrow and waited for her to say something else, maybe to explain why she was there, but she only stood on the porch, fidgeting and trying desperately not to stare at his naked chest.

"Want to come in?" He pushed the door open wider and stepped aside.

Katie gulped and nodded before making a conscious decision. "Yep." Then she was across the threshold. Her fingers twisted and untwisted and knotted in front of her while she stood just inside the entryway.

He closed the door behind her, his bare arm brushing against hers as he passed. "You can come farther in. I probably won't bite."

Immediately, her desire pictured his mouth on her neck, on her shoulder, teeth grazing her skin. Lost in the arousing vision, she just blinked at him until she realized he was teasing her. "Oh, ha, ha."

"Can I get you a beer?"

The words tumbled out of her mouth. "Yes. Please. That would be great. Thank you." She had no plan, was running purely on instinct—but there was a heady amount of freedom in it. One thing was certain: there was no turning back now.

———

Ben moved slowly into the kitchen, worried that any sudden movement might spook her. He was not going to take the chance that she'd honest-to-god bolt from the house without telling him why she had come in the first place.

He took two bottles from the refrigerator and watched her closely while he removed the caps. She was, it seemed, trying to pull her fingers clean off her hands, and she kept shifting her weight from one foot to the other. Her tousled hair fell over her shoulders, making her look a little savage and sexy as hell. She wore no makeup and had on a simple white t-shirt and a pair of cut-off jeans.

And he had never seen anything so beautiful.

There went that fire, blazing up a little higher. He sucked in a deep breath and strolled with a faked nonchalance to perch on the arm of his couch, next to the girl about to vibrate out of her skin with nervous energy.

He held out the bottle. "Here you go." He clinked his bottle against hers. "Cheers."

It took considerable control not to spit out his beer when she chugged half her bottle at once.

"Thirsty?"

She shrugged, her cheeks blazing. Her eyes flitted around the living room before landing on his bare chest. He swiveled on his seat until Katie was directly in front of him, standing almost between his legs. "Now. What brings this vision of wanton beauty to my door so late on a Saturday night?"

Katie lifted her chin, then rolled her shoulders. "I want to talk to you."

"It couldn't wait until Monday?" He took a swig from his bottle.

Her head swung from side to side. "No, I need to do this as soon as possible." He watched her eyes drift from his chest over his bare shoulders, landing on his mouth. She nibbled on her lip again.

God help him.

"You couldn't have texted or called?" Another drink. The woman had something on her mind, and he was bursting with curiosity to hear it.

Her eyes locked on his, and she shook her head again. "No. This is something best discussed face to face." Without breaking eye contact, Katie downed the rest of her beer.

Ben was enthralled by everything happening here—the way her lips pressed against the opening of the bottle, the intensity of her gaze as she looked him over, lingering on his mouth, the staccato pulse he could see beating in the notch of her collarbone. His stomach clenched in anticipation, and he hoped against hope that she'd reveal the reason for her visit soon before he lost control and kissed her senseless.

He took the empty bottle from her hand, letting his fingers trail along her wrist. As he eased it from her grasp, he was rewarded with a burst of goosebumps covering her arm. The look on her face was difficult to read, but there was a fire in her eyes that intrigued him.

"Well, Parker." He walked the empty bottles to the kitchen counter. "You've got me curious. What did you have on your mind tonight?" When he turned, he was startled to see she had followed him and was less than a foot away. She hesitated but then took a deliberate step forward, the tip of her tongue pressed against her upper lip. Ben's knees nearly gave way.

"I…" she trailed off, raking her eyes over him and stepping closer. He stood as still as he could under the circumstances and waited. When Katie spoke, her voice was thick and shaky. "I have never done anything like this before. I honestly have no idea what made me come over tonight." She looked up at him, her eyes round and terrified, but still she moved closer, their bodies nearly touching.

His breath caught in his throat, and he swallowed hard. "I'm damn curious about that, myself." She kept licking her lips then pressing them together, and he couldn't stop watching them. "Wait—you've never done what before?"

Her answer came out as a throaty whisper. "Have you ever laid awake at night, wanting something so much that you can't function? You can't sleep, your stomach is in knots, even breathing becomes difficult." Her head tipped to the side, and she reached out, timid and halting until her fingertips grazed the contour of Ben's shoulder. Her eyes followed the movement of her hand, her bottom lip trapped between her teeth. "Something that consumes you. Makes your heart race from wanting it?"

Ben was having trouble focusing on anything but her touch on his skin. "I might have some idea," he croaked.

His head swam, and his muscles twitched under the trail of fire she left behind. Did she have any idea of the effect she had on him? He worked to train his gaze on her face, drowning in the sensations washing over him.

Still, he waited.

He watched in wonder as her eyes blazed with a hunger he

knew all too well. She leaned into him, teasing, feathering her mouth against his, and Ben moaned.

"Fucking Christ, Parker, what are you trying to do to me?"

Just when he thought the heat of his longing would burst into a fireball, she ran the tip of her tongue over his lip, capturing it between her teeth. A strangled growl erupted from the back of his throat, and his restraint crumbled.

He surged forward and crushed her against him, covering her mouth with his. All thought ceased, and he indulged in the taste of her, the feel of her skin under his hands, grasping the tangles of her hair and pressing into the small of her back until their bodies fused together.

Katie met Ben move for move, gasping when his teeth scraped along her jawline and retaliating by nipping at his ear and his neck. Their mouths became more insistent, their hands exploring, clutching at each other with an urgency he'd never experienced before. Ben lifted her, and she wrapped her legs around his hips.

"Oh, dear god." The words tumbled from Katie's lips when Ben kissed and nibbled a searing trail down her neck. Her fingers dug into his back, and he couldn't seem to hold her close enough. He gripped at her shoulder blades, feeling her bare skin under her shirt, then he lifted it over her head when they came up for air.

Setting her down and smoothing her bangs from her forehead, he wanted to see that wildness that had driven her to him. He buried a hand in her hair and eased her head back so he could look into those eyes, watch them while he stoked the fire in her, and his chest felt like it would burst. This feeling rushing through him was new and powerful.

"Parker, I..." Ben's throat closed, and he could only stare at her in amazement. He took her lips again, unable to get enough of the taste of her. Then he slid the strap of her bra off her shoulder, running his tongue up the curve of her neck and dying a little when she shuddered in response.

With all the self-control he could muster, he untangled her hands from around his neck and stepped back. She watched him, the confused look on her face telling him she was trying to figure out why in god's name he was stopping her. One corner of his mouth lifted, and he shook his head. "I don't know if this is a dream, but I can't say I care right now..."

Katie's hands fell to her sides, and she locked her eyes on his, seemingly intoxicated by what she saw there. He tugged at her belt loops and pulled her a step closer, then released the button on her shorts, letting them fall to the ground around her feet. He lowered himself in front of her slowly, starting from her shoulders, sliding his hands over her breasts while his mouth tasted her soft flesh. His fingers clutched at her hips to hold her still as his mouth traveled lower, and she shivered when his warm breath brushed over the soft skin of her belly.

Ben's fingertips slid inside the leg of her panties, and he was immediately rewarded when she trembled and gasped. "Jesus, Mary, and Joseph," he muttered with his lips still pressed to her hip. He moved slowly and deliberately against her, his fingers gliding back and forth, dipping inside and back again. Oh god, did she feel good. Her nipples strained against the fabric of her bra, and he couldn't resist scraping his teeth over one. She groaned, then undid the clasp, tossing the garment across the room.

Fuck, yes.

He closed his lips around her, using his tongue and his teeth to push her farther. Christ, the way her whole body was quivering in his hands was almost too much for him to take. Pressing his palm against the small of her back, she arched into him until her knees trembled and her hands clutched at his shoulders, every breath coming faster with a rasp and a whimper until she threw her head back with a long, shuddering moan.

Never had he seen a more exciting sight than this woman set free before his eyes. He wanted to take a bite of her, to feed on this new fire in her until it ravaged them both. It was at this moment that Ben knew he was truly and utterly lost.

"You don't play fair, Collins."

Standing, he pulled her against him and stroked her hair. "I never said I did. And I make no apologies for it. Now come here…" In one fluid movement, he swung Katie off her feet and into his arms, where she squealed in surprise.

He carried her to his bedroom and set her down next to the bed. Taking in every feature as he gazed at her, he couldn't believe she was finally in his arms. When he kissed her this time, it was slow and deep, wanting only to make this moment last in case it was, in fact, nothing more than a dream. "If I forget to say it, I am so glad you came over."

Katie pushed at the rest of his clothing, urging him to get it out of the way, and Ben accommodated her request before helping her do the same.

"You are breathtaking." He bent to nip her breast again, then guided her onto the bed, propping himself on his elbow next to her. When she reached for him, he patiently pushed her hands away. "No, not yet." If she touched him now, he knew it would be all over for him. And he wanted to stretch this feeling out for as long as possible. His gaze drifted over her naked form slowly, drinking in the sight of her. Ben nibbled at her neck, rained hot kisses over her collarbone. When he skimmed his teeth over her nipple again, the way she arched against his mouth set him ablaze.

"Oh, sweet Jesus…" he moaned, his tongue tracing lazy circles over her skin. "I want to take my time discovering all of your secrets, finding each and every spot on your body that drives you wild. I want to taste you and feel you and make you lose touch with reality. And then, once you recover, I'll do it all over again."

———

Katie's body was nearly pulsating with desire, and she needed more. The way Ben looked at her with awe and an insatiable hunger, was quite a heady feeling. Never had she felt as powerful as she did with Ben's eyes and hands on her. His fingers followed every line of her body, from her shoulders to her ankles, over every dip and curve. Through the haze of her arousal, Katie couldn't believe how much pleasure he seemed to get from this exercise. His eyes stayed on her, drinking in every reaction her body offered. At times, his expression glazed over, lip between his teeth as his eyes devoured her, a moan coming from so deep inside him that it was as though he was the one being stroked to the brink over and over again without quite crossing the line. His deft fingers and quick tongue elicited responses from her that she never knew were possible. No one had ever paid so much attention to her pleasure, and it was a provocative new reality.

"Oh my god, I think you're going to kill me," Katie groaned.

The heat of his mouth drifted up the inside of her thigh, teeth nipping her sensitive flesh, and he chuckled. "No dying. I am enjoying this far, far too much to lose you now."

The roughness of his beard between her legs was a distinct contrast to the hot, wet kisses he planted with increasing fervor, and Katie's whole body quivered. Every stroke of his tongue and touch of his lips revealed a new sense of elation and chipped away at any control she had been trying to hold on to. She jerked and arched into each caress until she couldn't take any more.

"Ben...please," she begged, her fingers tangling in his hair.

Then he was above her, his own eyes intense and wild with greedy passion. When she put her hands on him at last, she sighed, caressing him slowly as she guided him to her. Every ounce of restraint seemed to break away inside of him, and he choked back a growl of pure longing. He pressed into her, slowly, so slowly, until any rational thought she was still holding onto was overcome by a base animal need. He gripped her hair, capturing her lips, and she lost herself in the passion of him, the need she felt from him and for him evident with every stroke.

Katie wrapped herself around him, giving him everything she had and demanding the same in return. His name escaped her lips over and over, blasts of cannon fire racking her body until she cried out. She clung to him, unable and unwilling to release her hold. When they had both remembered how to breathe, Ben stroked her hair and rained kisses on her face, her shoulders, her throat.

"Holy hell." He couldn't seem to keep his hands from her skin, nuzzling his lips in the crook of her neck. "You...are something else, Parker."

She stretched with a satisfied groan, then wrapped herself around him, scraping her teeth along the edge of his ear. "I hope that's a good something."

After kissing her slowly, his lips soft and warm, his tongue sweet and gentle, Ben sighed. "I couldn't stop thinking about you, thinking about this. I was afraid I was imagining it when you showed up at my door." His hands roamed freely over her body. "But I've gotta say—the reality is so much better than anything I could have come up with."

"I was terrified, you know." She drew one fingernail across the curve of his bottom lip. "I almost turned around and left."

"I know. I watched you."

Raising up on one elbow, she blinked at Ben with surprise. "You what? You watched me? Oh god, that's not humiliating at all."

"It was adorable."

She flopped back onto the bed. "Ugh. That was not the goal —I wasn't going for 'adorable.' I was trying to be sexy and irresistible."

"You were—you *are*. And captivating, and exquisite." The look in Ben's eyes had changed, and it filled Katie with a warm, molten desire that she wanted to drown in. He pulled her against his chest, pressing sweet, leisurely kisses to her lips. Everything about this moment felt so right. Nothing else mattered besides the man whispering her name and the heaven of his arms around her.

Liberated. Free and wanton. That was how Katie felt, and she loved it. This man who stimulated her mind before her body was gazing at her like she was the most beautiful woman in the world. He touched her reverently, his tongue teasing until her nipples were hard and aching, sighing when he discovered just how ready she was for more. His hands were gentle and coaxing, fingers sliding and circling, awakening her with the slightest movement.

Abruptly, Ben pulled away, leaving Katie gasping for more. He cleared his throat and smiled serenely, propping his head on his hand. "So... what was it you came over to talk about?"

Katie let out a shaky laugh and tried to remember how to breathe. "I'm sorry, was I not clear about that?"

Ben resumed his expedition, his mouth traveling over her body with slow, tender kisses. "Mmm, I may have been a little distracted. To be honest, I don't think I was listening at all." He rolled, pulling Katie on top of him, a wicked light in his eyes. "I think you should start over. From the very beginning."

TWENTY

Katie awoke sometime later to a rosy sunrise shining through the windows. Ben wasn't in bed but judging by the aroma of coffee wafting into the room, she knew where to find him. Wrapping the sheet around herself, she wandered into the living room to reclaim her clothes.

"Well, good morning." Ben's eyes roamed over her, and he smiled. "Can I interest you in a hot beverage?"

Katie ambled into the kitchen, the sheet trailing behind her, where she greeted Ben with a lingering kiss.

"Mmmm. Yes, please. I would love some coffee. But I should probably put clothes on."

Sliding his hands inside the folds of the sheet to find her bare skin, thumbs circling her nipples, Ben nuzzled her neck. "I would strongly discourage you against that."

Her body reacted to his touch immediately. "Very tempting… but I need to at least get my phone charger out of my car. Give me five minutes, and I'd be more than happy to let you seduce me back into bed."

She spun away from Ben, a mischievous glint in her eye, letting the sheet unwind and fall to the floor. The corner of his mouth twitched, and he licked his lips as he watched her.

Katie moved lazily, gathering each item of clothing from where it had been discarded the night before. Ben's gaze on her naked skin thrilled her. Knowing that he wanted her, that she had the power to say yes or no, that he would take her again in a heartbeat if she asked, when she asked, was a very potent drug that went straight to her head. There had never been a moment in her life when she would have been so brazen, but this man gave her fresh confidence. Who needed coffee with this provocative sensation coursing through her veins? "Don't go anywhere." She smiled over her shoulder, then threw the front door open.

She had barely taken two steps out of the house before every muscle locked in place and the air was sucked from her lungs. The sight that greeted her couldn't be seen as anything but a violent warning that He was near.

The doors of her car were standing wide open, and the body listed to the side. Ice water ran through her veins, rendering her unable to move from the porch. Her car now felt menacing, threatening her with the revelation that He knew. Somehow, He *knew*. She had felt so powerful in her decision to come to Ben, but sitting in front of her was a brutal reminder that she held no power. Not really.

He held all the cards, and she wouldn't be allowed to forget it.

Silently, Ben appeared behind her, wrapping his arms around her waist. "Couldn't you find it? I'm sure I've got a charger…"

When she didn't answer, he must have followed her line of vision. "Holy shit, Parker!" Ben started toward her car to look at the damage, but Katie held him back.

"Ben. Wait, I…" Trying to take a mental step back and detach herself from the situation, Katie willed herself to calm down. "Let me go look first."

He frowned. "Like hell. There is no way I'm not coming with you."

They approached the open passenger door with caution, Katie's heart battering her chest. It was unlikely the perpetrator was still close by, but she was, nonetheless, terrified of what she might find. Her stomach dropped as she peeked inside.

He had shredded the upholstery, the batting inside pulled out and flung all over the car. The dashboard had been gouged with the word *bitch*, and all the wires were either pulled out or cut.

Her hand flew to her mouth, a strangled sob bursting from her throat before she could stop it. Taking a step back, she walked around the car and noticed that two of the tires had been slashed, explaining the unusual tilt. Angry gashes marred the paint all the way around, every surface showing some sign of an attack. With her energy depleted, her shoulders slumped, and she turned away.

She couldn't look at the car again. Not yet. She didn't know what to do next. What would a rational person do in this situation? She could only look at Ben with wide eyes. "Can you get my phone?"

Cocking an eyebrow, Ben lifted her arm, showing her that her phone was, in fact, already nestled in her palm.

"Huh. Look at that." The corners of her mouth lifted but formed a grimace rather than the smile she had intended. She dialed and waited for her brother to answer. "Hey. Uh, can you meet me at Ben Collins's house on Maplecrest? Yeah, you can make jokes later." Her voice dropped to a whisper. "Nick, He was here. It's bad. Okay. No, I'll call the sheriff."

Pacing as she talked, Katie gave a preliminary report to the sheriff's office, trying to distance herself mentally from what had happened. If she could forget that this was targeted at her, it would be easier to handle. There was no question in her mind that she'd fall apart if she faced the reality of the situation right then. After being reassured that deputies were on their way, she ended the call and dropped her head in her hands.

Ben guided her to his porch steps, sitting next to her with an arm wrapped around her shoulders. She tried to keep it together, to maintain her stoicism, but his tenderness and patience broke down her resolve, and she buried her face against his chest, letting the tears come.

Stroking her hair, Ben held her while she cried. When she felt there was nothing left, she pulled out of his arms, her heart aching as the silence stretched out between them. She knew there was no easy fix for the nightmare she was living but felt a quiet desperation to hear Ben offer comforting platitudes.

"Parker, I…" He fumbled with his words, chewing his lip. With his hands on her shoulders, he looked deep into her eyes. "I'm sorry this is happening to you. I know that sounds weak, but I am sorry. Your strength is amazing, and I am awestruck at how you've been holding it all together. But you don't have to face this alone anymore. You know I'll do everything in my power to keep you safe."

Katie stared at Ben open-mouthed as frustration replaced her fear. Everything she had feared was materializing around them. She fucked up, she could see that so clearly now. It had been a mistake to bring him anywhere near this. And she could see only one way to fix it.

She started pacing, running her hands through her hair. "This is not your fight, Ben, and I can't have you putting your-self in danger for me. I brought Him here; He followed me to *your* house, and that terrifies me. I won't let you get hurt. It—maybe it would be best if we stayed away from each other for a while."

She spun away to walk toward Sheriff Jacobson's car as it arrived, but Ben grabbed her arm.

"Hey, wait just a goddamned minute! What about what I want?" His jaw was set as he met her gaze. "Look, I can't tell you what to do, and I can't force you to be with me, but stop for one second and listen."

Her eyes narrowed, but she stopped trying to pull away from him. Ben wiped at the tears on her cheeks with his thumb.

"Not sure if you've noticed, but staying away from you is no longer an option for me. You have no control over whether I get hurt here, Parker. And I'm not stupid enough to think this is something I can magically fix for you, but I am here, and I will back you up in whatever you want to do. Tell me what you need from me, and I'll do it. Just don't ask me to give you up."

"But—"

"Damn it, Parker, will you shut up and let me be here for you?" He shook his head with a rueful smile. "You're so stubborn. Let me stand with you and help you fight this and let me make you smile when you want to crawl into a hole and hide. Just…" His arms fell to his sides. "Let me."

Ben's earnest expression melted all of Katie's anger. Where the hell did this man come from? She placed her hand on his cheek to make sure he was real. When he turned his face inward and kissed her palm with genuine tenderness, Katie nodded.

"I like you, Parker. A lot. So much more than a lot. You just got here, and I'm not ready for you to leave." He framed her face in his hands and kissed her lips. The intensity behind his eyes made Katie weak in the knees. She didn't want him to stay away. Quite the opposite.

Nick's truck screeched to a stop in front of the house just as the sheriff and his team started assessing the car. Fury and fear fought for control on Nick's face as he barreled across the yard and gathered his sister in his arms.

"Are you okay? Were you hurt?" Acknowledging Ben, Nick shook his hand. "Hey, man. You good?"

Ben nodded morosely. "Yeah. Jesus, Nick. This is some crazy shit."

While Nick and Ben talked about what they knew, Katie turned her attention to the sheriff and his team buzzing around her car. The crew was already taking photos from every angle, dusting for fingerprints, taking samples of everything that looked suspicious. Jacobson inclined his head once in greeting as Katie walked over.

"How are you holding up?"

She wrapped her arms around herself and shrugged. "Oh, you know. Same shit, different day." Katie offered a sad smile. "I hate this. Every time I think I can live a normal life, the bottom drops out again. It's exhausting."

The sheriff nodded. "We're doing everything we can, Miss Parker. And I assure you that we'll canvas the neighborhood, find out if anyone saw or heard anything out of the ordinary, and collect any video of suspicious activity. My team is already gathering every bit of evidence available to put this to an end. He can't hide forever."

She watched the men and women bustling around, but her mind was miles away. Would this ever end? It didn't matter where she went; it wouldn't be far enough. He was getting closer and bolder, the escalation of violence extreme, to say the least. Now she saw where all of this was headed, and it sent a chill down her spine.

Things had become complicated, just like she knew they would, and she feared the night before had been a colossal mistake. She wanted to be with Ben. Watching him talk to Nick, catching her eye with a reassuring smile over his head, made her heart flutter. Their connection was real, but the timing couldn't have been worse.

And she didn't know what she was supposed to do—what she *could* do now.

TWENTY-ONE

On Monday morning, Katie leaned against the counter in the breakroom, drumming her fingers against a warm mug of coffee. She held very still, afraid that if she moved, she'd burst with the pent-up anxiety she was carrying. The night before had been fraught with nightmares if she slept at all, and her brain worked overtime to play out every horrific possibility while she was awake. Nick tried to talk her into staying home, to lock the doors, and just take a day to recover and stay safe. What he didn't seem to understand was that working on projects and meeting deadlines would give her a sense of control that had been stolen from her.

When Ben walked in a few moments later and squeezed her hand with an affectionate smile, she felt the tension drain away.

"Morning, Parker. Ready to get some shit done and take over the world?"

It was all she could do not to jump into his arms and rain kisses over his face right then, but she watched him continue through to their offices with her heart full. No one affected her the way he did. She'd had boyfriends who made her blood race, others who put her on edge, but being with someone who could quiet her anxiety with just a smile was a new experience. And it was one she wanted to hold on to with both hands.

Lost in daydreams while fresh coffee brewed, Katie jumped when the door to the break room banged shut. Patsy stormed into the room, pointing an accusatory finger at her.

"All right, Katie—spill it."

"What are you talking about?"

Patsy rolled her eyes. "Come on, don't play dumb. I saw you at the carnival."

"Yeah, I saw you there, too. We spent the morning together."

"Good god, woman—did you bang Ben or what?" She rubbed her hands together, a wicked gleam in her eyes.

"Oh my god." Katie groaned.

"You two were very cozy Friday, playing games, riding the roller coaster, watching fireworks. You went home with him, didn't you?" Eyes wide and hopeful, Patsy clasped her hands against her chest. "Please tell me you went home with him."

Katie turned her back before answering.

"I did not go home with Ben on the Fourth of July. You're letting your imagination get the better of you." Of course, her answer was twisted up in semantics: Katie hadn't gone home with Ben on the Fourth, that was true, but there was no way she would volunteer what happened the following night.

Patsy sidled up with raised eyebrows. "Kaaatieee…there's no point in trying to fool me. Everyone in Enderlin could feel the sexual tension between you two. You were practically twanging."

"Jesus, do you hear the things you say?" Katie shook her head and sipped her coffee, still avoiding eye contact. "I swear to you on everything sacred that I did not go home with Ben Collins on Friday. Can we drop it now?"

Patsy groaned, dragging a hand down her face. "Such a

wasted opportunity. How could you not take a bite out of that sweet, sweet ass?"

"Whose sweet ass are we biting?" Ben's amusement was clear in his voice as he entered the break room. Katie's face burned scarlet, and she stared at the floor while her friend stammered out lame explanations.

"Oh, well. We were talking about...Ryan Gosling!" Patsy looked at Katie, begging her for back up. "There was some debate about whether he or, um, Chris Hemsworth was more nibble-worthy."

Ben held up his hands and shook his head. "Keep me out of this. I'm a Ryan Reynolds man, myself." Turning back to face Katie, Ben flashed a grin and a quick wink at her. The corner of her mouth twitched, but her friend didn't notice.

Patsy fanned herself with her hand and pretended to faint against Katie's shoulder. "Oh Ben Collins, I do declare, you just gave me fantasy material to last a lifetime."

Through peals of laughter, Katie swatted at Patsy, who scampered out of the room, leaving Katie and Ben alone at last.

"So... what did I walk in on?" Ben leaned against the counter close enough that his shoulder brushed against Katie's. It sent an immediate shock of electricity down the length of her arm, and she was sorely tempted to lean into it. Just not here.

Katie groaned. "The Inquisition, Ben. Thank you for showing up when you did. I'm convinced the physical torture was going to start any second."

Glancing at her from the corner of his eye, Ben cleared his throat. "What, uh, what was she grilling you about? Something tells me it had nothing to do with any celebrity butts."

"You'd be right about that." Katie leaned in close. "She was trying to get me to admit that I had gone home with you. So, it was actually your sweet ass being discussed."

Ben pursed his lips and frowned as he processed this information, and Katie was torn between melting into his arms to kiss him or dissolving in laughter. After a moment, he sipped his coffee and shrugged.

"Well. Not sure if that's flattering or disturbing." Glancing around the room quickly, he leaned in for a kiss and murmured against her lips. "But we can certainly discuss that option later."

———

Katie poked her head out of the kitchen when she heard Ben switch on the radio. He was cleaning up after dinner while she washed the dishes. Watching him move around the room, her heart swelled. They'd been nearly inseparable since the Fourth of July weekend, and the smile hadn't left her face for weeks. They still butted heads at work, still pushed each other's buttons, still drove each other insane. But being with Ben was both easy and exciting, and she was crazy about him.

But a dark, persistent thought kept pushing its way to the front of her mind, dampening her high spirits. She leaned against the doorframe. "Ben?"

"Hmm?" He pecked her cheek when he passed into the kitchen with the last of the dirty plates.

Katie picked at her fingernails. "It's been a few weeks since He trashed my car, and nothing else has happened. I know I should be glad, but I don't think He's ever gone this long without contacting me." She looked up, tears swimming in her eyes, her voice barely a whisper. "I keep waiting for the other shoe to drop, you know? He wouldn't have just changed his mind after all this time. I can only think He's planning something horrible. Something that will hurt the people I love and destroy me."

He gathered her against his chest and rubbed her back, planting a kiss on her forehead. "Listen, Parker, we are taking every precaution and being vigilant. We'll see him coming from a mile away if he tries anything now. Maybe that's all that happened. He sees everything you've done—the self-defense classes, the alarm system at your parents' house, researching a private investigator—and he knows you're not afraid, so he's lost interest. Bullies and sadists get off on seeing their victims suffer. Now that you're back in charge, it's no fun for him."

"Maybe you're right. I really want to believe you're right. So, let's call it cautious optimism and be grateful for small victories." She placed a hand on his cheek and whispered, "Thank you. For everything."

"For you, anything." A crooked grin spread across his face, and he kissed her forehead again. "But we aren't done yet. Those dishes aren't going to wash themselves."

Katie laughed and snapped her towel at his retreating form. Shaking her head, she returned to the task at hand, feeling a small sense of relief as she settled into the ease of such a mundane task.

"Hey, is there anything special you want to do this weekend?" She dried her hands and stepped out of the kitchen. "This is probably the first one without a big deadline waiting on the other side."

Her voice trailed off as she took in what was happening in the living room. The song playing on the radio seemed to have taken hold of Ben. Without realizing he was being watched, he was swaying his hips and bopping to the music. Katie leaned against the door frame, arms crossed.

When he caught her watching, eyes wide and lip between her teeth, his arms dropped to his sides. "What?" he huffed.

"Just enjoying the show."

Narrowing his eyes, Ben tossed the rag on the table and twisted the volume knob on the radio. "You want a show, huh? I'll give you a show."

Puckering his lips at Katie from under raised eyebrows, he

wriggled his shoulders and shimmied back and forth. "You want a little of this?"

Katie's eyes popped wide. "Please stop."

"Maybe some of this?" He spun around and blew a kiss over his shoulder. He swayed his ass left to right and back again, dipping lower and lower with each pass.

"Oh my god." Katie laughed, but she couldn't tear her eyes away.

Now Ben was advancing on her, his hands behind his head, moving his hips in a seductive roll.

"Is it hot in here, or is it just me?" He continued undulating his body as he unbuttoned his shirt and shrugged it off his shoulders.

Katie's hands flew to her mouth as he drew closer and closer. "How is this even happening right now?" She gasped through her giggles.

Even though his face was a comical exaggeration of sexy, Katie wasn't completely immune to his charms. He pulled his t-shirt off and spun it in the air above his head, wriggling around Katie while she dissolved into laughter.

"Where are the dollar bills, baby? You know you can't resist me."

Curling a finger through his belt loop, she pulled him against her and whispered, "If you don't stop gyrating and take me to bed right now, things might get ugly." Katie scraped her teeth on his earlobe, and he growled.

"Your wish is my command."

Burying his face in the crook of her neck, Ben wrapped one arm around Katie's waist and lifted her off her feet, making her squeal. He started to carry her to the bedroom, but she wiggled out of his arms.

"Wait! Lock the doors first."

"What? Why? It's seven o'clock."

She turned him toward the kitchen and swatted his butt. "I

don't care: humor me. I'll be much more relaxed knowing they're locked."

Ben heaved a theatrical sigh and rolled his eyes. "Fine. I'll get the back door, you get the front, and I'll meet you in the bedroom. But hurry. I want you naked and in my arms in about thirty seconds."

He disappeared into the kitchen, and Katie spun toward the front door, hand already outstretched for the deadbolt. But she didn't get more than a few steps before the smell of smoke and the faint sound of sirens caught her attention. With her stomach in her throat, she pulled back the curtain from the front window and screamed.

"Parker? What is it? Are you okay?" Ben was at her side in an instant, but even he couldn't calm her shaking. He cautiously opened the door, and black smoke billowed in, making them both cough. "Holy shit. What the hell is that?" He dashed out the door, heading for the hose at the side of the house, while his neighbors staggered over with buckets of water.

Katie knew what she was looking at but couldn't make sense of it. Hanging in the tree was the burning remains of a stuffed strawman figure. Except it was obvious to her that it wasn't meant to be a man. Frozen on the front porch, she recognized the wavy, chestnut wig that hadn't caught fire yet, waving across the blank face: blank except for two bright blue buttons sewn on for eyes.

The world around her wavered and took on the quality of a nightmare. The flashing lights of the fire truck made the faces that had gathered on the sidewalks look otherworldly. Her arms and legs felt like they were filled with lead, and she couldn't do more than watch Ben and his neighbors as they tried to get out of the way of the firemen. Glowing embers and tufts of smoldering batting dotted the grass, leaving charred black patches when the hose doused them with water.

Her legs suddenly refused to hold her up anymore, and

she dropped to the stoop in a heap. She knew things were too quiet, knew He was just biding His time until her guard was down. Neither she nor Ben had seen or heard anything all evening. It was early enough that the summer sun was still shining—didn't anyone else see Him putting this in the tree? If He hadn't attacked her in the parking lot and followed her to her car, she would think He was a figment of her imagination.

The firemen had quenched the fire and were taking down what was left of the effigy. There was no real resemblance to Katie, but she knew without a doubt that it was supposed to represent her.

Despite the lingering heat of the evening, she shivered.

TWENTY-TWO

"**B**ut how the hell did he even get that close? Is he a fucking ninja or something?" Nick drained his beer and slammed the mug on the table hard enough to rattle the rest of the glasses scattered across the surface. "If I ever get my hands on this bastard, he's gonna wish he'd never been born."

Katie stared at the scratched tabletop, tracing the letters left behind by people who had been there long before. Squeezed into the booth next to her, Ben was rubbing his palm in slow circles on her back. She knew he was trying to keep her calm and be the face of serenity, but she could see his jaw clenching and releasing as he bit back the angry tirade brewing below the surface.

After the deputies had taken their reports, looked for evidence, and interviewed everyone milling around on the sidewalk, Katie was still unable to keep her hands from trembling. Her nerves were shot, and there was no way she felt safe at Ben's house, not now. Nowhere felt like a refuge anymore. In an attempt to distance themselves from the terrifying events of the night, they tracked down Nick and Cael, who were having drinks at Maxie's. Now the four of them were gathered around the table to hash out what, exactly, had happened.

Touching her hand lightly, Cael drew Katie's attention. "Hey. You're awfully quiet."

"What is there even to say? I feel sick." She buried her head in her hands. There were no more tears, no plans to make. Nothing she did made a difference; she had nowhere to hide. He would always be one step behind her, waiting for the right moment to—to what? Her stomach twisted, and an icy finger traced up her spine.

Ben wrapped his arm around her shoulder and pulled her against his side, kissing the top of her head. "It'll be okay. You're safe now."

Shrugging out from under his touch, Katie snorted. "No, Ben, I'm not. I have never been, and I will never be."

"Don't say that. Together, we can—"

"We can't do anything. Haven't you been listening to me?" Katie slammed her hands on the tabletop, and the bar around them became quiet. "He'll just keep coming. We've been so stupid thinking we can outsmart Him or stop Him or deter Him in some way. He won't stop. We can't stop Him. And like I told you before, He will keep coming and coming until He's dead. Or until I am."

"Those can't be the only options, Kat." The blood rushed from Nick's face, and he leaned across the table to grasp his sister's hand. "We don't know what his goal is. He's getting brazen, sure, but that just means he's taking more risks, and we're going to catch him any day now."

The laugh that burst from Katie was dark and without any trace of humor. "You're delusional. I'll be dead before that happens. I know it, you know it." Her voice dropped to a whisper, and one tear rolled down her cheek, splashing on the back of her hand. "He's so close. I can feel Him watching me even now, like He's just over my shoulder, waiting."

Silence fell over the little group, and the men cast their eyes around the room. But Katie kept her eyes down. He was there, she felt it in her bones, and she'd only drive herself crazy trying to pick Him out of the crowd. Even in her nightmares, His face was nothing more than a shadow, a hazy blob in the depths of a sweatshirt hood. But His voice…that was what haunted her, awake or asleep. The sound of His voice, His hot breath on her ear, His hands tightening around her throat; these made up her waking hell.

"Parker," Ben brushed his arm against hers, as though afraid to offer comfort, "we're not trying to make light of the situation. I swear we're not."

"It's bravado, Kat, nothing more." Nick passed a hand over his face, and Katie was shocked at how tired and sad he looked. "As hard as we're trying to convince you that things aren't a complete shit show, we're trying twice as hard to convince ourselves."

With a chuckle, Cael rubbed at the back of his neck. "We're kinda pathetic. We were just hoping you hadn't noticed yet."

Looking around the table, Katie felt some of her fear and anger slip away. She knew she was lucky to have such good people around her. They were doing their best in a situation that none of them had any clue how to navigate. Smiling at Cael and Nick and nestling against Ben's shoulder, she sighed. "The jig is up, boys. I've known the whole time."

"Hello, Ben." Katie's head snapped up at the familiar voice just as the blood drained from Ben's face.

"What are you doing here, Elizabeth?"

Her smile was sickeningly sweet as she looked around the table. "Well, you've been avoiding my calls. So I went to your house looking for you—god, what a horrific mess out front— and your neighbors told me where to find you. Ignoring me isn't going to change our situation."

Katie felt Ben stiffen next to her, and she placed a hand on his arm. "What situation?"

"Oh, honey." Elizabeth's condescending laughter sent a

cold chill down Katie's back. "He hasn't told you, has he? Why, Ben, that's hard to believe. Lying is so not in your nature."

Sliding out of the booth, Ben took hold of Elizabeth's elbow, his voice low and dark. "Can we please talk about this outside?"

"Don't you want to share the happy news with your friends?" She yanked her arm out of his grasp, laying one palm flat against her stomach and the other around his waist. "Ben and I are going to have a baby!"

Katie felt as though all the air was sucked out of the room, leaving her gasping. Searching his face, taking in his downcast eyes and tensed shoulders, Katie knew it was true.

Disgust was obvious in Ben's voice as it rose in volume. "Why? Why did you come here, Elizabeth? Are you so hell-bent on making me suffer for not choosing you that nothing matters more than humiliating me?"

Ben turned to Katie with pleading eyes, his hands outstretched. "Parker, please listen. This isn't what it looks like. I—I was going to tell you. I just didn't know how or when, and then everything else started happening, and all I wanted to do was protect you. Elizabeth means nothing to me. You are the one I care about. Please believe me."

Elizabeth screeched and grabbed Ben's arm, pulling him around to face her. "I mean nothing to you? Nothing? We have history, you and I, and, apparently, I mean enough to you for us to be in this predicament."

"All right, let's just take a deep breath here. The two of you have a lot to work out but screaming at each other is not going to solve anything." Nick turned to Elizabeth, laying a hand on her shoulder. "We can all sit down and talk, try to—"

"Don't you touch me." Elizabeth jerked away from him. "You all think I'm stupid, don't you? You're ganging up on me, trying to gaslight me into thinking all of this is my fault."

Covering her ears, Katie couldn't think straight. The noise

was getting out of hand, with Elizabeth attacking Ben while he tried desperately to defend himself and Nick trying to be heard over them both. Maybe, if she sat very still and waited long enough, she would wake up and learn that this whole evening had been nothing but a nightmare. There was no way she could believe this had become her real life.

A soft touch on her hand startled her, and she looked up to find Cael grimacing. "Want to get out of here? Step outside for some fresh air and a little quiet?" He hooked a thumb in the direction of the yelling. "I don't think they'll miss us for a few minutes, and you look like you could use a break."

Her vision blurred with fresh tears as she nodded, and the two of them headed for the back door. It seemed that their departure didn't register with Nick, Ben, or Elizabeth, as they were all caught up in their screaming match. Once Cael and Katie stepped out into the dark silence of the parking lot, the weight of the whole night crashed over her, and she nearly fell to the ground sobbing. Cael wrapped his arms around her and let her cry into his shoulder.

"Hey, hey, it's going to be all right. I promise. Please don't cry." He jangled his keys in front of her and stepped back. "Let's go for a ride. We'll roll the windows down and blast some music, and you can shout at the top of your lungs and just let everything melt away."

Sniffling, Katie rubbed at her face with the back of her hand. "I don't know. I left everything in there on the table—my purse, my phone. And won't they all wonder where we went?"

He steered her toward his car with a reassuring arm wrapped around her shoulder. "Don't worry, we'll be right back. We won't be gone for more than fifteen or twenty minutes. It'll be fine."

Looking back at Maxie's with the sad realization that no one had followed them, that Ben hadn't even noticed she was gone, she made a decision. "God, yes, please. Get me the hell out of here."

————

Katie stared out the passenger window of Cael's car, aware of the passing scenery but too deep in her thoughts to really see any of it. Swiping at a tear with the back of her hand, she sighed. Ben had been lying to her. How could he hide something from her that was so monumental to their relationship? Things probably hadn't ended with Elizabeth, either. He just managed to juggle them both so successfully that neither of them knew. Who was she kidding? The two of them probably sat around and laughed their asses off at her stupidity.

She felt like such a fool. Hadn't she learned her lesson with Derek? If it seems too good to be true, it invariably is. And, boy, did Ben seem too good to be true. A handsome face, a few well-placed compliments to go along with their electric attraction, and she was putty in his hands. Another tear slipped down her cheek.

"Wild night, huh?" Cael turned the radio down. "How are you holding up?"

Katie turned toward her friend and snorted. "How am I holding up? Barely, Cael. I am barely keeping it together right now. Do you think anyone would miss me if I went into hiding for, oh, the next ten years?"

Cael glanced at her a couple of times; his brow furrowed. "Um, yes. You would definitely be missed." He cleared his throat and turned his attention back to driving. "I would miss you."

"Thanks." She relaxed back against the headrest and frowned. "Am I overreacting?"

"What?"

Sighing, she raked her hands through her hair. "I'm just saying that maybe they hadn't decided what to do about the pregnancy yet, so weren't telling anyone. My relationship with Ben is pretty new, too. Isn't it possible that he wanted to see where things went with us before telling me, in case I reacted exactly the way I did?"

"You're joking, right?" Katie watched Cael's knuckles turn white as he gripped the steering wheel. "Why are you trying to make excuses for his behavior? Don't you think that if he cared about you, really cared about you, that he would be open and honest?"

She massaged her forehead with her fingertips, eyes closed. "You're right. I know you're right. Boy, Derek must have done a number on me if I still automatically think everything is my fault."

"It's okay. I suppose I get it. But please remember that you're perfect, and Ben is an idiot."

Katie scoffed and rolled her eyes. "Right. Thanks, though. That's nice of you to say."

The car stopped, and Katie looked out the windshield into complete darkness, realizing she had no idea where they were. "I thought we were going back to Maxie's. How long have we been gone? Maybe we should call Nick and let him know I'm okay."

Cael sat silent, his hands resting in his lap, and his expression unreadable. He turned off the car and tucked the keys in his pocket before twisting his head to look at her. Dread bloomed in her stomach like shards of ice. Something wasn't right.

"Ben doesn't deserve you. I hope you can see that now. Derek was an asshole and was the farthest thing from worthy to even look at you, much less touch you the way he did."

"Jesus, Cael. That's a little harsh and, to be honest, none of your business." She was having a hard time looking at him as she responded. There was something strange and a little frightening in his eyes as they sat in the inky blackness in the middle of nowhere. "I appreciate you getting me out of there tonight, but I'm feeling better, and I can't avoid this forever. Can you take me back now, please?"

His lips curled into a chilling smile, and he tipped his head to the side as he looked at her. "I'll never understand what you see in him. In any of them. You're blind to what's right in front of you, aren't you? Everything you could ever want, and need has been within reach your whole life."

Frigid tendrils of fear wrapped around Katie's spine, and her breath caught in her throat. What the hell was happening? The answer was skittering in the front of her mind, but she couldn't believe it. Was Cael, her friend, the one who'd been the cause of her nightmares for years now? No, no way. He'd never do that to her. She swallowed, and her throat threatened to clamp shut. "I want to go back, Cael. Take me back. Now."

He lunged for her, gripping her arm and pushing his face close to hers. He bared his teeth and snarled, his twisted features equally foreign and familiar—and terrifying. "Oh no, Katherine, I don't think I will."

Suddenly she felt like she was falling through the earth. *That voice.* It was the same gravelly rasp that had been haunting her.

"I've waited far too long for this moment with you."

A sob burst from her throat as the truth blasted through her. "It was you. All this time. Cael, why?"

He sat back in his seat, scratching his chin. "Why? You should know why, Katherine. Because I love you." Stars exploded in Katie's vision as his fist came out of nowhere and made contact with the side of her face.

Stunned, she scrabbled at the door, trying to find the handle that would let her escape, but her eyes wouldn't focus. Then his hand grasped a fistful of her hair, pulling back slightly before smashing her head into the window.

It was like a bomb had gone off inside her skull and her ears began to ring. She could feel the hot stream of blood running down her face and into her eyes, obscuring her vision even further. For some reason, her hands wouldn't do what she was telling them, and she couldn't fight him off when Cael dragged her over the center console and yanked her from the car.

Her feet scrambled for purchase beneath her, but Cael was hauling her across the grass, half carrying and half dragging her, and she was no longer in control of her own body.

"What are you doing? Cael, stop, just stop for a minute."

Then he was heaving her into some kind of building, and she screamed, clawing at the frame to keep from going through that door. Even in her dazed state, she knew that if she crossed that threshold, she wasn't coming out again. Not alive, anyway.

"No! Cael, no! Let's just stop and talk about this. Nothing's happened, we can just go back and forget all about this." She whimpered. "Please, Cael. Please."

He paused in his attempts to wrench her hands free, and hope filled her chest. Maybe she'd gotten through to him. Maybe he had changed his mind about whatever he had planned and would let her go. She held her breath waiting to learn her fate.

"We can't go back, Katherine, not now. Besides, I don't want to. I've been dreaming of this night for years. Come with me, it's time."

He lunged and got his shoulder under her body, pushing with an unexpected strength. He pulled the door closed behind him, sealing Katie's terrified screams inside where no one else could hear her.

TWENTY-THREE

B en dragged a hand down his face and sighed. The night had gone from bad to worse, and he had no one but himself to blame. Standing at the bar, he stared into his glass of gin. He needed to talk to Parker. He needed to apologize and explain the situation—and hope that she still wanted to keep him around.

Every moment since Elizabeth stormed into Maxie's was blurred together, and he felt like he was drowning. Over the course of the hour that she'd been there, the argument devolved into complete chaos. Elizabeth jabbed him in the chest repeatedly, demanding answers and alternating between hysterical sobbing and disgusted screeching, while Nick kept trying to settle things down by shouting over them both. Somewhere in the middle of it all, Ben had lost sight of Parker.

All he wanted to do was talk to her, but every time he craned his neck around Elizabeth to catch Parker's eye, she refused to look at him. Time and again, he was yanked by the arm and spun away from the table, so Elizabeth could rail at him and cry and tell him how he'd callously abused her. Nick kept walking away but would inevitably return with more platitudes and useless ideas. Even in the scant instances Ben caught sight of Parker, he could see the heartbreak on her face. And it nearly killed him.

After what seemed like hours, Elizabeth finally appeared to run out of allegations to fling at him—and Max had threatened to drag her out by her hair if she didn't knock it off. She sniffled and stormed out of the bar, promising that this wasn't over. Nick had retreated well before she left, taking out his frustrations on the dartboards and muttering under his breath. The near silence was disorienting at first, but Ben's only priority was making things right with Parker. He dashed for the table, finding her purse and phone, but she was nowhere to be seen. He figured she was hiding out in the restroom until the altercation died down, so he grabbed a drink while he waited for her to reappear.

He had no idea how to fix this. The thought of losing Parker made his chest burn, but he had a strong feeling that his omission of Elizabeth's pregnancy, more than the pregnancy itself, would be the thing to drive her away. She'd never be able to trust him again.

Ben glanced up as the bathroom door opened, but it still wasn't Parker. The woman who exited passed by the bar, so he reached out to tap her shoulder.

"Excuse me. Was the other woman in the restroom all right?"

Raising her eyebrows, the woman hitched a thumb behind her. "There's no one else in there, sugar."

"Are you sure? Curly brown hair? Really blue eyes?"

"Darlin', there are two stalls in there. I was in one. The other was wide open and empty. There is no one else in there." She looked him up and down, and her expression softened. "Sorry. Your date must have skipped out on you." Patting his arm, she turned away to join her friends.

Just then, Nick approached the bar to refresh his drink, and Ben made his way toward him. "Hey, Nick—"

"I can't right now, Ben." Nick sighed and turned his back. "Give me a few minutes to get my blood pressure back down."

Something was scratching at the back of Ben's mind that he couldn't quite pinpoint. "Have you seen your sister?"

"Yeah, I saw her a little while ago. She looked miserable."

When he tried to walk away, Ben stepped in his path. "How long ago?"

"What?"

"When was the last time you saw her, Nick? I haven't seen her since right after Elizabeth showed up."

Looking around the bar, he frowned. "You know, I'm not really sure. She's probably hiding out in the bathroom or something."

"She's not in the bathroom. I already had someone check."

"Maybe she had someone take her home?"

Ben's throat was suddenly very dry. "Without her purse and her phone?"

Nick froze in his tracks. "She left those here?"

Holding up Parker's purse, Ben's heart started racing. "Nick, something is very wrong here. There's no way she'd leave all by herself, not after her stalker sent her a very distinct, threatening message. She knows he's close, and she's scared. Parker wouldn't put herself at risk like that, no matter how upset she was."

The expression on Nick's face morphed from irritation to fear in a matter of seconds. "I'll go look out front: you check the bathroom again and the parking lot." Both men were already in motion before the words were fully out of his mouth.

Ben shoved the ladies' bathroom door open, and his voice echoed off the walls. "Parker?" Waiting just a few seconds for a response, he already knew she wasn't there. A mounting panic was telling him the parking lot would yield the same results, but he sprinted for the back entrance anyway, silently praying he was wrong.

Bursting out the back, Ben only managed to startle a couple of guilty-looking young ladies sharing a cigarette. He rounded the side of the building at a jog, almost out of breath as he collided with Nick.

"Any sign of her?" The frantic shaking of Nick's head set off alarm bells for Ben. "Where's Cael? Maybe he saw her leave? Or she told him where she was going?" He turned to run back inside, but Nick grabbed his arm.

"His car's not here." He waved his hand toward the parking lot. "Cael already left. He probably gave her a ride home, and she was just so upset that she forgot to grab her things."

Ben wanted to believe that Nick's theory was true. He waited for the flood of relief in his chest, for the slowing of his heart, but it didn't come. When Nick's eyes met his, it was obvious he was holding on for the same thing. "Nick, how well do you know Cael?"

His eyes wide, Nick shook his head. "No way, Ben. No fucking way. She's known Cael since high school. He never said a bad word about her—he'd never do anything to hurt her. Hell, after she moved away, he was the only one who hung out with me and talked about her, like he understood how much I missed her. He was always checking in with me to see how she was, always worried about her. He even asked for her address so he could send her birthday cards and stuff…"

Ben watched the blood drain from Nick's face, and his own knees turned to jelly. Suddenly there was no air, and he clutched at his throat, forcing out the words neither of them wanted to acknowledge.

"It's Cael. He's been stalking her all this time. And now he's got her."

———

Katie was agonizingly aware of the ache in her jaw and the inside of her skull throbbing in time with her heartbeat. Her head felt heavy, but she knew she couldn't give in to the pain for a second.

She wanted to touch the side of her head and assess the damage, but she couldn't move her arms. The sun filtered through the grimy windows, casting a dull light over her surroundings. How long had she been tied up? The details of the night before were sketchy at best. Despite the excruciating pain in her head, Katie pulled at her wrists and ankles, but the duct tape held her tight. How the hell had she been so stupid? She'd walked right into Cael's trap, just as he'd been planning all along.

"Help!" Her throat was so dry the scream came out as a croak. Lifting her face toward the ceiling, Katie called out again, praying that someone would hear her. "Please, help me!"

There was a soft shuffling to her left, and she finally heard a voice.

"Ah, good. I was worried I'd done more damage than I'd intended."

Strolling into her line of vision with his hands clasped behind his back, Cael gazed at Katie, his head tilted. There was a distinct lack of urgency in Cael's movements, making her alarm inflate to full-blown terror as she watched him. Katie shook her head slowly, the awful truth still so hard to believe. "It was you, all this time?"

Cael sighed theatrically and slapped his palms against his thighs. "Do you know how long I've been waiting for you to catch on? Watching you flounder around, so close to finding out has been torture."

"Is—is this some kind of joke? This isn't even remotely funny."

Teeth bared, Cael swooped in close. "You're absolutely

right, Katherine." He put his mouth near her ear and snarled. "There's nothing funny about this situation."

Rage flowed off him in waves, and Katie was too shocked to make a sound. This person seething at her was no longer her friend. He was nothing more than a violent replica of someone she thought she knew.

Katie clamped her mouth shut and waited, holding her breath. Cael's face was inches away, his eyes searching hers. Her heart was trying to burst free, the noise deafening in her own ears. This had to be a mistake. Cael was her friend; it couldn't be him. Her head was spinning from the contradiction.

As suddenly as the anger had come over him, Cael's face softened. He trailed his fingers along her cheek, and she involuntarily flinched. Enthralled, he didn't seem to notice. Instead, he leaned closer and inhaled, closing his eyes in ecstasy.

"Oh, Katherine, I've waited so long for this." He stroked her hair and lifted a handful of curls to press them against his face.

Katie tried to keep the panic out of her voice but couldn't stop it from trembling. "For what, exactly, Cael?"

"For the moment I know that you know, of course," he cooed. "To see the look on your face when at last you realize that we belong together, that I am your soulmate."

He swept his hands down her arms, over and over, then sliding up from her shoulders to cup her face. "You can't know how long I've wanted to be with you. This feeling has built up until keeping it a secret, waiting for the right moment, was physically painful. I've been desperate for you to see me, to know who I really am. Now, at long last, we can be together."

Squeezing her eyes shut, Katie tried not to cry. "No. I don't understand."

Cael laid a finger on her lips. "Shh, Katherine. You will, my love. You will. Open your eyes, and let your heart and soul show you what you already know."

"Don't touch me." She jerked her head away from his touch. Anger and fear merged inside her, one feeding the other. "Cael, this is insane."

His facial expressions morphed quickly from adoration to sadness to rage, and each change heightened Katie's terror. Then all emotion was wiped away, and the cold, hard mask that took its place made her blood run cold.

"Insane? No. Not at all." Cael turned away, leaning against the kitchen counter, and shrugged. "It's simply a means to an end. I didn't want to hurt you, Katherine, and taking you by force wasn't my original plan. But when certain *complications* arose, I knew you wouldn't understand unless I could make you listen."

Katie shook her head, but the pain it stirred up caused her stomach to churn. She had to stay calm, to think. Squeezing her eyes shut to keep her skull from shattering, she pushed the dread deep inside.

"Cael, please call an ambulance. My head is killing me. I promise I'll listen to what you have to say; we're friends, aren't we? Just please call for help. I think I'm really hurt."

He crossed his arms and stared at her for a moment. It seemed he was mulling over her request, but then his eyes narrowed, and he sneered.

"Ha." The laugh shot out like a bark, making Katie recoil. "I wasn't born yesterday, Katherine. I'm sure you're uncomfortable, but you'll be fine." He strolled into the kitchen, taking a glass out of a cupboard and filling it with water. He then pulled a prescription bottle out of his pocket and shook a couple of pills into his palm, offering them to her.

She eyed them suspiciously. "What are those?"

"Something to ease your pain and let you rest. Open your mouth."

"No. Cael, take me to the hospital."

His face darkened, and he set down the glass of water. Shaking the pills in his hand like a pair of dice, he leaned close and scowled. When he spoke, his voice dripped with unspoken violence.

"Put the pills in your mouth, Katherine."

She turned her face away. "No. I need a doctor."

A low growl rumbled up from Cael's chest, and he lunged at Katie. With his free hand, he slapped her across the face, hard. Stars exploded in her vision, and her agony expanded ten times over. He gripped the back of her neck and pressed the pills against her mouth, trying to force her lips apart.

"Take the fucking pills. I will break your jaw and force them down your throat if I have to, but by god, you will swallow them."

Stunned by the attack, Katie whimpered but allowed him to place the pills in her mouth. He held the glass to her lips and tipped it gently until the cool water washed them down. Through her tears, she kept her eyes fixed on his face. He abruptly rammed a finger in her mouth and felt around roughly, gouging the insides of her cheeks, and scratching her tongue. When he seemed satisfied that the pills were gone, he stood back with a relaxed hand on his hip.

His fury had subsided, and he was smiling, pleasant and indulgent. "See? That wasn't so bad. I only want to take care of you, Katherine." He stroked her hair as if he was petting a dog but frowned at the blood he found when he pulled his hand away.

"Ugh. Seems your wound has split open again. Such a mess." He shook his finger in her face. "See what you made me do? I had it all cleaned up, and then you had to make me angry. Don't do it again."

Stupefied, Katie watched Cael walk out of the room. What the hell was happening? Everything was wrong, and she wasn't sure if this was real or a nightmare. The stabbing pain in her head told her it was real, but the whole situation screamed delusion.

As the pills took effect, Cael's returning form wavered in

and out of focus. It became hard to hold her head up. Panic raced through her as her eyelids drooped, and she knew she would lose consciousness soon.

"Ah. Is that better, then?"

Trying to form words, Katie only managed a mumble. "*Please* don't…"

He swiped her hair off her face and pressed his lips to her forehead. "Shh. It's okay. Just sleep. I'll clean your wound again, and you'll feel better. Trust me, I'll take care of you."

His voice faded through a rapidly narrowing tunnel, and she slipped into oblivion.

TWENTY-FOUR

Consciousness returned in waves. She was aware of little things around her, and then the dark swirled in to take it all away. The smell of food assailed her senses, making her want to gag. She thought she heard movement close by, but then it was gone again. Each time she clawed her way up from the drugs he gave her, she swore she felt fingers touching her arm or stroking her face before she was pulled under once again.

The next time the fog began to lift, she felt a cool, wet towel wiping her face. While a dull ache was still squeezing her skull, it was nothing like it had been. When Katie tried to lift her head, the muscles in her neck screamed in protest, making her gasp.

"Hmm, I wondered about that. Poor thing. A neck pillow would've been a good idea, huh?"

She continued to move her neck, trying to stretch out the stiffness. Her eyelids fluttered open to find Cael sitting in a chair directly in front of her, their knees touching.

"There you are. You must be starving by now. We'll eat in a few minutes."

He grinned and tweaked her nose before setting off for the

kitchen. Katie watched him go, her mouth agape, trying to determine what circle of hell she had fallen into. Still not convinced this was real life, her brain was nonetheless functioning with more clarity. As drowsiness continued to fade, Katie knew she couldn't wait around to see what Cael had in store. She needed to reason with him.

Or find a way to escape.

She wriggled her arms, testing the strength of the tape. There was a little give, enough to let air between her skin and the armrest, but that was all. Her ankles were just as secure. When had she lost her shoes? She'd loved those shoes. Where were they? The absurdity of her concern about her footwear while restrained by a madman almost made her laugh.

Casting her eyes around the room, she took stock of her surroundings: two small, rectangular windows covered in dark curtains and a small folding table, but no other furniture besides the chair facing her and the one she was lashed to. She could see Cael through the kitchen's pass-through. He was humming a light, peppy tune to himself as he moved about the space. Katie didn't know how long she'd been unconscious, but the bathroom she could see down the hallway was suddenly calling her name. She cleared her throat and tried out her voice.

"Cael?" She nearly choked on his name. "Cael? I have to go to the bathroom. Like, now. Can you come take this tape off?"

The noises from the kitchen stopped, but Cael didn't answer. Instead, he set down his utensils and stepped into the hall to face her, his eyes narrowed. He paced across the room, keeping his gaze trained on her face.

"You'd like that, wouldn't you?" His voice was a shard of ice she felt deep in her bones. "You would love it if I cut you loose and let you wander freely." He stopped in front of her, and his voice dropped to a menacing whisper. "That isn't how this is going to work, Katherine."

She swallowed hard, and her heart sped up at his sudden

anger. Nostrils flaring, a glint in his eye, Katie realized she didn't know this man. Cael, her friend, had left some time ago, and she was instead staring at a dangerous stranger. For the first time, true terror rooted itself in her chest.

Cael regarded her with narrowed eyes. "Well. It's unavoidable, and I'm not totally unprepared for the situation, but you know I have to be careful. I had hoped things wouldn't go this far, to be honest. You should have accepted the truth long before now."

Katie shook her head. "What truth? What are you talking about?"

Without answering, Cael spun on his heel and returned to the kitchen. "It's fine. But I don't want our dinner to burn, so give me a minute."

She listened to him bustle around, her mind racing. How the hell was she going to get out of this? Did anyone know where they were? Did *she* know where they were? She had no idea if anyone was out there looking for her. The reality was that she was going to have to be smart and find a way to rescue herself.

Cael returned, his gait slow and relaxed, and fear rippled over her skin. He brandished a knife in one hand then held up the other for her to see a small rectangular object. "I will cut the tape. I will take you to the bathroom. If you try anything, I will use this." He held up a small box and pressed the button to make the electric charge arc and crackle. "And you won't like it. Do you understand?"

Katie jumped at the sound and light. *A stun gun?* She could barely believe her eyes and started to shake her head. But then He held it close to her face, and she felt the heat of the current. Tears sprang to her eyes, and she pressed her lips together and nodded.

"Good." A bright smile lit up Cael's face as he set about slicing through her bonds, the stun gun always in her line of vision.

Swallowing hard, she knew she had to do something, and the only thing she could think of was to get him talking. "Is this your cabin, Cael?"

"God, no," he scoffed. "Do you think I'd own a shithole like this? No, I found it online."

"Oh, yeah? Like one of those rent by owner websites?" Her heart lurched with hope. The sheriff would have no trouble tracking them with that kind of trail.

"Nice try, Katherine. You'd like to think I was that careless, wouldn't you?" He sat back on his heels and smiled. "No, I encountered a local doomsday prepper, purely by accident, and he couldn't stop bragging about his off-the-grid cabin. I asked to see his set-up so I could build my own sanctuary. He brought me here, excited to find a kindred spirit who also saw the imminent destruction of society. He is now a permanent feature of this property." He paused, a far-away look in his eyes. "Buried under a large oak tree about a hundred feet behind us."

Her shoulders sagged and Cael chuckled. Leaning in, he put his mouth against her ear. "No one knows we're here. No one will find us. Do you think I wouldn't take every precaution? That I wouldn't search high and low for the perfect location, hidden from the road and the sky, its owner so distrustful of the government that the property doesn't even have an address?" His breath was hot on her skin and yet a chill made her tremble. "I assure you we are invisible to anyone who may come looking. You and I can finally be alone together, as we were always meant to be."

Once he'd removed the tape on her wrists and ankles, Cael took a firm grasp of her elbow to guide her. Katie stepped into the bathroom and turned to shut the door, but Cael shook his head.

"The door stays open."

Katie balked. "But—"

Darkness descended over his features, and he stepped

forward, slamming the door back against the wall. "The door stays open."

As soon as she was done, Cael was there with a pair of handcuffs and a pleasant smile.

"Come on, you need to eat something."

The last thing she wanted to do was eat. Her stomach was churning still, and she knew anything she ate would come right back up. And the way Cael's eyes lit up with a petrifying fervor any time he looked at her was making things worse. Trying to keep her breath steady while fighting her growing dread, Katie knew this was only the beginning of her nightmare.

He led her back to the chair and fastidiously wrapped duct tape around her legs, joining them with the chair once again. Standing slowly, he leaned in, dragging his hands through her hair. His eyes were closed in ecstasy as he brushed his lips across her forehead with a sigh. She turned her head away to hide her revulsion.

Oblivious, he pulled a small folding dining table over to her chair and bounced back to the kitchen. He carried two bowls back and set one in front of Katie.

"This is my very own recipe—I hope you like it." He beamed.

Katie stayed still while he dug into the food, her hand-cuffed wrists in her lap. She kept her eyes down, afraid to look at him, then he abruptly stopped.

"Why aren't you eating?"

"I'm not hungry," was all she could manage.

Cael calmly set his fork on the table. When he rose from his seat with the same cool demeanor, she knew she'd made a mistake. He spoke in a low, measured tone.

"You're...not hungry? You're not hungry. I didn't *ask* if you were hungry. I asked why you weren't eating." She studied him as he paced the room, hands on his hips.

"I can't believe your ingratitude, Katherine. I went to a lot of trouble to make this for you—for *us*—and you...aren't hungry." Cael's pacing stopped, and he sighed. "Just so you know, I didn't want things to go this way. I hoped you wouldn't make this difficult." His voice dropped to a whisper. "Seems I was wrong."

In a flash, he was at her chair. He clutched a handful of her hair and yanked her head backward, making her yelp. To her dismay, she saw the stun gun in his other hand. She could hear the hum of the charge building and knew things were much more dire than she had realized.

"No! Cael, you don't have to do this." Her choked screams transitioned to sobs. "I'll eat, I promise."

He considered her pleas for a moment, then shook his head slightly, his face composed as though they were talking about the weather. "It's too late for that. Let's look at this as a teaching moment. You need to learn."

Without another word, he rammed the stun gun into Katie's ribs and let loose the charge. Every muscle in her body tensed against her will, shooting pain through her. Her jaw clenched as she tried to scream and all that came out was a strangled, high-pitched groan. He pulled the stun gun away, and her muscles twitched, pain radiating out through all her limbs as she struggled to catch her breath.

"Why? Why are you doing this?" Her eyes met his, and she was terrified by what she saw there. He seemed to be excited by what he had done, by the pain he had caused her. His eyes were wide and shining as he licked his lips and grinned like a madman. Stroking her hair off her forehead, he tried to quiet her.

"Shh, shh, it's all right, my beautiful Katherine." He began rolling up his sleeves and whispered, his mouth pressed against her ear. "I know that was unpleasant but trust me when I say it is all necessary. This has to happen to make you see the truth." He stood over her, watching her face and delighting in his power. "And believe me when I say, the rewards will be worth the suffering."

———

Katie's head sagged onto her chest. Her body screamed in agony, her muscles feeling torn and mutilated. Cael had seen fit to 'make her see the truth' over and over for nearly an hour. He drove the stun gun into her flesh in different locations— her arms, her legs, her back—watching each reaction with a sick thrill.

"Oh, you are exquisite," he breathed against her tear-stained face. Then he forced her head back, savoring her torment. "This has been an unexpected delight. However, there are other matters at hand. We will have to revisit this." He dragged his tongue up her cheek, tasting her sweat and tears, moaning as he turned away.

A chasm of despair opened wide in her chest, but she would not allow herself to tumble into it. Humming to himself, Cael returned his new toy to the counter then pulled Katie's chair back up to the table. She sat still, keeping her eyes trained on her clenched hands. Now that she knew her pain excited him, she would do everything she could not to show it.

"Let's try this again, shall we?"

He slid her bowl closer to her and waited for her to pick up her spoon. With trembling hands, she choked down a few bites of the now-cold meal. The stun gun had left her weak and nauseated, and Katie desperately hoped to keep the food down. If her stomach rejected it, there was no telling how he would respond.

When she had eaten all she could, Cael took the dishes and folded the table out of the way. "In this life, Katherine, there are unquestionable truths. One of these is that each person has a soulmate, another person on this earth to complete him and be his above all others." He clasped Katie's bound hands in his own, fixing her with an indulgent, benevolent gaze. "You, Katherine, are my soulmate. And I am yours."

Lifting their joined hands, he closed his eyes and crushed his lips against her knuckles.

"Do you have any idea how fortunate we are to have found each other? Some people wander incomplete and alone their whole lives." He trailed his fingers along her jaw. "But we—we were brought together through divine providence. I was meant to find you so we could share eternity."

Katie was struggling to make sense of what he was saying. It was the same nonsense he'd been writing to her for years, but somehow the meaning behind them still eluded her. Pressing her lips together, she watched Cael grow more intense, rubbing her hands against his mouth.

"But you knew that, didn't you? Your soul's been calling to me, pulling me to you since the moment we met. You don't have to hide our love anymore. From this moment on, I am yours, Katherine. And you are mine."

Her mouth dropped open, then clamped shut, and her head shook back and forth of its own accord, rejecting his words. When she found her voice again, the words burst out of her in a rush before she could catch them.

"No. You're wrong. We aren't soulmates, Cael. I don't love you, and this—this crazy shit will never change that." She allowed the fury to build up inside her, fueling her tirade and pushing all fear to the back of her mind, making her forget what he had already done.

What more he was capable of.

Katie leaned forward, showing her disgust plainly on her face. "You need help, Cael. You're fucking sick."

His eyes grew cold, and he increased his grip on her hands painfully. "You're lying. I—I've felt the connection between us. I know you love me!" His hands petted her hair, over and over, his voice rising in pitch, whining like a child. "That's why all of this is necessary. I have to free you from everything standing in our way. You *are* mine."

"No. Stop saying that. I love Ben."

Cael backhanded Katie across the face hard enough to make bright lights pop and zoom in front of her eyes. For a moment, she couldn't breathe, her head spinning from the pain. When she finally gulped in some air, she watched as a small, cruel smile spread over Cael's face.

"You will be mine, Katherine. And Ben will never have you."

Throwing her arms up in defense as Cael readied himself to launch at her, they both froze when the front door swung open and slammed shut. "Jesus, Cael, it took me forever to find this place. Mars might have been closer."

Katie's stomach turned to lead at the familiar voice. Elizabeth strutted into the room, impeccably dressed, scrolling through her cell phone. Looking satisfied with whatever she had just read, she dropped it into the purse dangling from her arm and looked around the room. When her eyes found Katie, trapped and wounded, there was a brief flash of alarm before her features twisted into a wicked smile.

"Well. Don't we look cozy?" Elizabeth pushed her lips out into an exaggerated pout. "Oh, no. Are you hurt, Katie? Maybe a little scared?" Then she threw her head back and laughed.

Cael walked backward to join Elizabeth without taking his eyes off his prisoner. "What are you doing here? I thought we agreed that I'd come to you?"

She rolled her eyes and huffed. "You were taking entirely too long. Besides." Pushing past Cael, Elizabeth strolled toward Katie and leaned forward to take a closer look at her face. "I wanted to see the fruits of our labor. While I wasn't expecting you to rough her up quite so much, I'm certainly not disappointed."

Confused, Katie couldn't do anything more than stare. Was she still unconscious? None of this made any sense. Why would she dream about Elizabeth showing up instead of Ben or Nick—or the police? But when she glanced at Cael, his face told her that this was all very real. His brows were drawn down, and his arms crossed as he stared at Elizabeth. Casting her eyes between the two of them, the truth became clear, and her heart dropped.

"Oh, Cael, I think she's finally catching up." Looping her arm through his, she leaned her head on his shoulder. "I don't know what you see in such a dense and boring girl, but to each his own. As long as she's out of my way, I couldn't care less."

Cael pushed her off him, his nose wrinkled in disgust. "I didn't do any of this for you, Elizabeth, and don't talk about her like that. You shouldn't have come here."

"You weren't answering my calls or texts, and I believe you owe me something."

Tears sprang into Katie's eyes. "How could you help him? Do you have any idea who he is and what he's done? That he's been stalking and tormenting me for years?"

Elizabeth shrugged and began examining the little cabin, poking her head into a doorway directly across from the kitchen. "Honestly, I don't care. He approached me outside the diner the morning I found you and Ben there together and offered to help get you out of my way. And that was an offer I really couldn't pass up."

"You should stop talking now, Elizabeth." Cael's voice was low and threatening. "Let's step in the bedroom, and we can discuss what you're owed."

"Wait. I don't understand." Katie squeezed her eyes shut to try to sort out what she was hearing. "Why would you need me out of the way? If you're having Ben's baby, you'll be in his life no matter if I'm around or not."

Elizabeth shook her head. "You poor moron. I'm not pregnant."

"What? But you said—"

"I said a lot of things. That doesn't make them true. I needed some way to keep Ben around until I could figure out how to get rid of you. It wasn't well-thought-out, and I couldn't back out once I told him. If he knew I'd lied about that…well."

So many thoughts were racing through Katie's mind she was having trouble following them. Elizabeth wasn't pregnant? What had Cael promised to get her help with his scheme? She glanced at him and was surprised by his agitation. He was chewing on his fingernails and shifting his weight from one foot to the other, frowning. When Elizabeth rounded on him, he flinched.

"All right, you little weasel. Do you have the ultrasounds or not? If I'm going to string Ben along long enough to comfort him through Katie's disappearance, I need to be convincing." Elizabeth winked at Katie as though they were sharing a private joke, and Katie's stomach lurched. With a heavy sigh, Elizabeth poked Cael in the chest, punctuating her words. "Look, I don't give a rat's ass what you two do after I leave. You can dress her like a doll and fuck her or peel her skin off and eat it. I don't care. But you damn well better have what you promised me or, I swear to god, I will make your life a living hell."

Cael's face burned bright red, and he kept glancing at Katie from the corner of his eye, as though trying to gauge her reaction. His shoulders curled forward, and he stumbled back a couple of steps under Elizabeth's attack. Katie watched his hands clench and release, clench and release. And then she felt a shift in the room's atmosphere. The hair on her arms stood on end, icy tendrils weaving between her ribs.

Elizabeth had no idea who she was dealing with. She hadn't seen what Cael had done to someone he professed to love. What would he do to someone he didn't give two shits about? Keeping one eye on the stun gun lying on the kitchen counter, Katie knew she had to warn her.

"Elizabeth." The name was barely more than a whisper. "Elizabeth, you need to go. You need to run. Now."

Crossing her arms and cocking her hip, Elizabeth sneered at Katie. "Oh, really? Why? Are you going to attack me? Scratch my eyes out, perhaps?" With a chuckle and a roll of her eyes, she turned her attention back to Cael.

In the same instant, she and Katie registered a drastic change in him. The embarrassed flush in his cheeks was gone, the tension drained from his posture. He stood tall, his back straight, wearing a tranquil expression that did nothing to dispel her fear. And when Katie caught sight of his dead eyes, her blood ran cold at what she saw—or didn't see. There was no fear, no love, nothing to indicate the existence of any kind of compassion or humanity at all. Elizabeth must have seen exactly what Katie did because the smirk dropped from her face, and she faltered backwards, trying to get away from him. But she wasn't quick enough.

In the blink of an eye, Cael lunged at Elizabeth, wrapping his hands around her neck and choking off the scream she didn't have time to let loose. Her eyes wide, she scratched at his fingers, trying to find a way between or under them to make him release his hold on her.

"Cael! No!" Katie screamed and tore at the tape still securing her ankles. "Stop! You'll kill her!" But time stood still when she caught sight of his face. In the middle of this melee, this violence, his lips curved into a satisfied smile, and his eyes came to life with a gleeful shine.

Unable to do anything to stop him, Katie watched in horror as he propelled Elizabeth backward, her eyes bulging and legs flailing. The two figures disappeared through the open doorway with a series of loud bangs and thuds. Sobbing and helpless, Katie wrapped her arms around her head, trying to cover her ears as the thrashing sounds from the other room slowed and then stopped completely. In the sudden silence, there was nothing but her own ragged breathing.

Cael emerged from the other room like a man sleepwalking. He picked up Elizabeth's discarded shoe, looking at it like he had no idea what it was, before tossing it through the opening behind him. Pulling the door closed, he stood with one hand on the knob, his chest heaving as he caught his breath. Then his head turned slowly toward Katie.

"Now. Where were we?"

TWENTY-FIVE

Afraid to look away, Katie stared into his cold eyes and drew in a stuttering breath. "Oh god, what did you do, Cael?"

Passing both hands over his hair before straightening his shirt, he raised his eyebrows. "What do you mean? To her?" He hitched a thumb toward the now-closed door.

She nodded, afraid to hear him confirm what she already knew.

"Nothing that bitch didn't fully deserve." He shrugged. "She wasn't a good person, Katherine."

This wasn't real. This couldn't be real. Cael said the words as though they should have been common sense. He was so composed, as though nothing had happened. Watching him busy himself with cleaning up the kitchen dishes, Katie's hopes of reasoning with her captor vanished.

Clearing her throat, Katie called to him. "Is she—is she dead, Cael?" She had to know for sure. "Did you kill her?"

He stepped out of the kitchen, wiping his hands on a towel. "Would you think less of me if I said yes?" Cocking his head to the side, he looked at her like he really wanted to know her answer.

She closed her eyes and groaned. It was true; Elizabeth was dead, and he killed her. He had hinted at what he could do, what he *would* do, but now the danger she was in was unmistakable and very, very real. Pressing the heels of her handcuffed hands to her forehead, she willed herself to stay calm.

"You can't seriously be upset about that." He clucked his tongue and put his hands on his hips. "Of course, you are. Oh, my Katherine. That is so like you, to care about everyone, even the vermin who despise you." Kneeling in front of her, he tucked a strand of hair behind her ear. "Only one of the many things I love about you."

Katie flinched from his touch, and her stomach tightened, threatening to vomit the contents all over them both. The way he was caressing her face, her arms, and her hands, disgusted her, and she only became more repulsed with every touch.

"Stop it. Stop saying you love me. You don't do this to someone you love." The fear that had dominated her for the last few hours was quickly being replaced by rage. Locking her eyes on him, she glared with all the hatred inside her. "And I don't care what you say or what you do, I will never love you. How could I? You're a monster."

He blinked rapidly, seemingly shocked by her venom. Gripping her hands, he leaned closer and whispered urgently. "Don't say that my beloved. I know it's shocking, I freely admit that, but it was also necessary. I couldn't let her come between us. Our souls belong together. I've known it since the first time you smiled at me. You must have felt it, too."

Katie scoffed. "You're delusional. I'm not your soulmate. I don't know how many times I need to tell you that! And you don't belong to me. You belong in a mental hospital."

"You're lying." He froze in place, his voice tight and deep. "You love me. I know you love me."

"No. I don't." She shook her head and lifted her chin in defiance. "I don't love you; I never have, and I never will. I love Ben."

He winced as though she'd struck him. "You're lying," he muttered again. But any hurt she saw in him shifted into fury at the resolve in her eyes.

"No." With amazing speed, he spun away to grab the stun gun. He jabbed it into her side before she had a chance to react, shouting to be heard over her screams.

"You've brought this on yourself."

Over and over, he pressed the gun into her flesh, sending excruciating jolts of electricity ricocheting through her body. His voice grew louder and more manic with the delivery of each shock.

"Ben has ruined everything, ruined what we could be together. He doesn't deserve you. He could never love you the way I do! Admit you belong to me and end this agony for us both."

It took several minutes for Katie to realize the inhuman shrieks filling the cabin were hers, and her mind, at last, registered the blinding pain coursing through her. She was filled with the agony of every bruise, every burn, and every shock for the torture it was, and her mind felt like it was fracturing under the torment.

Hovering at the edge of consciousness, just when Katie thought she couldn't survive any more pain, Cael stopped. He dropped to the floor, the gun slipping from his fingers. Grasping her knees, he turned his tear-streaked face to her, panting from the exertion of his attack. Katie's sobs rocked her body when she was no longer able to hold them in.

"Why do you make me do this to you? I only want you to love me, Katherine, to choose *me*." Cael's voice was choked with emotion. "Please, please love me."

He laid his head on her lap, wrapping his arms around her waist, clutching in desperation. They stayed that way, locked together and weeping, until Katie had no more tears.

Startled awake by a hand tapping her cheek, Katie flinched. Consciousness made her acutely aware of all her aches and pains—the bruises and burns crying out all at once—and she wished for the relief of nothingness again.

"Wake up." The harsh tone of Cael's voice instantly set Katie on edge.

The handcuffs were gone, but she found her wrists bound with a thick plastic zip tie. Her chair was the lone piece of furniture in the room, and she couldn't tell from the pale light filtering through the curtains if it was day or night. How long had she been his captive? It might have been hours, days, weeks—the repeated torture was pushing her to the brink of insanity. To ground herself to the present and keep herself from falling apart, she focused on the rhythmic patter of rain on the roof.

Rain. Katie frowned, knowing that her one chance of rescue might have been a hunter or hiker stumbling upon this cabin and hearing her screams, bursting in to save Little Red Riding Hood from the Big Bad Wolf. But a rainfall that sounded this heavy would make the woods treacherous and muddy and would keep everyone out of the area. Any hope of salvation dissipated.

With a pang of heartache, she thought of Elizabeth. There would be no one to save her, whether Katie was rescued or not.

Cael stood in front of her, arms crossed, his cold eyes piercing her. As she waited for him to say something, her stomach twisted and knotted painfully.

"I think I've been going about this all wrong."

His brow furrowed as he paced. Cael seemed to be working something out, and Katie knew it couldn't be anything good. With his newfound appreciation for the power —and the arousal—he felt by hurting her, Cael could only be devising creative new ways to get what he craved.

Steepling his fingers under his chin, he stopped and regarded Katie.

"We were brought together through the design of the universe, but maybe I need to let things happen in their own time." He cupped Katie's cheek and ran his thumb over her cracked and bleeding lips. "It took me so long to find you. I can wait a little longer if it means an eternity together."

Keeping silent seemed her best move at this point. Contradiction and arguing only got her pain. Besides, she had come to understand that there was nothing she could say to dissuade him from doing what he wanted. Knowing what he'd done to Elizabeth, the extent of the physical danger she was in was obvious. There were just two ways she might leave this cabin: On Cael's arm as his partner and soulmate or in a body bag.

"I've waited, Katherine. God knows I've tried to be patient." He let his fingers brush along her collarbone, sliding under the edge of her shirt to feel her skin. "Watching you with the others, knowing what you let them do to your body, I've shown exemplary restraint. And I've been so alone all these years, waiting for you. But soon, we'll be together. Our souls, our minds, and our bodies."

As he continued to caress her, his hands roaming freely, Katie's chest tightened around her lungs until she couldn't breathe. He seemed to have abandoned the stun gun—for now. But awareness of the many other ways he could violate her exploded in her mind. She never would have imagined Cael capable of such a depraved, violent act before, but now she recognized there was nothing he wouldn't do.

Ignoring the sour taste of rising bile, Katie cleared her throat. "How long have we been here, Cael?"

The movement of his hands halted. "What difference does it make?" He pressed his lips into the hollow below her ear, nuzzling her neck. "What does time matter for us?"

Katie thought quickly through her fear, scrambling for a

way to distract him from what she was sure he was about to do.

"Well, of course, it doesn't matter, but I want you to tell me how this all began. I need to know everything if I'm going to fully...*give* myself to you." Trying not to tremble, she pressed her cheek against his. "And I want to understand. I think—I think it will help if you explain it to me."

Pulling back, Cael grasped Katie's shoulders. His face was pure joy, and his eyes lit with a hopeful fire. "Really?" He kissed her forehead and scampered to the kitchen, returning with another chair and two bottles of water.

"Oh, my love, I will explain everything. I should have known—you require a much more delicate touch. Brute strength would never work with you. I see that now." Nodding at his own revelation, he opened one of the bottles and held it out to Katie. She snatched it with her bound hands and gulped the cold water. He scooted his chair closer so he could stroke her hair and chuckled under his breath.

"Where to start? There's so much to tell." He tapped his fingers against his chin and pursed his lips. The water bottle half empty, Katie waited for him to speak. At least while he was talking, he wouldn't hurt her or put his hands on her. Maybe she could even convince him to loosen her binds. Then she could find a way out of this nightmare.

"I knew, felt it deep inside, in my bones, that you were meant to be mine the first moment I saw you." He sighed, reliving the memory. "I never really cared about making friends in high school—was never very good at it—but I wasn't opposed to it, either. I agreed to hang out with Nick out of sheer boredom, but he hadn't told me he wouldn't be alone, that his kid sister was tagging along. When I first caught sight of you, the world stopped. In your face I saw not just your beauty, but your strength, your glowing soul, and I knew there would never be anyone else for me. I think you knew it then, too, because you turned and smiled at me, and I was positively bewitched by you." His breathing sped up, and he bit his lip, leaning forward. "I had forgotten all about Nick. There was only one goal, one purpose in my life from that moment on. You. Whether it was for five minutes or for eternity, I knew I had to be with you."

Katie shifted in her chair, the intensity of his gaze burning into her. Trying not to panic, she offered him what she hoped was a serene smile. "All the cards and gifts I got in San Francisco, at college, were from you, weren't they?"

"My aunt lived in Oakland and flew me out to help her work on her house. But that left me plenty of time to visit you." Somehow, he managed to blush as he spoke, leaving Katie dumbfounded. How was it possible that he could look like a shy, lovestruck kid after callously murdering a woman only a few hours before?

"Of course, that all changed after you graduated." Lacing his fingers behind his head, Cael leaned back in his chair. "I decided it was time—that you were ready to learn the truth. Across all the miles, you somehow still drew me to you. I came to San Francisco and followed you to some trendy bar. Oh, my heart sang when I found you through the crowd, and everything else faded until you and I were the only beings in existence." He paused, a frown creasing his forehead. "You drew me to you, like a moth to the flame that would inevitably destroy it. I didn't see him until I was so close, I could touch you."

He cleared his throat and sat rigid in his seat. "It was soon clear that you weren't just with him, but that he possessed you, *owned* you. That was one of the most difficult nights of my life, watching him touch you. So, I made it my mission to learn everything I could about Derek. I followed him. I tracked him to his work. I even befriended him at a pick-up basketball game by the beach. He was formidable, I'll give him that: charming, handsome, admired by everyone. But in the end, I knew Derek was a minor obstacle that I could easily overcome." The way the corners of his mouth curled into a smile chilled her. "And I did."

Something about the way he said those words caught her attention and set alarm bells ringing inside her head. "What... what do you mean by that?"

Cael shrugged. "Oh, I'll get to that, my beloved." He rose from his chair and circled around until he was behind Katie's chair. "I will tell you, though, that becoming his friend changed nothing. I knew you were meant to be mine, and I would never be at peace until we were together. He had to be dealt with."

He lifted her hair off her neck, tracing the exposed skin with his fingertips. Katie tensed at his touch, and it was all she could do not to squirm. But when his roaming hands clutched her breasts and his lips pressed hot and insistent against her neck, she couldn't hide her revulsion any longer.

Before she could stop herself, she launched out of the seat. Her shoulder connected with Cael's chin, making him grunt and fall back a step. In her frenzied attempt to get his hands off her, she had forgotten that she was still anchored to the chair legs. She realized too late that her feet were immobilized, and she toppled forward. With her hands still bound by the zip tie, she was powerless to stop her momentum and hit the floor, elbows first, with a loud *bang*! The contact sent a jolt of pain up her forearms to the tips of her fingers, the bones feeling like they had shattered into a thousand pieces. It knocked the wind out of her, and she floundered on the floor, gasping for air.

Through a haze of pain, Katie watched the unhurried approach of Cael's black dress shoes. She struggled to draw breath and became uncomfortably aware of how still he was when he stopped inches from her face. Then he crouched next to her, seeming to delight in her discomfort.

"Why do you have to make this so difficult?" He brandished a knife, waving it in her face, and chuckled when she tried to wriggle away from him, the chair dragging behind her. With quick, fluid movements, he slashed with the knife and released the tape binding her ankles. Before she could react, he had flipped her onto her back and straddled her hips.

Cael loomed above her, his shadowy features transforming him into the visage of Death himself. She screamed, hefting her weight from side to side in an attempt to throw him off her. His eyes were wide, and his smile crazed in the semi-darkness, and the louder she screamed, the more maniacal his appearance became.

Finally, he seemed to grow tired of her display and slapped her face. "Enough!"

With a *thunk*, he buried the knife in the floorboard next to Katie's head. She felt the vibrations through her whole body and was immediately shocked into silence.

His expression dangerous, Cael gripped Katie's throat, pressing his thumbs into her flesh hard enough to make her choke. She couldn't do more than claw at his hands in her panic with her wrists still bound, but in her mind, she saw her lifeless body lying on the floor next to Elizabeth's. He leaned forward and whispered in a menacing tone, his mouth only inches from her ear. "That is quite enough."

TWENTY-SIX

Rising to his feet, Cael hauled Katie upright with him in one deft move. He shoved her back on the chair and stared as she coughed air back into her lungs.

"You seem to be trying to make me hurt you. I thought we were making progress. I thought you were starting to understand." He ran his hand through his hair and paced away from her. "Everything I've done has been for you. All the lying, all the planning, was to bring you to me. And how do you thank me?" Maintaining eye contact, he bent forward and yanked the knife out of the floor.

"All I've ever wanted was for you to see me as your other half. The love letters I wrote you, the flowers, the photos—you are a part of me, Katherine. You feel the same way, I know you do. You must."

Abject fear kept her from responding. She didn't know what to expect from one moment to the next, and that alone was terrifying. Tears blurred her vision, but she refused to look away.

His shoulders hunched and he swayed on his feet, his face shrouded in shadow while the knife hung loosely at his side.

He mumbled, "I just...can't you..." When he lifted his

head, his eyes were red, and his cheeks wet. "Just love me, Katherine. Everything I've done has been for you, can't you see that? I need you. I need you to love me; is that so much to ask?"

In that instant, Katie realized this man was a stranger to her. He was no longer Cael, her friend, or even Cael, her stalker and tormentor. He was pathetic and deranged and needed help. For a moment, compassion bloomed inside her, and she was flooded with a need to comfort this broken man.

But then his arm moved, pale light glinting off the blade still clutched in his hand. His 'love' for her was nothing like love. It was a need to possess, to control, and would end in her death if she didn't do what he wanted. Something inside Katie clicked into place and hardened, and she saw a chance to survive, if she could be brave enough to take it. She forced her lips into a smile and tried to relax her shoulders.

"I'm sorry, you just surprised me." She pulled in a deep breath and raised her eyebrows at him. "Kiss me now. I'm ready this time."

A ghost of confusion crossed his face, but it was gone almost immediately. The hope and excitement that took its place almost made Katie feel guilty for what she was about to do. *Almost.* She had to focus on everything he had put her through, everything he had done.

What he had done to Elizabeth.

He tormented Katie for years, terrified her, caused her anguish and pain, all based on an obsessive delusion.

And she was going to feed that delusion to save herself.

It was a difficult task to keep an inviting smile on her face while watching the knife getting ever closer. Katie wasn't sure what her plan entailed; she only knew she had to catch Cael off guard by giving him what he wanted. But how much was she willing to give?

She swallowed hard and steeled herself for his touch. This time when his lips met her skin, she held perfectly still. Revulsion reared up in the pit of her stomach, but she pushed it down. She had to if she was going to convince him his plan had worked and that she was finally his.

Cael groaned from the back of his throat as his kisses moved along her neck, exposing more skin as he went. He slipped the strap of her bra down over her shoulder, and Katie clenched her teeth to keep from screaming. Everything inside her was fighting to pull away, but she refused to give in. Her bound hands trembled, and her heart was pounding, but she knew she had to be patient to have any hope of getting out of this situation alive.

"I've dreamed about this moment so often, Katherine. You can't imagine how exquisite it feels to touch you at long last." His mouth traveled along her jaw; his hands buried in her hair. "Everything I've done has brought me here, to this moment."

He pressed his lips against Katie's, unsure at first, but then with more insistence. She struggled not to retch as she allowed Cael to kiss her, her hands clenched so tightly she expected her nails to break through the skin on her palms.

While he moved his mouth against hers passionately, forcing his tongue past her stiff lips, she squeezed her eyes shut and tried to separate herself from what was happening. She willed her mind somewhere else, somewhere far away from this nightmare where he was groping her, and she couldn't get away. But inside, she was screaming.

The reality of the situation was that she was at Cael's mercy. She knew that he could easily overpower her, and there was nothing she could do to stop him. And that realization made her blood run cold.

Blissfully satisfied, Cael beamed at her, and he sighed. "That was just as earth-shattering as I anticipated. It was all worth it. Everything I did, the terrible things I had to do were necessary to bring us together."

Pushing her nausea down, Katie tried to smile at him. "Of

course, I understand. You had no other choice." Elizabeth's face flashed in front of her eyes, and she shivered.

He leaned back in the chair, gazing into the distance with a dreamy smile on his face. "I suppose you should know all of it, Katherine. Every step was for you, after all. You saw what happened with Elizabeth. I was completely justified." One corner of his mouth lifted in a sardonic smirk. "And let's just say Derek got what he deserved."

"Oh god." Katie groaned. "So you did kill him."

Cael heaved himself out of his seat, waving his hands in the air. "Don't be so naïve. Derek was no saint. You of all people should know that."

He stopped and leaned against the counter, watching Katie with his head to the side. "It wasn't part of my plan, you know. I had never considered just getting rid of him. My strategy was more nuanced, designed to steer you to my arms."

"What did you do?" She was barely able to push out enough air to be heard, and her hands trembled at the prospect of hearing the details of his death firsthand. But she had to know the truth.

"It was perfectly orchestrated—not by me, but I could see the hand of the universe in every step. Fate presented the opportunity to me on a silver platter." Cael tapped his finger against his chin. "To be honest, it was Derek's own behavior that sealed his fate. He was so self-absorbed and so used to having everything go his way, he never saw it coming."

Katie clasped her fingers together to stop them from shaking. Her chest felt tight, making it difficult to breathe. The terror that had been enveloping her quickly fell away, replaced by rage, and she found her voice.

"You're a monster." Hot tears spilled onto her cheeks.

Blackness overtook Cael's face again, but this time Katie's own anger was so palpable that she hoped he came at her.

There was no way he'd get the better of her with the hatred coursing through her veins.

"Yes, Katherine. I killed him. With his own vice and avarice. He was so riddled with flaws and weakness that he was his own undoing. I didn't plan it, but I wasn't about to walk away when the idea presented itself. He couldn't help but brag about his sexual conquests, about his cheating, to anyone who would listen, including me. Of course, when he picked up a couple of sluts after a basketball game and invited me to share a glass or two of Scotch with them, how could I say no?"

Here he paused, his gaze lost in the distance on something Katie couldn't see. He shuddered and turned unfeeling eyes on her.

"After the bar, he invited everyone back to his place, always ready to show off his wealth and privilege. The women were fawning all over him while I poured us some more drinks, allowing me to *enhance* his a bit. With roughly ten crushed pain pills."

Then he threw his head back and laughed.

"He and I drank our Scotch, chatting and laughing until he began to slur his words. I told the women he'd had too much and that they should leave to let him sleep it off. He was so out of it that he couldn't talk or move, and he struggled to keep his eyes open. I think he wanted me to call for help, judging by the way he grunted and flapped his hands at me. Of course, there was no way I was going to lift a finger to help that piece of shit. Then I had the pleasure of watching as he realized that something was very wrong and that it was my doing. It was fascinating."

With his hands clasped behind his back as though presenting evidence at a trial, Cael strolled toward Katie, a faraway look in his eyes. He stopped a few inches from her knees, looming over her.

"I finished my drink slowly, explaining to him why he didn't deserve you. Every now and then, as I described the connection you and I share and how I could never allow anyone to come between us, he would whimper or groan. Before long, Derek lay still, eyes closed, taking only shallow breaths. And then, just before he expired, the strangest thing happened." He tilted his head and looked to Katie to gauge her reaction. "His eyes fluttered open just a bit, he stared right at me for a second, and one single tear rolled down his cheek. Like I said: fascinating."

Rage bubbled in Katie's chest. Fear was no longer the ruling emotion, and she wanted nothing more than to destroy the fiend in front of her. Her muscles were coiled and tense, building up energy like a rubber band about to snap.

Cael closed his eyes, a smirk curving his lips. "That moment was particularly delicious. Knowing he understood that you, ultimately, were the reason for his death. You and his own boorish behavior."

Unable to hold her wrath back any longer, Katie sprang out of her chair with a screech.

Leading with her head, she rammed into Cael, her shoulder boring into his chest and her head driving up into his chin. She pushed him backward, his feet scrambling to keep him upright until he smacked into the kitchen counter. He collided with such force that the dishes in the adjoining cupboard rattled, but he didn't fall.

Her rampage was far from over, and the adrenaline racing through her would not be stopped. With a guttural roar, she hunched forward and put all her weight behind the upward thrust of her zip-tied hands, connecting with Cael's jaw once again. She heard the satisfying clack of his teeth before he finally crumpled to the ground, unconscious.

Katie stood over him, panting from the exertion with tears streaming down her face, but still feeding off the anger that his confession had unleashed. In that moment, her greatest desire was to surrender to her primal urge to destroy this demon and send him back to the hell he came from. But a different voice spoke up quietly, urgently, from the back of her mind.

RUN.

She cast around for the knife he'd been wielding a moment ago to cut her wrists free but didn't see it anywhere. It was possible Cael had it on him somewhere, but there was no way she was getting close enough to him to check. While the knife would be useful, time was of the essence, and she didn't have the luxury of wasting it to search.

She pressed her forearms against her stomach, trying to stretch out the plastic tie enough to wiggle her hands free, but it held firm. Remembering a lesson from her self-defense classes, she raised her arms above her head and brought them down hard against her hips to snap the plastic. She grunted with the effort and felt the jarring impact travel through her legs, but she knew she couldn't stop. Drawing in a deep breath, Katie pushed her hips forward and tightened her stomach muscles in anticipation, then exhaled and drove her elbows down one more time.

The zip tie snapped.

Without looking back, Katie ran for the front door. She slammed into it in her haste, the resounding *bang* of the collision echoing through the cabin. Convinced Cael was right behind her with his hand outstretched to grab a fistful of her hair and bury his knife in her back, she cried and fumbled with the doorknob. Despite all her yanking and shoving, the door wouldn't yield.

When she stopped to inspect it, her heart sank at the discovery of two padlocks securing it from the inside. She realized he must have put those on after murdering Elizabeth and while Katie was unconscious. Twisting and pulling at the locks with all the strength she had left, Katie grunted out her frustration, but nothing budged.

She crept silently on her bare feet around the cabin, searching for another way out. The bathroom window was barred, and the others were all painted shut. She stared at the closed bedroom door. There could be another window inside or even the keys to the padlocks. But Elizabeth was also in there. Glancing back at Cael's prone form, she swallowed and slowly opened the door.

It was darker than out in the main part of the cabin, but the light spilling through the opening was enough to see inside. There was a bare double bed pushed into the corner to her left, an open closet next to it. Directly across from Katie was a window, but this one was boarded up from the outside. A three-drawer dresser sat under the window, and Elizabeth's body was on the floor in front of it.

She was on her back, arms splayed out to her sides, one leg bent and tilted toward the other. Katie's hand flew to her mouth, and she squeezed her eyes shut. Elizabeth's fancy purse was near one of her outstretched hands, as though she had simply laid on the floor and was reaching for it. But as she approached the dresser, she caught sight of Elizabeth's face, and a heaviness settled in her chest. Head tipped to the side, her eyes wide and unblinking, there was an unnatural relaxation to her features that made Katie shiver. No matter what she had done to her or to Ben, Elizabeth didn't deserve to die like that. No one did.

Her frantic hunt for the keys in the dresser and all the kitchen and bathroom drawers turned up nothing, and a wave of anguish engulfed her. She buried her hands in her hair, pacing wildly and trying not to fall apart. Then she remembered that Elizabeth had come in with a cell phone. *A cell phone!*

Dropping to her knees, she upended the purse, watching the contents scatter around her. She shuffled her hands through the dead woman's belongings, unable to find the one thing that could mean her survival. Where could it be? She knew Elizabeth had dropped it into her purse, so where was it now?

Katie crawled on all fours, sweeping her hands along the floor. Then she spotted the phone peeking out from under the bed and her heart soared. She was saved!

But when she had the phone in her grasp, she realized that it couldn't help her. The screen was shattered to the point that pieces were missing, what she could see of the inside smashed and mangled.

All the strength leached out of her, and she slumped forward, her head touching the floor. She'd been so hopeful, so sure that she could simply make a phone call and she'd be rescued. The disappointment was crushing. A knot of despair grew and grew in her chest until it burst out of her, forcing her head back and emerging as a guttural howl of pain.

No one was coming to save her, and time was running out.

She had to find the keys. There was no question in her mind that he would have kept them very close, in one of his pockets.

The question was whether she dared to take them from him.

TWENTY-SEVEN

She shook her hands loose, shifting from one foot to the other, trying to calm her frayed nerves. Cael was stretched out on the floor, one arm extended to the side, lifeless. He wasn't moving, but that didn't mean he wasn't gathering his strength to pounce once she got close. Would she be able to fight him off again? She'd caught him by surprise before, and that was the only reason she had gotten the upper hand. It was luck, and luck alone, that knocked him unconscious. If her fists had hit him a bit to the right or the left…

Katie knew she had to do something, and panicking was not it. Stiffening her spine, she slowed her breathing and reasoned that if she could find the keys to the padlocks, she might find the keys to the car, too. One foot in front of the other, she crept across the floor to Cael's still body, giving his outstretched hand a wide berth.

She stared at his sprawled, slack-jawed form for several seconds, examining the movement of his chest, watching his fingers and legs for any sign that he was conscious. When she felt satisfied that he was still out, she crouched down and crawled cautiously toward him.

Patting each of his pockets with the lightest of touches,

Katie's heart leapt when she felt a set of keys. But were they the right ones? There was only one way to find out. Holding her breath, she slipped her hand into the pocket of his dress slacks, trying not to wake him. Her fingertips inched closer and closer to the object she desperately needed. Only a millimeter more, and she could loop her finger through the ring and get the hell out of there.

Without warning, Cael's hand shot out and clamped onto her arm, keeping her from the item that meant her freedom. She screamed, whipping her head up, expecting to see pure fury on Cael's face. Instead, his eyes were glazed and unfocused, and his grip was already weakening.

"Katherine..." Her name fell from his lips in a low mumble, and she saw that she still had a chance.

She didn't think about her next steps, didn't have a plan, but she let instinct take over and moved with lightning speed. Jamming her hand into his pocket, she snatched the set of keys from their hiding place. Cael rolled groggily and reached for her, his mouth contorted in a menacing snarl, and she swung her fist and connected with a force that shot pain through her fingers and all the way up her arm. The blow knocked him back long enough for her to spring to her feet and haul ass to the door.

The second key she tried unlocked one of the padlocks, and she hurled it across the room before glancing quickly over her shoulder. A bolt of horror shot through her at the sight of Cael on his hands and knees, trying to get his feet under him. His face was twisted, blood dripping from his lip, and he was no longer as dazed as he had been just thirty seconds ago.

The keys slipped out of Katie's fumbling fingers and crashed to the floor. Her body suddenly seemed to weigh a thousand pounds, and she couldn't make her hands move fast enough. Through panicked tears, she fit the last key into the padlock and had the door open in a flash. Shuffling steps approached behind her as she crossed the threshold into a blast of fresh air, and the voice that bellowed her name was far closer than she had hoped.

"KathERINE!"

She flew out the door, certain she felt fingertips brush against her hair. The suffocating darkness of a moonless night gave no indication of where she was or which way would mean safety, and yet she ran. Clouds obscured the stars, and Katie stumbled, blind, onto what she hoped was the path to the road. The grass was wet and slippery under her feet, but she kept moving until her eyes adjusted to the gloom.

Now that she could make out some of her surroundings, she realized with dismay there was no discernible trail to follow. She spun in a circle, searching in the gloom for a way to refuge.

Her heart stopped. Cael was staggering toward her, brandishing the knife, gaining on her with every step.

"Katherine. You have nowhere to go. No one is coming to save you. You're mine."

Katie flung herself into the foliage, not knowing if it would save or doom her. Wet leaves slid under her bare feet as the rain came down again, drenching her. Branches scratched her face and snagged on her clothes, but still, she ran. Twice she tripped and landed hard on her knees in the rocks and mud. There was no time to rest or nurse her wounds, however. Any kind of hesitation would mean her death.

Cael continued to shout obscenities and threats, his voice gaining strength and bridging the distance between them with more clarity. "Katherine, you fucking bitch! You've ruined everything. Believe me when I say I will relish hearing your screams as I open you wide and pull out your insides."

Tears and rain mingled on Katie's cheeks as she tried to catch her breath. She was so tired, bruised and torn, and still reeling from Cael's latest stun gun attack. Nevertheless, she kept moving, the promise of seeing Ben's face again driving her forward.

Where was she? She had grown up here, had trekked through these woods more times than she could count, and had always found comfort in their depths. But now nothing was familiar, and she begged the powers that be to send someone, anyone, to save her.

The ground suddenly disappeared beneath her, and she tumbled down the steep slope of a ravine. Roots and branches stabbed her and yanked at her hair with every roll, the taste of blood and dead leaves in her mouth. When she finally crashed to a stop at the bottom, she clapped a hand over her mouth to stifle the sound of her ragged sobs. She hoped against hope that if she could just lie here quietly, Cael would rush past, oblivious. But he'd already found her, his relentless pursuit continuing.

"I'm coming, Katherine. It will all be over soon." Cael's voice boomed from the top of the ravine as he began picking his way down to what she feared would be her final resting place.

With a wail of despair, Katie realized he would never stop. This would never be over until she was dead. Her 'destiny' had changed the moment she defied him. There would be no reconciliation, no penance to gain his favor: only punishment in the form of torture and a slow death. She heaved her aching and bleeding body to the other side of the gully and began a frantic climb for her life.

The rain fell harder, running down her face in rivulets, blinding and choking her. Cael was still advancing, now only a few steps behind her. She could hear him swearing each time his dress shoes failed to find a grip on the muddy slope.

"Stop running! You know how this must end now." He grunted with the effort of staying upright as he traversed the steep incline. "We could have been happy. If you had only trusted me, had loved me, we could have had an amazing life together."

Katie's fingers dug into the loose mud to haul her

wounded body up the embankment, but she ended up sliding back six inches for every foot of progress she made. Her arms were weak, exhausted, and her legs were shaking from the effort of gouging into the wall of earth to push herself higher. She could see the top, at last. The edge of the road several feet ahead was visible and hope alone kept her moving. But the question remained: would there be any help for her there?

Her mind twisted and turned from one possibility to the next. Running across the blacktop to the woods on the other side could deliver her into the same situation she was currently fighting to survive and force her to wander blindly. Staying on the road would make her visible to potential rescuers but vulnerable to her attacker's physical strength. The stun gun had wreaked havoc on her muscles, making every movement ten times harder than it should be and depleting her energy. While she had temporarily taken Cael out of commission at the cabin, he seemed to be back at full strength and was gaining on her by the second.

"Cael, stop. Please, stop. You don't have to do this!" Her voice gave out on her, tears strangling the words as she held out hope that there was some small, rational part of her friend left.

The sound of his laughter froze her blood, tentacles of panic gripping her brain. "I know I don't *have* to do this. But I want to, Katherine, very much." His voice was tranquil now, no longer showing the effects of struggling over the wet ground. "You have no idea how I ache to see the light fade from your eyes, to feel the warmth of your blood as it flows through my fingers. Is there anything more intimate, anything more powerful to bind us together for eternity?"

Scrabbling for the top of the gorge, afraid to look behind her, Katie's fingers barely brushed against the cement, unable to grab hold of anything. Her feet slipped in the muck as the rain poured through the leaves above and cascaded down the slope.

Out of nowhere, a hand clamped down on her ankle, making her scream. She twisted, trying to kick herself free, and was petrified by the look on Cael's face, blazing at her out of the darkness.

His eyes were wild, his lips pulled back in a grimace, the blood oozing from the corner of his mouth making him look like a newly risen ghoul. He pulled on her ankle, using it to hoist himself closer as an unnerving cackle rose from his throat.

"It's time, Katherine. There's no more running, no more fear, only the peace of death. And I will grant that to you as my final act of love and devotion."

Too late, she caught the glint of the blade. His arm launched at her with lightning speed, slashing a long stripe of pain across the flesh of her thigh. Katie screamed and thrust out her other leg, summoning every ounce of force buried deep within her bruised and beaten body. Her heel caught him square in the chest, toppling him backward to the bottom of the muddy ravine.

Without waiting for him to land, she flipped onto her stomach and began the arduous climb toward what she hoped would be safety. The storm seemed to mirror her frenetic energy as she fought the unstable ground, trying to save her life. In a burst of noise and movement, the clouds unleashed a downpour with a deafening clap of thunder, and the wind shook the trees in a violent show of force.

Katie dug her naked toes as far into the earth as she could, heaving herself closer and closer to the top, moving through sheer force of will. Her hand slapped onto the cement, and her heart leapt. She was going to make it.

The urge to look behind her was strong, but she refused. Her focus was on getting up to the road; she would figure out the next step once she was on solid ground. The skin on her knees scraped against the edge of the blacktop, but Katie barely noticed. Blood seeped through her clothing from where

Cael had sliced into her, but the pain was nothing compared to her determination to live.

She crawled on all fours when she was on the pavement, not sure her legs would support her. Whipping her head back and forth, straining her eyes to peer up the road in both directions, she tried to determine her best chance of survival. But her muscles were shaking with the lesser effort of crawling, and she knew she would never outrun Cael. Straight across the road loomed more dark woods. Katie knew she had to keep going forward. Her best chance would be to lose him in the trees somehow. She just had to get there first.

Before she could move, Cael's maniacal laughter gusted to her on the wind.

"No." She pushed to her feet, swaying as she turned to face her pursuer. The pain and the sorrow of it all was suddenly too big to control, and it forced a strangled scream from deep in her chest. Unable to do much more than watch, she stood in the road trying to suck air into her lungs while he pulled himself out of the ravine. She was so tired. Her knees shook, but she held her ground, even as she wept. "But why, Cael? Why do you hate me?"

Suddenly, his crazed, homicidal expression melted away. Cael straightened himself and scrutinized her with wide eyes. Then his head tipped to the side, his brow wrinkled in confusion. "What? Why would you say that? I don't hate you."

"Then why? What do you want from me?"

"Just you." He reached for her, adoration shining through his eyes. "It's always been you."

Headlights whipped around the corner, startling them both. Their eyes locked in a split second, each making a quick decision. Just as Katie turned to dash into the woods on the other side of the road, Cael lunged for her. The headlights drew closer and closer, cutting through the rain and turning it into a cascade of diamonds. Cael's hand closed around Katie's wrist, and she screamed. Red and blue lights whirled to life as the sheriff's cruiser screeched to a halt. The passenger door flew open, but she could only make out a vague shadow behind the glare.

"Let her go! There's no way out of this for you, Green."

Relief and terror flooded through Katie as the familiar voice poured hope into her soul. Her scream rivaled the thunder. "Ben!"

With a snarl, Cael yanked her toward him, pinning her back against his chest. He dragged her backward, pressing the cold, wet steel of the knife to the pulsing artery just below her jaw. Through clenched teeth, he whispered in her ear, "We could have been happy. Now your lover will get to watch you die in the street, unable to save you."

Katie squinted against the flashing lights, searching for Ben's face. There were other figures moving behind and around him, fluid and shadowy, but she only cared about him. She just wanted to see him, to hear his calming voice, feel the warmth of his smile one more time. Cael's fingers dug into the flesh of her arm even as the point of the knife broke through her skin. Feeling warm blood trickle down her neck, she knew this was the end.

"Parker." Ben's calm voice broke through the commotion surrounding her, and her heart stilled. "Parker, I'm here. Everything's going to be okay."

Cael's laughter vibrated through her, and he dragged her a couple of steps further away. "He lies, Katherine. Who do you think he's trying to convince? You? Or himself?"

Ben was moving sideways in front of the car, maneuvering into a better position, but Cael moved right along with him. Always holding Katie in front of him as a shield, he never blinked or looked away.

Trying to take a breath, Katie opened her mouth, and a hopeless sob burst out. Ben flinched toward them, reaching out, but Cael only scuttled further out of reach. Puddles of water littered the blacktop, and his dress shoes skidded before he regained control. The knife slipped, slicing into Katie's cheek. She screamed.

"Parker!"

"Don't move." Cael pointed the knife at Ben, his breath coming hard and fast now. "Don't take another step. Let me walk her out of here without you following, and she'll live. Or keep coming at me, and you'll see her pretty guts all over this road. Your choice."

"Collins, get back in the car and let me handle this." Sheriff Jacobson's voice cut through the pouring rain, steely and low, and Katie could make out his shape crouched behind the open driver's door. "I've got more backup on the way, including a hostage negotiator."

Cael threw his head back and laughed. "The only negotiation is happening right here, right now, with Katherine's life as the sole bargaining chip. It appears to me, though, that we've come to a stalemate."

"You're a dead man, Green. Mark my words." She couldn't see Ben's face, but the danger in his voice was enough to make Cael hesitate. Then he shook his head and pressed his cheek against Katie's.

"No, no, I don't think I am, actually. Let's talk through a few options here, okay? First, you could rush me and try to wrestle the knife from my hand. But I'd slit her throat from ear to ear before you took your first step."

The adversaries had been rotating this whole time, Cael dragging Katie back toward the woods. Ben was no longer backlit, and when she saw his face, she was nearly over-whelmed by the riot of relief, terror, and love that exploded inside her. His face was almost unrecognizable: his eyes cold and his expression made of stone. Staring down the monster who held her captive, his mouth was set in a grim line, his jaw muscles working. She'd never seen that look on his face before, and it chilled her to the core. If they both made it out of this alive, she hoped to never see it again.

"Another choice open to you is for the good sheriff to take his best shot at me." He leaned away for a moment and raised his voice. "Go ahead, but you and I both know there's no shot you could take that wouldn't sacrifice Katherine in the process."

Turning his attention back to her, he jostled her around until his lips were against her bloody cheek, the knife now pushing up under her chin. Katie's stomach churned when she felt his tongue snake out to taste her blood, and a groan bubbled up from deep in his throat. "Of course, removing the hostage from the equation will allow them to get their man, but then robs me of the pleasure of taking your life myself."

"Parker..." She could feel Ben's pain through his strangled tone, and she wanted nothing more than to take him in her arms and soothe him. But Cael was still edging further out of the pool of the car's headlights.

He smiled and taunted Ben further. "Then your third possibility is to simply talk me down, as it were. Convince me to let her go and give myself up. Come on, Collins, use your wit and charm to disarm me and save the woman you love. Then, when she's dead, you can spend the rest of your pathetic life wallowing in the knowledge that you failed her."

Ben was silent for a moment, his hands clenched at his sides, seemingly oblivious to the rain streaming into his eyes as he glared at Cael. Faint sirens started up in the distance, and Ben smirked.

"Well, well, Green. Seems there's a fourth option you missed. Those reinforcements are closer than you thought. They've been tracking your path through the woods this whole time. The trees behind you are full of snipers. You lose."

It was obvious to Katie that his words had an immediate effect on Cael, judging from the way his whole body tensed and rooted him in place. "You lie. You're a liar. You wouldn't jeopardize her life that way, not even to get to me."

Shrugging, Ben took a step toward Cael, catching Katie's

eye for a fraction of a second. But that second told her every-thing she needed to know. Hope bloomed inside her, and she prayed that Cael couldn't feel her heart race in anticipation of whatever Ben had planned.

"They're some of the best marksmen in the state. I trust that they'll be able to take you out without a scratch on Parker. Do you trust yourself the same way?"

Cael shuffled back and forth, unsure which direction would afford him cover, the knife shaking in his hand. "I'll kill her. You know I will."

"Your head will be in a million pieces on the ground before we even hear the shot." Ben had continued moving closer, now barely a few feet away from Katie. Cael didn't seem to notice now that panic had taken him over. "You're done, Cael. If you let her go now, you just might live."

"Please, Cael. Please." Her voice cracked with rage and fear and fatigue. "Just let me go. What did I do to make you hate me?"

His erratic breathing stilled, and the knife fell away from her neck. Cael spun her to face him, gripping her wrist. "Oh, my darling. I could never hate you." His features softened, his wide eyes pleading with her to understand. "All I ever wanted was for you to see me, to see that we were meant to be together. Everything I've done was for you. I love you, Katherine."

A burst of movement caught Katie's attention, and she turned to see a snarling Ben charging at Cael. From that instant, it seemed everything around her moved in slow motion.

Swinging her around to his side, Cael raised the knife, headlights glinting off the metal. She watched the sheriff rise from behind the door, waving an arm and shouting for Ben to get out of the way. Laser-focused on Cael and running with his shoulder down, Ben either didn't hear or didn't care about the sheriff's orders as he slammed into Cael with the force of a truck.

Katie had been whipped around Cael with such speed that when Ben collided with him in a jumble of shouts and cursing, the momentum kept her moving and she slipped right out of Cael's grasp. The seconds seemed to stretch to minutes, to hours, her eyes locked on Ben as she fell. He was reaching for her and calling her name, completely unaware of a maniacal Cael looming behind him, the knife lifted high above his head, ready to strike.

Landing on her back with monumental force, all the air was forced out of her lungs. Then her skull slammed into something hard, and darkness engulfed her.

TWENTY-EIGHT

F eeling like her head was wrapped in a thick woolen blanket and stuffed with cotton, Katie slowly regained consciousness. She didn't know where she was, and her eyes refused to obey her command to open.

"Katherine?"

The muffled voice seeped into her awareness. She couldn't place it, however, and wasn't even sure it was coming from outside her own mind.

"Katherine."

The voice was louder now. Or was it closer? Maybe her brain was becoming clearer, and she was only hearing it better.

"Katherine."

A hand wrapped around her wrist as the voice sounded once again, and everything flooded back to her: the cabin, the stun gun, the hands and lips on her against her will, Elizabeth. She saw the glint of the knife as it slashed toward her and heard that maniacal, chilling laughter as if it were being broadcast all around her.

"No!" She tried to yank her arm out of his grasp and screamed with all her might. Both of her wrists were trapped now, held by large, firm hands. There was tape on her arms, but she swore she would not be strapped down ever again. She thrashed her body back and forth, arching up off the bed, yelling with all the breath she had in her lungs, but she couldn't break free.

"It's all right, Katherine, you're safe here. I'm Dr. Hopkins. You're in Enderlin General. No one is going to hurt you."

The words were lost on Katie. She heard them, she understood each of them, but her frantic mind wouldn't register their meaning.

"No, no, no!" Her shouts turned to sobs when her body lost the strength to fight anymore. He was gone. Just as she predicted, falling in love with Ben Collins had meant his death. In her mind's eye, she could see Cael's face so clearly, and could almost hear the sound of the knife ripping Ben away from her. She fell back on the pillows with a whimper. "Oh, Ben, I'm so sorry…"

Then his voice was in her ear, and he stroked her forehead. "Shh, Parker, I'm here. I've got you. You're safe."

As she opened her eyes, the unexpected light made her head throb. "Ben?"

He pressed a kiss to her cheek, then sat back so Katie could focus on his face. "Hey, there. Glad you could join us." One corner of his mouth lifted, and Katie sprang up, throwing her arms around his neck as she dissolved in tears again.

"Oh, god, I saw the knife. I thought you were…" She clapped a hand to her mouth, holding back the dread she'd been drowning in. Taking a few deep breaths, she regained her composure. "All this time, the nightmare I was living, it was Cael. I thought he was my friend. He killed Derek. Just watched him die. Oh my god, Elizabeth. Ben, I saw him…I couldn't stop it." Her choked crying drowned out the rest of her words.

Gathering her against his chest, Ben stroked her hair and kissed the top of her head. "Shh, I know. The sheriff's team found her." He held her at arms' length, forcing her to look in his eyes. "There was nothing you could have done. You have to know that. What happened to Elizabeth was not your fault, Parker."

She sniffled and laid back on her pillows. "I should have tried harder to warn her, to convince her to run. She had to be so scared, and I didn't do anything..." Dizzy and spent, she couldn't hold her head up any longer. Closing her eyes, she let the tears slide away to soak into the pillow.

Ben enclosed her hand tenderly in his. "She didn't deserve what happened to her, but I'm convinced Cael had always planned to kill her. Nothing you did or didn't do would have changed the outcome."

"Ben, there's something else." With her heart lying heavy in her chest, she tried to think of how to tell him about Elizabeth's deception.

"The pregnancy wasn't real. I know." He smiled sadly at Katie's gasp of surprise. "I always suspected it was a lie; she wouldn't give me any details about doctor's appointments or show me ultrasounds. It was all a little too convenient."

After a series of quick raps at the door, Katie was thrilled to see her parents and her brother hovering just outside the room.

"Hey, Kat." Drawing closer, Nick swiped the back of his hand across his eyes and snuffled. "You scared the hell out of me, you know. No one knew how badly you'd been hurt, and if you'd... Well, don't do that shit again; you hear me?"

He stared into her eyes for a moment before crushing a rough kiss on her forehead. Clearing his throat and sniffling, he stood near the door, staring at his feet.

"What—what the hell happened? It's all so hazy I can only remember bits and pieces."

Her gaze flitted around the room, waiting for someone to explain things. They all watched her as though she might crumble in front of their eyes if anyone said the wrong thing.

Karen came forward and took one of Katie's hands. "Oh,

Kat. We were so worried. I don't know what we would have done if we had lost you." She blinked away tears and pasted a smile on her face. "Well. You're here with us now, aren't you? Everything will be okay." Brushing a kiss over Katie's temple, she moved out of the way for David.

"Hi there, kiddo. Rough few days, huh?"

She gaped at the surrounding faces. "Few days? How long was I gone?"

A look passed between her parents. Her dad turned back to her, patting her hand and smiling. "You're safe now, sweetheart. That's what's important. You get some rest, and we'll come by again tomorrow."

The small group filed out of the room, giving Ben pointed stares. "I'll be right back." He cleared his throat and hurried out the door.

Lying in the soft bed, clean and warm and dry, Katie wasn't convinced this was anything more than an elaborate dream she had concocted to escape her waking nightmare. She looked down at her hands, laying against the brilliant white sheets. They were cut and scraped and bruised, and the pain in her thigh felt real enough. She examined her arms and saw the burn marks from the stun gun glaring out at her from under the IV lines. Those were no hallucinations. Cael's face, excited and aroused during her torture, flashed in front of her eyes, and she squeezed them shut, willing him gone. Silent tears rolled down her cheeks as she acknowledged she'd never be able to erase the image from her mind.

At the sound of the door closing, she jolted up in the bed, ready to run or fight if she needed to.

"Hey, it's only me." Ben stepped toward the bed, his hands up, as though trying not to spook her. "You're safe here, Parker. No one's going to hurt you."

Katie nodded and relaxed back into the pillows while Ben pulled a chair next to the bed. "I'm so glad you're here," she whispered, pressing her palm against his cheek. "I didn't know if I'd see you again."

Covering her hand with his own, he turned to brush his mouth against the inside of her wrist. "Same here."

A lopsided grin played around his lips while his thumb traced a lazy circle on the back of her hand. Katie was relaxing in the bed, her eyelids feeling heavy, but she still had questions. She frowned. "Ben? How long was I gone?"

His thumb hovered over her skin for a moment, and he cleared his throat. "Almost four days. You disappeared from Maxie's, and we didn't find you until two nights ago, in the dark and the rain. I thought you were a ghost when I saw you on the road." Ben choked out the last word and stared at the floor.

Gaping at him, she was unable to wrap her mind around what he was saying. "*Four* days? That can't be right. How is that possible?"

There was no way for her to know if it was day or night in that dark, dingy room. Time there flew by and stood still at the same time, trapping her somewhere between reality and hell. When she looked at Ben, he was chewing his lip and couldn't meet her eyes. Anxiety squeezed her chest.

He pursed his lips and grimaced. "Jesus Christ, Parker, we all thought we'd lost you. We didn't know where to look for you and that—god, that nearly killed me." After a deep, shaky breath, Ben locked his eyes on hers. "What do you remember about what happened?"

Katie wasn't sure she wanted to focus on that. It felt like all the pain and the fear was lying just below the surface. It would only take a tiny scratch to open the wound and send it flooding through her again. And she wasn't sure she'd make it out on the other side. "I didn't see it coming, that's for sure."

Ben settled into his chair, keeping Katie's hand tucked in his as if he thought she might disappear if he let go. She couldn't say she minded, though. It was a comfort and gave her back some of the courage and strength she lost in those woods. As long as Ben was with her, it would all be okay.

She explained the ruse Cael had used to lure her out of the bar. Knowing now that Elizabeth's role that night was strictly to divide the little group, she was ashamed she'd fallen for it. Recounting the moment she realized the truth was a lot harder than Katie expected. Even after everything he had done, she still thought of him as her friend. She knew now that had never been the case.

When she got to the part where Cael attacked and murdered Elizabeth, Ben's calm demeanor faltered. His body seemed to deflate, and his shoulders drooped. "Jesus, Parker."

"Knowing what he did to her, I lost it when he told me about Derek. I acted without thinking it through. But I know that if I had hesitated, well, I'd be dead right now. I don't know where the strength came from, but I'm glad it was there."

Ben hung on every word through her explanation of how she overpowered Cael and escaped into the night. He brought her hands to his mouth and kissed her knuckles, his gaze never leaving her face. "You are some kind of badass; you know that, Parker?"

She scoffed. "Some badass. I stumbled around in the dark and the mud and fell in a gully and still almost died. And then you were there." Katie swallowed the lump that had formed in her throat. "My hero."

He chuckled, then suddenly had trouble meeting Katie's eyes. "The sheriff—he didn't have any leads. We had no idea where to start. Did he drive you out of town? Get you on an airplane? No one in the bar noticed anything suspicious. You left your phone behind. There was no paper or electronic trail to tell us where he might have taken you. We were flying blind, Parker."

The comprehension of how well Cael had covered his tracks sent her stomach into turmoil. She would never have been found. He could have kept her there as long as he wanted, done anything to her. She shuddered. "What happened after—where is he? Did the snipers…?"

A shadow passed over Ben's face, and he took a deep breath. "Well. About that. There were no snipers."

Katie's head snapped up and she gasped. "What? You're joking."

"The backup we were waiting for was in the wrong place, on the road that led to the cabin. It would have taken another fifteen minutes for them to get to us. Jesus, I thought I was going to have to watch you die, right there in front of me—and there was no way to stop it."

Ben rubbed his hands through his hair, as though trying to scrub away the memory.

"I took a chance. Things had already gotten so far out of his control, I just pushed him a little farther. Then he shoved you out of the way, and I was so scared that after I found you alive, I was *still* going to lose you. I let my guard down and Cael took his chance. Thank god Sheriff Jacobson was there or —well, I'm just glad he was there." He glanced at her sideways. "The sheriff took his shot just as Cael was about to stab me in the back. He, uh—he didn't suffer. I thought you might want to know."

Cael had taken so much from her, had tormented her for months, for years. He had made her afraid of her own shadow, had taken Derek's life, and watched as it slipped away. Had he been tried for his crimes, he would have been convicted; there was no doubt in Katie's mind about that. But to die alone and in fear in the middle of the road? No one deserved that.

A nurse stopped in to check Katie's vitals and to see if she needed anything. When she earnestly expressed her desire to go home, the nurse explained that she had suffered a concussion. Now that she'd regained consciousness, they needed to keep her for observation one more night, but she should be able to leave the next day. It wasn't what she wanted to hear, but Katie understood and appreciated the caution.

After the nurse left, Ben stood and stretched. "I suppose I should let you get some sleep. I'll head home and—"

"Don't go." Before he could finish, Katie grabbed his hand. "There's enough room on this bed, I swear. I just..." She looked away to hide her fear. "I don't want to be alone."

Crawling onto the bed and curling his body around hers, Ben held her long after they both drifted off into a peaceful, dreamless sleep.

TWENTY-NINE

"Ooh, tough luck, fellas." Patsy pouted at the two men frowning at her from across the pool table. "I believe the wager was twenty bucks, right, Katie?"

Slinging an arm around her friend's shoulders, Katie laughed. "Absolutely right, Patsy." When her opponent slapped the bill in her hand, she shook her head. "Kev, you've seen us here every Wednesday night for the last six months, at least. Why in the world would you challenge us? For money, no less? You should know better."

Ducking his head, Kev and his partner slipped away into the busy happy hour crowd. Katie and Patsy shared a smile before dissolving into giggles.

"Oh, man." Patsy sighed. "Is it wrong that winning felt good? Because I really enjoyed taking his money."

A rugged man with blond curls and a full beard approached from the bar, carrying two shot glasses. "Hey, Pats, you got one more game in you?"

Patsy beamed at him. "For you, Matthew, you bet your sweet ass. You don't mind, do you, Katie?"

The couple barely seemed aware that Katie was still there,

so she kissed her friend's cheek as she handed her cue to Matthew. "Don't be too rough with him."

Standing on her toes, Katie scanned the crowd, searching for one particular face. When she found it, she felt her heart expand, and she wound her way closer.

Ben opened his arms to welcome her without interrupting his conversation with Nick and a group of serious-looking men very intent on whatever her father was saying. She scooted into his embrace and tried to catch up on the discussion.

"No, no, you've got it all wrong," David interjected. "We're trying to improve the square, trying to make it easier for foot traffic to reach the shops and attractions. We don't want to change anything; we're looking to make safety and accessibility improvements, that's all."

Nick nodded, stroking his chin. "Oh, okay, I get it. Trying to bring in more tourists? Make it a day trip kind of destination. A 'let's go visit Enderlin and bask in its small-town charm' kind of thing?"

David clapped him on the back. "Now, you've got it."

Ben leaned close while the discussion wound on, speaking softly so only Katie could hear him. "Feeling like a little peace and quiet right about now?"

"Oh, god, yes."

Ideas flew around the circle of planners, allowing Ben and Katie to ease their way backward and out of the conversation. With a quick glance around to make sure no one was watching, they made a break for Maxie's back door, gulping in the fresh night air. Giggling like children, they leaned against the building, holding hands.

"It's crazy in there, huh?"

Katie nodded. "Crazy. But you have to admit, this town loves Dixie and all she's done for Enderlin. I'm not surprised so many people showed up for her retirement party."

Ben brushed his thumb absently over the back of her hand.

"It still doesn't seem real. Dixie stepping down and naming me as her successor is beyond my wildest dreams. A year ago, could you imagine we'd be here?"

"Never. But, then again, a year ago…" Her eyes focused on a dark memory that was far away but still lurking just under the surface of her consciousness. "A year ago, I wasn't sure I'd be anywhere, let alone here. It seems so long ago, but somehow, it's still raw. I wish to god I could let it go." A chill ran through her, and Ben pulled her tight against his chest. Even in the summer's heat, she appreciated his warmth.

"Parker, no one expects you to just get over it. What you went through…well, that kind of thing takes time. Every day, I wish I could have saved you from all of it. Jesus, Nick beat himself up for months, thinking he should have somehow known. None of *us* are fine, and we didn't experience what you did." He kissed the top of her head and slid his hand up to stroke the back of her neck. "You're working through it. That's all you can ask of yourself."

Katie knew he was right. The words made sense. It's what she would have said to someone else in her position. And yet, it had taken more than three months for the nightmares to subside after the ordeal. During that time, she had woken in a cold sweat, screaming, at least three times a week. Now it was maybe once a month. Katie saw Cael's face in a crowd occasionally, too. Anytime that happened, her heart would stop, and she'd be paralyzed in fear until reality set in again. Sometimes she could hear the crack and sizzle of the stun gun in her mind, and it was like she was still trapped in that dark cabin.

Thankfully, her family, her friends, and especially Ben had seen how she was struggling and encouraged her to see a therapist. With her counselor, she could go into detail about what happened in a way she couldn't with the people who loved her. The idea that they wouldn't believe her, or that they would distance themselves if they knew the specifics, was a real fear that she still carried. Meditation, grounding techniques—these had helped Katie regain her sense of self. Without the support of the people in her life, Katie knew she wouldn't have made it through the first months after Cael kidnapped and tortured her.

Ben felt her quivering and rubbed her back. "Hey, you're safe." Holding her at arm's length, he made her look into his eyes. "Parker, you are the strongest woman I have ever known. You didn't let him win, did you? He didn't make you hide—not by stalking you and not by hurting you. The fact that you turned this horrible experience into something good is a testament to your unending fortitude."

Letting the corner of her mouth curve up slightly, Katie shrugged. "Anyone in my place would have done the same."

"God, Parker, no. No, they wouldn't have. A lot of people go through scarring events, but you're the only one I know who could turn that experience around to create a trauma center to help others." He took her face in his hands and kissed her. "You amaze me every single day."

A wave of love overtook Katie as she gazed into Ben's deep green eyes. This man had been with her every step, never pitying her or letting her feel sorry for herself. He had been kind and encouraging and patient. When she could no longer handle being under the same roof with her well-meaning but overprotective parents, he moved her into his place without batting a lash. He had put her first and carried her when she couldn't get through the day, and he had urged her to follow her instincts when the idea of the trauma center first presented itself. Every phase of her recovery included Ben holding her hand, following her lead. Loving her.

He pulled her necklace out from under her shirt and swung the chain in front of her face. "When are we going to tell people?"

"Soon, I promise." She tucked the necklace out of sight. "I didn't want to take away from Dixie's retirement and your promotion. You both deserve to be celebrated for all you've done. Let's wait another week. Then we'll casually slip it into the conversation one night at dinner."

Ben cleared his throat and pantomimed passing dishes around, playing out the scene he anticipated in the near future. "Could I have the potatoes, please, Nick? Oh, and by the way, I've asked Parker to marry me, and she said yes—the fool."

Throwing her head back, Katie burst into laughter. She snaked her arms around Ben's neck and pressed herself close to him. "I orchestrated the whole thing and duped you into proposing in the first place. Don't you take credit for all my scheming."

With his hands tangled in her hair, he lowered his lips to hers. His touch lit a familiar fire that spread from the pit of her stomach to the tips of her toes. The kiss deepened, and they lost themselves in each other.

The back door opened, spilling light and noise into the parking lot, and the two reluctantly separated. Katie twined her fingers with Ben's as they slowly made their way back inside.

"You're going to run into some trouble once we're married, you know."

Ben raised an eyebrow. "Oh? What trouble might that be?"

"You won't be able to call me Parker anymore. We'll both be Collins, and that would be far too confusing for everyone involved." She turned to face her fiancé. "What are you going to call me then?"

Gazing into the ocean of her blue eyes, Ben didn't hesitate to answer.

"That's easy. I'll call you mine."

THE END

ACKNOWLEDGMENTS

"Thank you" can never express my gratitude to all the people who left pieces of their hearts in this book. Left to my own devices, it probably would not have been written, much less published and let loose in the world. But I am beyond fortunate to have crossed paths with some amazing people whose encouragement and love I don't feel I deserve. Without everyone listed below, this would still be nothing more than a dream and a wish. I'm sure I missed some names, but just know that if you ever said a kind word, read a chapter, gave me feedback, taught me about writing, or simply kept me company while I plunked away, I appreciate you more than I can adequately express.

Thank you to Nancy Schumacher, Caroline Andrus, and the entire team at Melange Books. This book, quite literally, would not exist without every one of you.

Thank you to my mom and my sisters for their encouragement and unconditional love from day one. (And Mom, I hope that one day you'll be ready to read the spicy bits.)

Thank you to Sam Tschida, my first editor, whose constructive criticism was invaluable to helping shape this story into something resembling a novel.

Thank you to Gina Denny, my *last* editor, whose deft polishing of my little piece of coal made it truly shine.

Thank you to Metamorphosis Literary Agency, my agent Amy Brewer, and especially to Katie Salvo: my first agent, my editor, my friend. You talked me off the proverbial ledge more times than I can count. The luck of the draw brought me to you and without your encouragement, insightful editing, and unending patience, this would still be a dream.

Thank you to every member of the Central Iowa Authors group and everyone who joined us for NaNoWriMo, whether in person, virtually, or in spirit. Finding this collection of creatives was one of the best things to happen to me and you all taught me so much. I want to specifically acknowledge Lynn, Krystal, Mary, and of course, Rick. Thank you for showing up, for welcoming everyone, and for herding cats with grace and kindness.

Thank you to my Galentines: Stephanie Caffrey, Jamie Seitz, and Sarah Bigley. I don't know how we found each other, but I'm beyond thankful that we did. Your uplifting hearts, your creative spirits, and your friendship have changed me for the better, and you mean the world to me. Thanks for spending hours - *so* many hours - hanging out and writing and laughing and sharing your amazing selves with me every week. You have ALL the strengths, and I love you ladies.

Thank you to my children, Maddie Rasmussen, Simon Purcell-Clark, and Garrett Clark. Not only do you make me incredibly proud of who you are every single day, but your honest feedback, your love, and your rock-solid faith in me have been invaluable. I am the luckiest girl in the world, and I love each of you so, so much.

And last, but most…

Thank you to my husband, Andrew. Look at us. It is no stretch to say that this book would never have existed without you. You talked me through plot holes, kept me going when my brain told me this would never happen, and had faith in my writing - and in *me* - long before I did. Every love story I will ever write begins and ends with you. Nuboo.

Don't miss out on your next favorite book!

Join the Satin Romance mailing list
www.satinromance.com/mail.html

———

THANK YOU FOR READING

———

Did you enjoy this book?

We invite you to leave a review at your favorite book site, such
as Goodreads, Amazon, Barnes & Noble, etc.

DID YOU KNOW THAT LEAVING A REVIEW...

- Helps other readers find books they may enjoy.
- Gives you a chance to let your voice be heard.
- Gives authors recognition for their hard work.
- Doesn't have to be long. A sentence or two about
  why you liked the book will do.

Sharon L. Clark is a romantic suspense author hailing from Des Moines, Iowa, where she never outgrew her enormous imagination and continues to feed both her hopeless-romantic heart and her villain-wannabe brain.

An avid reader from a very young age, Sharon still enjoys living vicariously through the heroines in adventure novels, falling in love again and again through romances, and getting the tar scared out of her now and again. After attending the University of Northern Iowa Sharon met her husband, Andrew, and together they have raised three pretty cool humans and a handful of dogs. It wasn't until she was nearly an empty nester that she decided to focus on writing, and let other people see what goes on inside her head: the good, the bad, and the bizarre.

I'll Call You Mine is her debut novel, but you can check out her short stories and other musings on her website or see what she's up to on her other social channels.

SharonLClark.com

facebook.com/SharonLClarkAuthor

x.com/sharclark36

instagram.com/sharclark40

linkedin.com/in/sharonlclarkauthor

www.ingramcontent.com/pod-product-compliance
Lightning Source LLC
Chambersburg PA
CBHW031000260626
47169CB00002B/631